DEA

Plato yanked the
Kettering onto the
remembering to reach in and switch the motor off.
Cautiously, he took a slow breath.

Plato leaned down to grab the old psychiatrist's
hands. Kettering had always seemed like a sun-
dried raisin of a man. Talking to him, you felt as if
a sneeze or a harsh word might send him spiraling
into the air.

But now Kettering suddenly seemed even heavier than Andre Surfraire, the late chief of surgery.
Plato wrestled the body along the garage floor,
panting and wheezing with effort. His head was
starting to pound, and his vision was growing
dim. With every step he took, he paused to cough
and gasp for air, waiting for his sight to clear
again.

And finally, Plato was stumbling blind, yanking
on someone's hand and trudging along a few
inches at a time, not knowing why but remembering that it was somebody important, that there was
some reason he had to keep walking, keep dragging this heavy *thing* behind him. And then he
lost even that, stumbling forward and lurching
into something solid. He fell, vaguely hearing a
sound like jangling bells or broken glass.

And then, nothing . . .

Aldridge Used Books
864 Alamo Dr.
Vacaville, CA 95685
(707) 452-9022

D0383433

① SIGNET

PAGE-TURNING MYSTERIES

☐ **PRELUDE TO DEATH A Blaine Stewart Mystery by Sharon Zukowski.** Caught between family loyalty and the search for justice, New York P.I. Blaine Stewart finds herself in Key West risking all to clear her brother's name in the murder of an unofficial poet laureate and widow of a famous Cuban expatriate artist. As the case gets hotter, Blaine can't help wondering if all her efforts will end up a prelude to her *own* death. "Breathless, hot-blooded, edge-of-your-seat . . . a page-turner."—Edna Buchanan, author of *Suitable for Framing* (182723—$5.50)

☐ **LEAP OF FAITH A Blaine Stewart Mystery by Sharon Zukowski.** When socialite Judith Marsden paid Hannah Wyrick, a surrogate mother, to carry her test-tube baby, she had no idea that Wyrick would disappear two months before the delivery date. Accompanying Wyrick is Marsden's son, heir to 29 million bucks. How is New York P.I. Blaine Stewart supposed to find a baby who hasn't been born yet?
(182731—$4.99)

☐ **PARSLEY, SAGE, ROSEMARY, AND CRIME by Tamar Myers.** Shocked to find out that she's the number one suspect in the murder of a film's assistant director, Magadalena Yoder is in a scramble to track down the real killer. What a stew to be in—especially since her only clue is a grocery list headed by parsley. (182979—$5.99)

☐ **THE ANATOMY OF MURDER A Cal & Plato Marley Mystery by Bill Pomidor.** When the cadaver lying on a steel table in Dr. Calista Marley's anatomy class turns out to be her husband Plato's favorite former patient, its enough to turn him positively green. The coroner listed her cause of death as heart failure. But Cal's sharp eye soon spots evidence that the lady may have been cleverly murdered.
(184173—$5.50)

Prices slightly higher in Canada

Buy them at your local bookstore or use this convenient coupon for ordering.

PENGUIN USA
P.O. Box 999 — Dept. #17109
Bergenfield, New Jersey 07621

Please send me the books I have checked above.
I am enclosing $＿＿＿＿＿＿＿ (please add $2.00 to cover postage and handling). Send check or money order (no cash or C.O.D.'s) or charge by Mastercard or VISA (with a $15.00 minimum). Prices and numbers are subject to change without notice.

Card #＿＿＿＿＿＿＿＿＿＿＿＿ Exp. Date ＿＿＿＿＿＿＿＿＿＿＿
Signature＿＿＿＿＿＿＿＿＿＿＿＿＿＿＿＿＿＿＿＿＿＿＿＿＿＿＿＿
Name＿＿＿＿＿＿＿＿＿＿＿＿＿＿＿＿＿＿＿＿＿＿＿＿＿＿＿＿＿＿＿
Address＿＿＿＿＿＿＿＿＿＿＿＿＿＿＿＿＿＿＿＿＿＿＿＿＿＿＿＿＿＿
City ＿＿＿＿＿＿＿＿＿＿＿ State ＿＿＿＿＿＿＿ Zip Code ＿＿＿＿＿＿＿

For faster service when ordering by credit card call **1-800-253-6476**

Allow a minimum of 4-6 weeks for delivery. This offer is subject to change without notice.

TEN
LITTLE
MEDICINE
MEN

Bill Pomidor

A SIGNET BOOK

SIGNET
Published by the Penguin Group
Penguin Putnam Inc., 375 Hudson Street,
New York, New York 10014, U.S.A.
Penguin Books Ltd, 27 Wrights Lane,
London W8 5TZ, England
Penguin Books Australia Ltd, Ringwood,
Victoria, Australia
Penguin Books Canada Ltd, 10 Alcorn Avenue,
Toronto, Ontario, Canada M4V 3B2
Penguin Books (N.Z.) Ltd, 182–190 Wairau Road,
Auckland 10, New Zealand

Penguin Books Ltd, Registered Offices:
Harmondsworth, Middlesex, England

First published by Signet, an imprint of Dutton Signet,
a member of Penguin Putnam Inc.

First Printing, January, 1998
10 9 8 7 6 5 4 3 2 1

Copyright © William J. Pomidor, 1998

All rights reserved

 REGISTERED TRADEMARK—MARCA REGISTRADA

Printed in the United States of America

Without limiting the rights under copyright reserved above, no part of this publication may be reproduced, stored in or introduced into a retrieval system, or transmitted, in any form, or by any means (electronic, mechanical, photocopying, recording, or otherwise), without the prior written permission of both the copyright owner and the above publisher of this book.

PUBLISHER'S NOTE
This is a work of fiction. Names, characters, places, and incidents either are the product of the author's imagination or are used fictitiously, and any resemblance to actual persons, living or dead, events, or locales is entirely coincidental.

BOOKS ARE AVAILABLE AT QUANTITY DISCOUNTS WHEN USED TO PROMOTE PRODUCTS OR SERVICES. FOR INFORMATION PLEASE WRITE TO PREMIUM MARKETING DIVISION, PENGUIN PUTNAM INC., 375 HUDSON STREET, NEW YORK, NEW YORK 10014.

If you purchased this book without a cover you should be aware that this book is stolen property. It was reported as "unsold and destroyed" to the publisher and neither the author nor the publisher has received any payment for this "stripped book."

In memory of John P. Schlemmer, M.D.

1929–1997

The Boss—and the best Chief of them all.

Chapter 1

INTEROFFICE MEMO

From: Lionel Wallace, M.D., Chief Executive Officer, Riverside General Hospital
To: TREND Task Force Members (All Department Chiefs)
Date: Friday, March 27
Re: Planning Retreat at Camp *Success!*

Please remember that the retreat for the Team-Related Education of Nurses and Doctors (TREND) at Camp *Success!* takes place this weekend. Attendance is mandatory for all clinical department chiefs. Training in team building will be a major theme of the retreat. Major reductions in funding among the various departments will also be discussed. Attached is a list of equipment required for the trip.

"I'm going to kill him," said the chief of obstetrics and gynecology.

On a cold and windy Friday afternoon in March, the Council of Chiefs was gathered in the lobby of Cleveland Riverside General Hospital. Oddly enough, not a single white coat was visible in the small cluster of doctors and nurses. Not a single stethoscope or suit jacket or Rolex watch.

Instead, most of the chiefs were bent double under the load of heavy frame backpacks, sleeping bags, canteens, and duffel bags. All eight members of the party were staring dolefully through the hospital lobby's front window, huddled together like a litter of puppies born in an animal shelter.

Decked out in their jeans and nylon jackets and camping gear, the Council of Chiefs looked as alien as a chamber orchestra playing Mozart on the moon.

"I'm going to kill him," the obstetrician repeated.

"How?" asked the chief of nursing services.

"Poison," guessed the chief of internal medicine.

"Slow torture," suggested the chief of psychiatry.

"The death of a thousand scalpels," grumbled the chief of surgery.

"Hardly," sniffed the chief of obstetrics and gynecology. She smiled ferally. "I'm going to scoop his heart out. With a blunt speculum."

"Won't work." The chief of pediatrics shook her head sadly. "Our dear hospital president doesn't *have* a heart."

Two young chiefs hovered silently at the edge of the crowd, cautiously noncommittal. Plato Marley, the acting chief of geriatrics, fingered his backpack uneasily.

"Tough crowd," he muttered to his wife.

Cal Marley, the chief of pathology, nodded. The oversized backpack dwarfed her tiny frame like a cabin cruiser hitched to a Volkswagen Beetle. But her back was unbent; she stood perfectly upright despite the heavy load.

"Good thing Lionel Wallace isn't here," she agreed. "I think we'd have a riot on our hands."

Lionel Wallace, the newly appointed president of Riverside General, was unaccountably absent. So was his vice president. Perhaps they were already at Camp *Success!* Better yet, maybe Wallace had read the weather report and canceled the weekend trip.

Plato Marley sighed wistfully. That was too much to ask.

He turned to his wife. "I guess we shouldn't tell anyone this whole trip was *your* idea."

"*My* idea?" Cal tossed her blond head and glared at her husband. "What are you talking about?"

"Don't you remember?" He spread his hands. "Last December, just before Wallace was appointed. You talked with him at the medical staff Christmas party."

Cal gasped. She remembered now. The president-elect had lamented the poor relations between the various clinical departments at Riverside. He worried over the need for cost-cutting measures. He asked Cal if she had any suggestions for improving teamwork between the teaching programs.

Cal had agreed with him—turf battles were always blazing between Surgery and Internal Medicine, between the medical and nursing staffs, with all sides jockeying for more funding and greater flexibility. Unfortunately, she didn't see any obvious solution. Turf wars were a part of every major hospital, and always would be—especially when budget cuts were looming.

Cal had jokingly suggested packing all the department chairmen up and sending them off to Camp *Success!*, northern Ohio's corporate boot camp. She had just seen an article about it in the *Plain Dealer* on the morning of the Christmas party. Camp *Success!* was the latest fad in business management—sending top executives out into the woods for encounters with nature, in order to build teamwork.

She and Plato had shared a good laugh about it over breakfast that morning, imagining fat accountants and lawyers and executives waddling through the Geauga County forest on scavenger hunts for buried notebook computers and cellular phones.

It had seemed hilarious at the time.

"I was just *kidding*," Cal insisted. "I never thought he'd really—"

"You don't kid around with Lionel Wallace," Plato sighed. "He has utterly no sense of humor."

"I know."

A large black minibus slid up to the hospital entrance with all the quiet dignity of a hearse. Its side panel was emblazoned with the Camp *Success!* motto: BUILDING TEAMWORK — ONE CHALLENGE AT A TIME. Beneath the motto was the camp's logo—a colorful abstract smear that might have been painted by a team of emotionally disturbed orangutans. The driver, whose black nylon jacket also bore the Camp *Success!* logo, jumped from the swing door and strode purposefully into the lobby.

He halted just inside the door, stood at attention, and fixed his gaze on the backpack-laden group. With his jet-black hair, dark sunglasses, and clean-cut good looks, he might have been a Secret Service agent eyeing a particularly suspicious crowd of White House visitors. Finally, his face softened and he stood at ease, feet shoulder-width apart and hands folded behind his back.

"Benjamin Disraeli once said that the secret of success in life is for a man to be ready for his opportunity." He smiled shyly at the floor, shrugging off their gratitude for this great pearl of wisdom. He looked up again. "My name is Claude Eberhardt, and I'll be your guide this weekend. I hope it will be a great opportunity for all of us."

He turned and led his charges outside.

Several chiefs groaned.

"A great opportunity," the surgery chairman echoed. "Opportunity for *what*?"

"For murder," the obstetrician replied with a grin.

"You brought your speculum?" the psychiatrist asked quietly.

"Of course." She patted her backpack. "Never leave home without it."

The guide started loading their backpacks into the luggage compartment of the bus.

The chief of internal medicine handed his pack and sleeping bag over, then turned back to the group and shook his head. "I just don't understand it—Lionel Wallace sending us on this trip."

"Why not?" asked the chief of nursing services. "You know what Wallace is like."

"I know." The internist's eyebrows were heavy and seamlessly joined—like a long woolly bear caterpillar. The caterpillar marched up his tall forehead. "But it's too innovative, too crazy—even for *him*."

"I agree," grumbled the chief of psychiatry, a short, dapper type with enough skin for two faces. The wrinkles deepened. "Lionel Wallace could never have dreamed up this scheme alone. He's as single-minded as a locomotive on a railroad bridge."

"All too true." The chief of surgery nodded sagely. "Someone must have put the idea into Lionel's head."

"I'd like to know who," grumbled the chief of obstetrics and gynecology. Her sharp, perfect teeth glinted in the morning sun as she strode toward the door of the bus. "I'd yank his heart out with a pair of blunt forceps."

Plato glanced down at Cal and winked.

"Don't," she pleaded in a harsh whisper. "Don't even *think* of it. Not a word. Not a syllable."

"Never," he pledged solemnly. "She couldn't *torture* it out of me. Not even with a blunt speculum."

"She won't *need* torture." She sighed, patting his arm fondly. "You're about as secretive as a Dictaphone. All she has to do is push the right button."

"Are you implying that—"

"Shh." Cal led her husband to the rear of the line. Discreetly, wordlessly, they lurked at the fringe of the crowd and handed their backpacks to the driver.

Just then, a plump blue-jeaned figure poked its nose out through the doors like a timid groundhog tasting the weather on a cold winter day. Lionel Wallace's long, sparse mustache twitched and his feeble eyes blinked in the chilly afternoon sunlight. Apparently, the hospital's president had come along for the ride.

He glanced with polite astonishment at the Council of Chiefs gathered on the sidewalk, as though he were meeting a party of trick-or-treaters. His eyes flicked over the obstetrician's shoulder, past the other members of the party, and finally settled on Cal.

"Ah, Dr. Marley!" he said happily. "You must come ride up front with me. After all, this little excursion was really *your* idea."

Cal gasped. Six heads swiveled from the hospital president to the two chiefs lurking at the edge of the crowd.

Before Cal could reply, Plato suddenly nodded and threw his shoulders back with a grin.

"Thanks for remembering me," he told the hospital's CEO. "I'm sure we'll all enjoy this weekend together."

Lionel Wallace glanced from Plato to Cal and back again, blinked five or six times, then nodded slowly. "Yes. Yes, of course, Plato. Quite. I'm sure we will."

Cal followed Plato through the gauntlet of chiefs, feeling six pairs of eyes sear the back of her neck as they stepped into the bus. Behind them, the obstetrician growled softly at Plato, like a Doberman marking a plump, juicy burglar.

Once inside, Cal sat between her husband and the hospital president. The chief of obstetrics followed, sitting directly across the aisle from the trio.

"An absolutely *splendid* idea," Wallace repeated. "Don't you think so, Dr. Oberlin?"

"Yesss," the obstetrician hissed through her teeth.

Her dark eyes flashed at Plato. "Thank you *so* much, Dr. Marley."

He smiled generously. "You're welcome, Dr. Oberlin."

Beside him, Cal clutched his arm, leaned closer, and whispered ever so softly.

"My hero."

"Accept the challenges, so that you may feel the exhilaration of victory."

On television screens scattered around the bus, smartly dressed actors were delivering inspirational quotes. The Council of Chiefs was bouncing along a narrow winding road somewhere in the hills of Geauga County, about thirty miles east of Cleveland. Most of the campers were asleep—lulled into a stupor by the vapid ramblings of the video monitors.

"Here we are." Cal pointed out the window of the bus. Across the street, a wide wooden sign dangled over a rutted dirt road. The sign read "TEAMWORK IS THE GATEWAY TO SUCCESS."

Plato glanced out the window and sighed. "Homey, isn't it?"

"I think this is going to be even worse than we imagined."

Cal didn't bother lowering her voice. Beside her, Lionel Wallace was curled into a fetal ball and drooling into his overcoat—probably dreaming of big insurance contracts and record profits and new hospital wings.

On the television monitors, an actor vaguely resembling George C. Scott frowned earnestly. "Never tell people *how* to do things. Tell them *what* to do and they will surprise you with their ingenuity."

Across the aisle, David Inverness shook his head. The internist had stayed awake and chatted with Plato and Cal during the long ride.

"Patton," he sighed.

Another actor wearing dark glasses and an old fedora filled the screen. "Winning isn't everything, but wanting to win is."

"All these slogans." Cal made a face. "I think I'm going to be sick."

"Barfing isn't everything," Plato intoned, "but wanting to barf is."

"Patton and Lombardi." David Inverness rolled his eyes. "They're quoting army generals and football coaches—to a busload of doctors."

Beside him, Marta Oberlin stirred and stretched. "Role models for the health care profession, I suppose. Decimate the competition." She glanced across the aisle. "Do you find General Patton inspiring, Plato?"

"Very." He winked at Cal. "I read him to my sick patients."

"It's a wonder they don't all die."

"They all do—eventually." He spread his hands. "That's the beauty of geriatrics."

"He's just kidding, Marta." The internist stirred in his seat. David Inverness hated controversy. The caterpillar crawled up his forehead again. "Aren't you, Plato?"

"Of course." He nodded.

"I know all about Plato's sense of humor." The obstetrician chuckled. "He was the hit of the house staff party last weekend. I was surprised that *you* weren't there, Cal."

Plato's jaw dropped. The party. The St. Patrick's Day party. *Oh, my God.*

"I didn't know about it," Cal replied slowly. "I was out of town last week."

She flashed Plato a puzzled look. He shrugged innocently, burrowing his chin into the collar of his coat.

"Too bad," Oberlin turned to the internist. "You remember Plato's little exhibition, David. Kind of a *Chippendale* motif. And in the middle of March, yet."

"Chippendale?" Cal dropped Plato's arm and sat up. *"Plato?"*

"Not at first." The obstetrician chuckled again—an ominous sound that differed little from her Doberman impression. "He had more than a couple of drinks before the tuxedo finally came off. That's what I mean by his sense of humor—it was the *way* he took that tuxedo off that was funny."

"I bet it was." Cal eyed Plato like he was some sort of dangerous alien life form: the Andromeda Strain in human shape.

"It was a—a *swimming* party," he sputtered. "At the health club. I—I had a cold, and I really didn't want to go in, but—"

"But Terri Lynn Jones convinced you," Oberlin noted helpfully.

"Terri Lynn Jones," Cal echoed.

"You've seen her, I'm sure." The obstetrician stared at the ceiling of the bus. "Psychiatry resident. Blond and gorgeous. More curves than the Cuyahoga River. Anyway—"

"Terri Lynn Jones had nothing to do with it," Plato insisted.

"Then maybe it was those two surgery nurses." Oberlin shrugged. "The ones that kept dunking you in the pool."

Plato frowned. "I don't remember any surgery nurses."

"The ones in the string bikinis."

"Oh." He buried his chin further inside his coat, like Beaker on *The Muppet Show*.

"You told me you were *sick* all week—that you didn't go out at all." Cal glared at Plato, dark whirlwinds looming in her brown eyes. "You said you lived like a monk last week."

Marta Oberlin chuckled. "One of *Chaucer's* monks, maybe."

"It was all perfectly innocent." David Inverness squirmed in his seat, obviously uncomfortable. "Really."

The obstetrician shrugged, oblivious to Cal's storm signals. Maybe it was just her sense of humor, which—as Plato recalled from the party—was even more bizarre than his own. Or perhaps she was getting back at him for supposedly planting the Camp *Success!* idea in Wallace's head.

"He had this skimpy green swimsuit on under his tuxedo," Oberlin continued. "And he did this little dance at the side of the pool."

"It was hardly a *dance*." Inverness shook his head. "Plato's shoelaces got tangled, and he hopped around trying to get his shoes off. So we all started teasing him."

"And he started this little striptease." Oberlin giggled— *giggled!* "It was cute."

"Don't listen to Marta." The internist glanced over at Cal. "It was nothing—Plato was a perfect gentleman."

Oberlin shrugged, finally silent. Cal harrumphed. Plato glanced at Inverness and sighed thankfully.

But that was just like David—always the peacemaker. At Council meetings, whenever tempers flared or arguments erupted, Inverness always began soothing, temporizing, compromising. He was allergic to conflict, squirming and wincing at harsh words and angry comments, as if they wounded him personally.

"I wish my ex-husband could have danced like that," Oberlin mused softly. "We'd probably still be married."

Inverness patted her arm and shot her a warning glance.

The residents called him Dr. Congeniality, and they were right. But like any nice guy, Inverness was prone to finish last. He never said no to his patients or his residents. His practice had the highest proportion of uninsured patients in the entire hospital. He haunted the floors day and night, caring for his sick patients personally while backing up his overworked residents. Even after he was appointed chief of staff and medical director, he remained the most personable, most approachable physician in all of Riverside General Hospital, seeming to have time for even the most trivial complaints or problems.

His wife and children had left him years ago.

Cal was still fuming, making those little chuffing noises under her breath like she did when she was angry. Like a well-mannered cat quietly working out a stubborn furball.

Plato's heroic gesture—rescuing Cal by shouldering the blame for the Camp *Success!* idea—was apparently all but forgotten.

"Anyway, I'm sure we all know about Plato's sense of humor," Marta concluded.

"We certainly do," Cal growled. She glanced at the obstetrician. "Maybe you could lend me that blunt speculum of yours."

"Anytime, dear."

Beside her, David Inverness squirmed in his seat.

The bus lurched and careened down the dusty dirt road into Camp *Success!* On the screen, the actors were still delivering their quotes and slogans and words of inspiration.

"Some men see things as they are and say 'Why,' " the television noted smugly. "I dream of things that never were, and say, 'Why not?' "

Across the aisle, David Inverness winced.

"Three bedrooms, ten occupants—and one bath," Cal griped. Standing in the common room of the Henry

Ford Cabin, she shook her head sadly. "I guess we're going to learn teamwork, all right."

The bus had jounced and rattled along the dirt road for nearly half an hour. They had crawled past the John D. Rockefeller Lodge, the Harvey Firestone Trail, and the Cyrus Eaton Challenge Course. Each landmark had been proudly described by their guide as the bus crawled past.

Finally, they drew up at the Henry Ford Trail, a mile-long winding path marked with brass plaques bearing more inspirational slogans and quotes. As the pack-weary hikers slogged up the trail behind their guide, Claude Eberhardt had paused to read each signpost aloud, like a priest reciting the Stations of the Cross.

Just as the campers were threatening to rebel, the guide had led them over one last hill to the Henry Ford Cabin. The sprawling pile of rotting planks and cedar shingles and rough-hewn logs made Plato and Cal's decrepit century-old home seem like the Taj Mahal.

"Rustic" was how Claude Eberhardt had described it. Marta Oberlin had used a less kind word.

"Do you *seriously* expect us to spend a weekend here?" The obstetrician's dark eyes flashed from their guide to Lionel Wallace and back again.

"Perhaps Claude can suggest some more suitable lodgings," Inverness remarked. His voice was calm and soothing, like an animal trainer caged with a lioness.

The Council of Chiefs had formed a half-circle around Wallace and the tour guide. Hemmed in against the crude stone fireplace, the CEO glanced at Eberhardt.

"They do have a point, Claude." During the walk, Wallace had chatted amiably with the guide, pointing to plants and trees and birds and quizzing Eberhardt about them. In deference to his companion's age and rank, Eberhardt had carried the CEO's backpack. The two already seemed like old friends.

Oddly enough, Wallace sometimes had that effect on people. Like the Board of Trustees, for instance.

Unfortunately, mere friendship wasn't going to provide a solution this time. Claude Eberhardt stared at his feet and shrugged. "Uh. Er. The other lodgings—Harvey Firestone Cabin and Rockefeller Lodge—are both full this weekend."

"Then you have no other place for us." Cy Kettering, the chief of psychiatry, unslung his backpack from his small shoulders.

"I'm afraid—"

"You must be aware that these quarters are completely inadequate." Kettering folded his arms and stared at the tour guide. Although he was hardly taller than Cal, the psychiatrist had a marvelously abrupt and confrontational style that put other physicians—and his patients—off guard. He puffed his saddlebag cheeks in disgust. "It's a miracle that this building hasn't collapsed. The floors are moldy with rot. The roof almost certainly leaks. The bedrooms smell like an old flophouse." He shook his head. "I wouldn't let my *dog* sleep here."

"We're not *asking* your dog to sleep here," Lionel Wallace pointed out. "I believe there is a rule against pets, anyway. Isn't there, Claude?"

Plato bit back a laugh. Beside him, Cal's eyes were bulging.

At his left, Marta was whispering to Inverness. "He didn't just say that. Did he?"

Inverness closed his eyes and sighed.

"They're remodeling the buildings one at a time," the guide explained lamely. "They just didn't get to this one yet." He gave a weak smile. "Camp *Success!* used to be a Boy Scout campground."

"Perhaps we should just head back," the chief of surgery suggested gently. "*After* we rest awhile."

Andre Surfraire had barely survived the hike up to the cabin. He had done plenty of hiking in his youth, outrunning Papa Doc and the Tontons Macoutes across the hills of Haiti. But that was several decades and a couple of hundred pounds ago. At fifty-something years of age, and well over three hundred pounds, the surgeon got winded every time he blinked.

He turned to Wallace. "How about it, Lionel?"

The president turned to Godfrey Millburn, his vice president and chief operating officer. Millburn had the dour, sad face of an undertaker, mounted on the body of a half-starved basketball center. He shrugged his bony shoulders under the backpack.

"We paid in advance. Nonrefundable." He glanced around the cabin. "Believe it or not, this outing cost us several thousand dollars."

"We have a dozen trainers on staff," Eberhardt hastily explained. "You'll meet them tomorrow. Between the team-building program and the food, Camp *Success!* spends quite a bit of money on a typical training weekend."

"Must be some great food," Plato muttered.

"If the mice haven't already eaten it," Cal replied grimly.

"Mice?"

She traced a plump rodent shape in the air. "I saw a big fat one in our bedroom."

The vice president leaned closer to Wallace and whispered something about a photo opportunity.

Wallace had seemed tempted to call the weekend off, but he nodded quickly. Turning to Claude Eberhardt, he stared at the guide for several seconds, then smiled. "I think we should give Camp *Success!* a chance. Eh, Claude?"

"Yes, sir." The guide nodded happily. "I'm sure you won't regret it."

"I'm sure he *will* regret it," Marta Oberlin said quietly. She gave her Doberman growl again, then flashed her teeth at Plato. "And you, too, my friend."

On his other side, Cal was glaring at him with silent rage. He recognized that look, the way a weatherman recognizes thunderheads looming on the horizon. At the very least, Cal's glare forecast a long, stormy conversation, with a steady downpour of choice words like "inconsiderate" and "thoughtless" and "dishonest."

Plato shuddered. He was *already* regretting coming here. Sandwiched between a jealous wife and a slightly unbalanced obstetrician, he felt like a mouse in a pit of vipers. It was shaping up to be a dangerous weekend.

But Plato had no idea just how dangerous the weekend would prove to be.

Chapter 2

"Tell us what you're feeling."

Claude Eberhardt's voice was a hushed whisper.

The Council of Chiefs was sprawled in a circle on the floor of the Henry Ford Cabin. Dinner had been a hasty affair, apparently prepared before their arrival and left in the cabin's tiny refrigerator—cold cuts and stale bread and a heaping tray of raw vegetables. The sandwich meat had disappeared all too quickly. Half of the campers had to subsist on rabbit food.

After dinner, Claude had gathered his team together for their first exercise: getting in touch with each other's feelings. He started with the safe bet—Godfrey Millburn, the yes-man—and worked his way around most of the circle. Gradually, the responses had become less cautious, the complaints more vehement.

Most of the room was cloaked in darkness; only a thin pencil of light shone from the door to the kitchen. At Claude's insistence, all of the department chiefs were holding hands.

"Tell us how you really feel," Claude repeated gently.

"I'm feeling *pissed off*," Marta Oberlin finally snapped. Her shrill voice punctured the quiet darkness like a star shell splitting a moonless sky. "We hike fifteen miles through the woods with full packs, starve to death on pine nuts and raw carrots, and sleep in a rat-infested cabin. All so we can learn teamwork by playing spin-the-bottle."

"You feel angry because you think this exercise is pointless." Claude nodded calmly. "That's valid."

"You bet your ass it's valid."

"What's 'spin-the-bottle'?" Lionel Wallace asked.

Nobody answered.

Godfrey Millburn stirred. With his small round head, sticklike arms, and long legs crossed before him, he resembled an enormous praying mantis. "Perhaps it would help if you explained your strategy, Claude. What's on tomorrow's agenda?"

The guide relaxed slightly. "I think you're all going to enjoy the program. We have one or two seminars planned, but most of the focus will be on active participation—a team-building nature walk, relaxation exercises, and of course the group challenge course."

"The group challenge course?" Cal frowned. "What is that, exactly?"

"You'll find out first thing tomorrow morning. I'll wake you all at sunrise, and we'll head out to the course." He gestured to the cabin door. "Somewhere out in those woods is a tightly sealed container full of fresh eggs and sausage and ham and pancake mix."

Andre Surfraire sat up painfully. "Did he say *sausage*?"

"The challenge course is one of our core exercises." Claude smiled proudly. "The concept is quite simple—it's basically a treasure hunt with eight stopping points. Each station has directions to the next site. But the team's tasks are strictly divided—only one person may use the compass, only one person may take measurements, and so on. The exercise is designed to foster interdependence and trust."

"Humph." Cy Kettering's face sagged thoughtfully. "I suppose that explains why you starved us this evening?"

"Sort of like Skinner's rats," Marta observed.

Claude raised his hands helplessly. "That was an accident. We had thought only *six* people were coming, not ten."

"Perhaps we could start looking now," Surfraire mused. "When does the sun rise tomorrow?"

"Six A.M.," the guide replied.

"Nine hours," the surgeon groaned.

"Part of the point of this weekend is teamwork, shared adversity." Wallace turned to the guide. "Isn't that right?"

"Exactly."

The CEO turned to the others and smiled. "We'll all get through this *together*. Perhaps we should adjourn and get some rest."

With a sigh of relief, the Council of Chiefs unclasped their hands and struggled to their feet. Lionel Wallace stepped onto the porch with the guide. Godfrey Millburn—now looking more like a walking cadaver than a praying mantis—shuffled off to one of the bedrooms.

The other chiefs huddled near the fireplace in a sort of guilty silence, like a gang of hopeful mutineers meeting for the first time.

"I think this weekend is working," Marta Oberlin finally said. "That guy is getting me so pissed off, I can't even remember what we used to fight about."

"Funding," Cy Kettering replied. "Privileges. The very real chance that Wallace plans to close one of our programs."

"I've heard that he wants to close *all* the programs." Patricia Kidzek, the soft-spoken chief of pediatrics, shook her head. "Get rid of the residencies one by one, and cut the salaried staff to a bare minimum."

"Ten little Indians standing in a line—" Kettering quoted. *"One went home, and then there were nine."*

"I've heard the same thing," Cal confessed. "That someone on the Board hired Wallace as an axman. They know the training programs are losing money. Wallace is hoping we'll sell each other out in order to keep our own residencies."

Plato nodded. "Until there aren't any residencies left."

"Then why did he bring us on this team-building weekend?" Oberlin asked. "If we stick together as a team, we can probably fight the Board, fight the cuts."

"Maybe he's *hoping* this weekend won't work—that we'll drive each other crazy," Kettering replied. "Maybe he already knew what a lousy place this is." He rolled his eyes. "Scavenger hunts for breakfast. *God!*"

"If he really planned that out," Plato observed, "he's a better administrator than he was a surgeon."

Anne Nussbaum, the chief of nursing services, pursed her lips. "That wouldn't be hard."

Before finding his niche in hospital administration, Lionel Wallace had been a general surgeon—had actually been Riverside General's chief of surgery. His lack of skill was legendary. In private, the old guard still referred to him as Cleveland's second Mad Butcher.

It was the Peter Principle in reverse—Lionel Wallace had been promoted beyond his level of incompetence—he couldn't *kill* as many people outside the operating room.

"Do you really think he's that clever?" Inverness asked. "This is *Lionel Wallace* we're talking about."

"You have a point, there." Cy Kettering shook his head. "Who knows—maybe his blundering manner is just an act."

"That would be *some* act," Marta Oberlin replied. "He's been doing it all his life."

Two hours later, Plato was still wide-awake. He was lying in a top bunk in one of the three bedrooms. Wads of Kleenex were crammed into his ears. His head was sandwiched between a pair of pillows. The pillows were folded between his arms.

It didn't help. Nothing helped.

From the two lower bunks, Andre Surfraire and Lionel Wallace were playing a chain saw duet, a symphony of snores that rattled the walls, shook the rails of Plato's bunk bed, and hammered his eardrums through the Kleenex and the pillows.

Wallace was sleeping in the bunk beneath Plato. Riverside's chief executive officer snored in a breezy tenor, a sharp counterpoint to the deep baritone rumble coming from Surfraire's lower bunk across the room. In the other top bunk, Godfrey Millburn was apparently fast asleep; Plato hadn't seen the vice president twitch or shift positions in the past hour.

Which wasn't really surprising. Millburn had slowly risen through the administrative ranks at Riverside General, bobbing to his present position with the quiet imperturbability of a dead body floating to the surface of a stagnant pond. He was completely unflappable—a tin soldier for the new health care industry, following orders without question, doing his job well, and supporting the chain of command.

Tin soldiers never questioned orders, never complained, and certainly never dreamed of stuffing socks in the mouths of their immediate superiors, as Plato was wishing he could do right now.

Oh, for a pair of Breathe Right nasal strips.

Plato unfolded his pillows, unplugged his ears, and sat up in his bunk. The noise was palpable, rattling his sternum like the bass beat at a Springsteen concert. Slowly, carefully, he rolled up his sleeping bag, descended the rickety ladder, and headed out the door.

Or *tried* to. Just as he reached for the knob, his sleeping bag hooked the flimsy wooden chair beside Lionel Wallace's bed. The CEO had been using the chair as a makeshift nightstand. It clattered to the floor, along with Wallace's water glass, travel clock, and seven-day pill dispenser. In the cacophony of snores, the disaster was barely audible.

Plato righted the chair and surveyed the mess. Luckily the glass was plastic, and nearly empty. The travel clock seemed intact. The pill dispenser was still closed. He picked up the items and replaced them on the chair, then passed through the door.

Out in the dimly lit hallway, Plato paused to gather his scattered thoughts. Behind the closed door, the chain saws still buzzed and rattled like something from a bad horror movie. But Plato remembered that a small moth-eaten sofa was parked out in the common room near the fireplace, at the opposite end of the cabin from the chain saw duet. The tiny sofa was calling to Plato.

Unfortunately, it had called to Cal as well. She was bundled up in her sleeping bag, head propped against one arm of the sofa, feet pressed against the opposite end. Her blond hair shone like spun gold in the flickering firelight. Her soft brown eyes were closed to slits, following Plato's moves with a narrowed gaze.

He smiled nervously—the defendant approaching the bench.

"Hi."

"Go away." She shut her eyes, tight.

Not exactly a promising start. Plato drifted closer, dragging his sleeping bag behind him like Linus's blanket. "Couldn't sleep, huh?"

"Nope."

"Me neither." He smiled again. "Wallace and Surfraire ought to be certified as occupational hazards. I
should report them to OSHA—my ears are still ringing."

"Poor you." Her words were as warm and tender as a
pair of ice cubes. "At least your bed isn't sopping wet.
There's a leak right over my bunk."

In the relative silence of the common room, Plato realized that it was indeed raining outside. Heavily, judging by the drumming overhead. Like the rinse cycle in
a car wash. A few stray drops were even blowing down
the chimney, hissing to steam when they reached the
red-hot coals at journey's end.

Plato moved to sit at the opposite end of the sofa. Cal
squirmed away, curling into a nervous hedgehog ball.

He patted her calf through the sleeping bag. Eyes
still closed, she cringed like a reluctant missionary being touched by a leper.

"Still mad about that party?"

"Your deductive powers are astounding, Plato." She
made that chuffing sound again. "How do you do it?
Telepathy?"

"Cally, I—"

"No, it *can't* be telepathy." The ice machine was going strong now. "If you could read my mind, you
wouldn't be here. You'd be up at Mentor Headlands,
about to jump into Lake Erie. With my blessings."

"Cally, I—"

"You and your two nurse friends. The ones in the
string bikinis. You all could jump in together."

"Come on, Cal. They dunked me, once." Plato
sighed, shaking his head. "There were fifty people in
that pool, and I think they dunked everyone. Including
Lionel Wallace."

"Lionel Wallace?" Her eyes finally opened. She
stared at him in surprise. "They dunked the CEO of the
hospital?"

"I don't think they knew who he was." He shrugged. "Anyway, they had a little too much to drink."

"I heard they weren't the only ones," Cal noted dryly. But she uncurled, just a little. "What did he do?"

"He laughed, just like everyone else." Plato waved a hand. "Didn't mind it a bit—I think he kind of liked it."

Her gaze narrowed. "I *bet* he did."

"At least until his toupee came off."

"Toupee?" Cal sat up, allowed one foot to touch Plato's hip. "I didn't know Wallace had one."

"Neither did most of us, I guess." He shrugged. "That's probably why he was parked in the shallow end. Keeping his rug dry—until the nurses dunked him."

One corner of her mouth turned up, ever so slightly. "What happened? Was he mad?"

"He came up laughing, didn't even know he'd lost it." Plato grinned at the memory. "Of course, *we* all did. He went underwater with a full head of hair, and he came up bald as a pumpkin."

Cal giggled.

"We all tried to act natural—nobody wanted to laugh at the hospital CEO. I guess we were hoping he'd just stick it back on and we'd all pretend nothing had happened." Plato stared at the fire. It was dying down a little. "Except he *couldn't* stick it back on."

"He couldn't? Why not?"

"Well, it was already stuck somewhere else. We didn't realize it until one of the nurses screamed."

Cal's eyes widened. "Oh, no."

"Oh, yes. It was stuck to her—well, stuck to her, umm, *swimsuit*. The top part." Plato stroked his beard. "The poor girl spotted it and almost fainted. I don't blame her. The thing looked like some kind of bizarre sea creature, or maybe a hairy gray jellyfish."

"Pah-*hah*!" Cal's laugh was like a shotgun blast. She slapped her knee and held her stomach. "Oh-ho-ho!"

"So, naturally, the nurse started screaming. Then the other one screamed. Then they both screamed together. Then one of them plucked it off and flipped it into the pool drain."

"The pool drain? Tee-hee-*hee*!" Tears glistened on Cal's cheeks. "Oh, no. Poor Dr. Wallace. Did he have to fetch it out?"

"He was already long gone—slipped out like an eel when nobody was looking. And the two nurses weren't far behind."

"Pah-*hah*! I bet they weren't." Her laughter faded to a light chortle, then to a giggle. Like a thunderstorm rolling away to the east. She rested both her feet on Plato's lap. "I wish I had been there."

"I wish you had, too," he replied honestly. He kneaded her calves in that spot she liked, just above the Achilles tendon. She stretched and sighed languidly.

"Still mad?" he asked again.

"I wasn't *mad*," Cal replied.

Plato raised a skeptical eyebrow. She sure had *sounded* mad. Her suggestion about Lake Erie didn't seem like the advice of a devoted, affectionate spouse.

"I was hurt. Surprised. Disappointed." She shrugged, her small shoulders shifting beneath the sleeping bag. "Why didn't you just tell me?"

Good question. Why *hadn't* he just told her?

"I wasn't going to go at all," he began. "I had that cold, remember. But Nathan Simmons kind of talked me into it." How lame it all sounded. Like he was telling his father why he had come home late from the senior prom. "After that, I sort of forgot about it."

Forgot wasn't the word. The hangover he'd suffered the next day made Plato wish the whole thing had never happened, that Nathan hadn't talked him into it, that the deadly medley of beer and wine and scotch he'd drunk at the party could have been purged from his system, that his head would stop throbbing and shrink to something smaller than the Goodyear blimp.

"You're *always* forgetting about things." Cal shook her head. *"Men!* What if you'd gotten into an accident on your way home?"

It never would have happened. Nathan Simmons had driven to the party. He was their family doctor and an old friend of Plato's. Dr. Caution. He drove an ancient Mercedes Benz, stayed off the freeways, and never drove faster than thirty miles per hour. Riding with Nathan was like riding in the pace car during the Indianapolis 500.

"What if something had happened to you?" Cal repeated.

"Like your knowing I was at that party would have made a difference." Plato rolled his eyes. "Were you going to fly back from New Orleans that night, just to make sure I got home safely?"

She shrugged.

"Besides—what about last January, when I was away at that family practice conference?"

"What about it?" She frowned. "I was home the whole time. At home or at work."

"That's not what Alice Devon said."

"Alice Devon?"

"She said you two went down to the Flats one night. Played pool at Jillian's." Plato waggled his eyebrows meaningfully. "Hustled a couple of guys, she told me."

"Her husband and her brother-in-law." Cal rolled her eyes. "Big deal."

"Why didn't you *tell* me?" Plato asked. "What if you'd gotten into an accident?" He sniffed loudly. *"Women!"*

Cal sighed, scooted a little closer. "Maybe we should put all this behind us."

"Maybe so." He leaned over. "Got any room under that sleeping bag?"

"Plenty."

An hour later, Plato woke up again. At least, *most* of him woke up. His left arm was completely asleep, apparently amputated at the shoulder by the pressure of Cal's head on his brachial artery. He struggled to sit up, to slide out from beneath his now-comatose wife.

"Mmffszvble," said Cal. She opened her eyes, blinked up at him, and fell asleep again. "Wazimah."

"Exactly," Plato agreed. He winced as blood rushed back into the pinched artery, shooting needles of pain up his arm. He leaned over, pulled Cal's sleeping bag up to her shoulders, and gently kissed her good night. She shrugged her shoulders up to her neck and nuzzled her pillow contentedly.

The fire was almost out. Plato tossed two more logs on and watched the hungry flames lapping at the new wood. Overhead, the rain had subsided to a steady drumroll. Hail, probably—the weather report had called for an overnight freeze.

He headed back toward his room, hoping that Wallace and Surfraire might have finished their duet. Turning the corner into the hallway, Plato caught sight of someone leaving the bedroom. The figure turned right and headed into the bathroom at the end of the darkened hall. He didn't turn the light on until the bathroom door was closed behind him.

Too short for Godfrey Millburn, and not nearly wide enough to be Surfraire. Must have been Lionel Wallace. Plato nodded. Before starting his chain saw last night, the hospital president had complained about his prostate trouble, warning his roommates that he would be up frequently during the night.

Surfraire had upped the ante, complaining about his digestion, his bowels, and his kidneys. Wallace had countered with a short speech on the state of his chronic bronchitis. Millburn had even chimed in, grumbling about the poor circulation in his feet.

Plato had gone to summer camp once, back in sixth grade. He and the other boys had stayed up half the night chatting about girls and baseball and girls and the camp counselor and girls and school and girls.

That conversation had been far more interesting.

Inside the bedroom, the symphony was going stronger than ever. Plato edged around Wallace's chair and climbed into bed. Nothing had changed. Across the room, Godfrey Millburn was lying in precisely the same position—flat on his back, legs stretched out straight, hands crossed neatly on his chest. Like a mummy patiently waiting for his sarcophagus.

From the bunk beneath Millburn, Andre Surfraire's bass was rumbling away. And Lionel Wallace's rich tenor was still carrying the melody.

Which brought up one simple question—a question that would haunt Plato for a long time to come.

If Lionel Wallace was snoring in his bunk, who had left the room just moments ago?

Chapter 3

" 'Travel thirty paces east-southeast,' " Marta Oberlin intoned. " 'Find the flat rock. Stand on it. Face south and see the oak tree. Count the number of paces to the oak tree. Travel the same number of paces past the oak tree, in the same direction. Dig down six inches to find the next clue.' " She shook her head. "God, this is *complicated.* Did anyone understand that?"

Most of the party shook their heads. The Council of Chiefs was shivering at the edge of an open field, midway through Camp *Success!*'s world-famous Challenge Course. Overnight, the rain had turned to sleet, and the sleet had frozen on the trees and the grass. The entire world was sealed up inside a thick layer of ice. The sun, just touching the tops of the trees, shot diamond sparkles through the forest and the field.

The chiefs were cold and wet and hungry. Claude Eberhardt had woken them at dawn with the bounding enthusiasm of a cocker spaniel, led them down to the challenge course, and then disappeared. He had to escort another party to the John D. Rockefeller Lodge, for a seminar on leadership tactics. He'd be back in an hour or so to check on his team's progress.

"We're *never* going to find our breakfast," Surfraire moaned sadly. "We'll be lucky if we don't miss *lunch,* besides."

"Let's just break it up into steps," Cal suggested.

In Camp *Success!* parlance, Cal had been appointed *Facilitator* of this particular treasure hunt. Claude had randomly assigned a different role to each of the chiefs. Marta Oberlin was the *Interpreter*—the only person actually allowed to read the clues. Plato was the *Pathfinder*—the keeper of the compass, who was to read the headings and point Surfraire—the *Calibrator*—in the right direction. The portly Calibrator was to waddle off the paces for each clue.

Other members of the party had similarly inane titles and different roles—digging for the clues, analyzing them, and so forth. Each role theoretically translated into a component of the Camp *Success!* team-building model—symbolizing the various identities which were present and essential in a productive, collaborative workplace.

Claude Eberhardt had explained the Camp *Success!* theory in painful detail, emphasizing the strict division of labor required for this morning's exercise. Cal and the others had tried not to laugh.

Once the guide left, his team had unanimously voted to ignore his instructions. Even Lionel Wallace hadn't objected. The Council of Chiefs would find breakfast as quickly as they could.

Which meant, for one thing, handing the compass over to Godfrey Millburn. The vice president was an avid camper and outdoorsman, and the only member of the party who could read a compass. Anne Nussbaum, the chief of nursing services, was of roughly average height and didn't waddle, so she would pace off the distances.

The rest of the party would read the directions and haggle over them together. David Inverness, of course, would mediate any disputes.

In the first half hour, they had navigated four of the

course's eight steps. But the clues were getting much harder.

Godfrey Millburn stood at the spot where they had found clue number four, and held the compass flat in the palm of his glove. Cal watched as the administrator waited for the needle to steady, then aligned the plastic arrow marked DIRECTION OF TRAVEL with the spot on the compass between east and southeast. Almost directly into the rising sun.

Plato nudged Cal and grinned. "Going to be a Girl Scout when you grow up?"

She smiled. "The Brownies were tough enough for me."

"Here, Ms. Nussbaum." Millburn looked up and pointed a long, spindly arm east-southeast. He turned to the nursing chief and made a somber gesture, like a funeral director ushering mourners. "Do you see the white boulder—across the field? Head straight for that, but stop at exactly thirty paces."

"Got it." She nodded firmly, her thin lips pressed together until they almost disappeared. "Thirty paces."

She cut across the edge of the field in perfectly measured steps, tracing a ruler-straight line toward the boulder. Halfway there, she stopped.

"Thirty paces!" Nussbaum sang out. She looked straight down, lifted one boot, and waved her arms. "Here it is!"

Cal nodded to herself. It was just what she expected from Annie Nussbaum. Riverside's division of nursing services had been a shambles before Annie took charge last year. Most people assume that the quality of a hospital depends on its physicians, but insiders know that competent nursing care is probably even more important. During a given hospitalization, nine-tenths of a patient's care is given by nurses—delivery of medications and intravenous fluids, performance of minor procedures, and the monitoring of a patient's condition. All are vital to a patient's survival.

Proper nursing care increases the patient's satisfaction and willingness to return to the same hospital next time—not to mention their likelihood of leaving the hospital vertically. Poor nursing care can be disastrous.

Needless to say, before Anne Nussbaum had taken charge, too many disasters had occurred at Riverside General, too many bodies had wound up in Cal's autopsy lab before their time. But the chief of nursing services had shaken up the fossilized nursing administration, forced several early retirements, and transformed the entire hospital's approach to patient care. She'd done twenty years of clinical work before getting her doctorate in nursing, and she had navigated the choppy administrative waters of Riverside General just as smoothly as she was navigating the challenge course at Camp *Success!*

"Great job, Annie!" Cy Kettering hurried up and patted her shoulder fondly.

"Very well done," Lionel Wallace agreed in a hoarse voice. The chief executive officer was the last to join the group, walking even more slowly than Surfraire. Wallace looked uncomfortable, twitching and shrugging inside his parka as though the coat were three sizes too small. Squinting up at Annie, his eyes were more bleary than ever. Riverside's president apparently hadn't slept well. He looked like he was ready to cry.

Andre Surfraire didn't. The surgeon beamed at Annie. "Perhaps we will have breakfast soon after all!"

" 'Face south and see the oak tree,' " Marta Oberlin read again. She faced roughly south. "That must be it. That tree there."

Godfrey Millburn shook his head sadly. "No, Dr. Oberlin. That's a willow. Off to the left—that's the oak they're talking about."

Annie Nussbaum was already counting off the paces. "Twenty-three!" she sang out when she reached the tree. The chief of nursing services led the rest of the group in a perfect line past the oak and into the woods, another twenty-three paces. She stopped.

Millburn stood in front of Annie and took a compass reading, then nodded his grudging approval. "Precisely. The oak is dead north."

"Let's dig." Patty Kidzek advanced with the folding camp shovel that the guide had left them. Claude had appointed her the group's *Excavator*, and Patty seemed to enjoy the job. The pediatrician had dug up the other four clues as well, taking a strange pleasure in sifting through the dirt and uncovering the clues.

She knelt on the icy forest floor, pushing leaves and twigs aside to clear the area where Annie had stood. Kidzek unfolded the little shovel and dug slowly and patiently, like a sea turtle burrowing a hole in the sand.

Lionel Wallace knelt beside her, scooping the ice and mud away and scrabbling with bare hands for some hint of the plastic tackle box that was probably buried somewhere nearby.

Patty's shovel smacked something hard. She smiled up at the CEO.

"I think that's it, Dr. Wallace."

The hospital president nodded. He scratched at the damp earth and uncovered a handle, then a box. Hot pink this time, with a blue base. He pulled it up and set it on the rim of the small hole, then started coughing.

More like *hacking,* really—like the life-wrenching gasps of a tuberculosis victim, where you're sure that a lung is going to come up sooner or later and it's only a question of when. Wallace crouched on his hands and knees, barking and choking and wheezing.

Alarmed, Patty Kidzek slapped his back between the shoulder blades. "Dr. Wallace? Are you all right?"

Wallace raised one hand. His voice was a wheezy rasp. "I'm okay. Just got a cold, I think."

Marta Oberlin lifted the box and opened it. As usual, this one contained another inspiring quote—something that would lend meaning to their small lives and make them more productive team players at Riverside General.

Right.

But even Marta Oberlin seemed to enjoy this quote. A smile played at the corners of her mouth. "This is a good one—it's from Mark Twain: 'Let us be thankful for the fools. But for them the rest of us could not succeed.' Could be the motto for Camp *Success!*"

Andre Surfraire glanced over her shoulder. "What about the next clue? What does it say?"

"Let's see," Marta began. " 'First, find the only maple tree within twenty paces of this spot.' "

"Does anyone know what a maple tree looks like?" Surfraire asked anxiously.

"Dr. Wallace?" Patty Kidzek, pediatrician and treasure-hound, was still crouching beside Riverside's CEO. "Sure you're okay?"

Lionel Wallace shook his head. He was still down on his hands and knees, head slumped between his shoulders. He seemed to be peering into the empty hole, as though another clue, another nugget of corporate wisdom, was buried there. His shoulders were shrugging—odd little hiccuplike twitches inside his parka.

Cal knelt beside him, too. "Dr. Wallace?"

He slowly turned to face Cal. Inside the fur-lined hood of his parka, the hospital president was a changed man. His face had undergone a sort of Dr. Wallace-Mr. Hyde transformation.

His nose and lips seemed to have puffed to twice their normal size. His eyes were red and watery. His face was one giant hive—angry and bloated and red, with only a few scattered patches of normal pale skin.

Even his *eyebrows* were swollen—a single low shelf that shadowed his bleary eyes. A thin trickle of drool dangled from his lower lip.

"Oh, my God." Cal gasped. *Anaphylaxis.*

As if to confirm her diagnosis, the hospital president tried to breathe again. His shoulders heaved as he bit the air. A thin, high-pitched whistle sounded—like a vacuum cleaner sucking air through a cocktail straw.

He closed his eyes, tottered on his hands and knees like a stricken bull moose, and keeled over onto his side.

"Is he hurt?" somebody asked.

"It's anaphylaxis," Cal announced. She jumped to her feet. "We need some epinephrine, *fast.*"

David Inverness crouched beside the hospital president and nodded quickly. "Anaphylaxis, all right. He's stopped breathing. Unconscious."

Plato stepped over Wallace, laid the body out flat, and began the routine. Airway-breathing-circulation. He checked the mouth with his finger, just to make sure the airway wasn't blocked, then pinched Wallace's nose shut, extended the neck, and began mouth-to-mouth breathing.

"He's tight," Plato said between breaths. "*Really* tight."

Anaphylaxis. Allergy gone mad. Some signal—like a bee sting, a bug bite, a food or a medication—triggered a massive, toxic allergic reaction. Hives, hoarseness, and wheezing were the milder symptoms. With full-blown anaphylaxis, the breathing tubes could completely shut down. The body suffocated itself.

Patty Kidzek was holding the president's wrist. "He's still got a pulse. A thready one."

"I've got some epi," Inverness said. "In my medical kit, up at the cabin. I'll try to—"

"*I'll* go," Cal said quickly. "Where?"

"In my backpack," the internist replied, seeing her

logic. He was at least fifteen years older than Cal. "Under my bed—the one on the right."

She was already gone, leaping through the woods toward the road. Behind her, Patty Kidzek's frantic voice echoed through the trees.

"I've lost the pulse. Better start compressions." A pause. "Ready? One-two-three-four-five-*breathe*! One-two-three-four-five-*breathe*!"

Cal timed her strides with the CPR count. She reached the road in under a minute, then jogged along it toward the Henry Ford Trail. The trailhead was almost a mile up the road. The Henry Ford Trail itself was a mile long. Even at her best running speed on the flat, Cal couldn't do a mile in under six minutes. That meant she was at least twenty-four minutes away from bringing the epinephrine back to the team. Probably a good bit more, since the trail was slippery and had plenty of hills and twists and turns.

Too long. Epinephrine was a potent antidote for anaphylaxis. But it couldn't bring dead hospital presidents back to life.

Maybe there was another chance. Cal cudgeled her brains for some idea, some clue. Another way to—

That was it! She remembered walking the Henry Ford Trail yesterday, and again this morning. Both times, Cal had been struck by how the trail seemed to loop and double back on itself. It seemed incredible that someone could have built a cabin—even a shabby, dilapidated cabin—a full mile away from any access road.

She spied her answer just in time. Over to the left, a narrow gap was visible in the wall of trees. With a little imagination, Cal could see a pair of ruts leading from the shoulder of the dirt road away through the grass.

If she was wrong—if the pathway led nowhere, or doubled back toward the road—Wallace would certainly die. If she was right, he might have a chance.

Cal jogged onto the path without a moment's hesitation. It was Wallace's only hope. She paced herself, following the faint trail through the trees, climbing a small rise, rounding a turn and climbing even higher, wondering if she'd made a mistake, feeling certain of it when the trail seemed to disappear, then looking up and seeing an impossibly beautiful sight—the slumping, ramshackle roofline of Henry Ford Cabin.

The path led around to the back of the building. The cabin was only about four hundred yards from the main roadway. Cal had saved at least twenty minutes with the shortcut.

She trotted around to the front porch, dove through the door, and hurried back to Inverness's bedroom. Tucked in a front zipper pocket was the medical kit—a big, old-fashioned leather monstrosity with "D.I." emblazoned on the buckle in gold letters.

Cal yanked the kit free and dashed out of the cabin. If anything, she made it back to the group in even less time. Plato was now giving the compressions, and Patty Kidzek was straining to blow air into Wallace's lungs.

But it didn't seem to be helping. The hospital president's face was dusky blue. His arms and legs were splayed and limp. Surfraire had already carved a tracheostomy in the center of Wallace's neck with a Swiss Army knife, pinching the hole shut with his fingers as Patty delivered the breaths. The neck wound was hardly bleeding at all.

Inverness snatched the bag from Cal as she trotted into the little clearing. His glance—a mixture of admiration and futility—said it all. Cal had tried her best, but the best wasn't anywhere near good enough.

Still, he grabbed a syringe and a long needle and an ampoule of epinephrine solution.

Marta Oberlin shook her head. "You're not going to find a vein for that, David."

He shrugged. "I'll just go into the heart—what the hell."

The obstetrician nodded quickly and tore Wallace's shirt open. While Plato continued his chest compressions, Inverness walked his fingers down the rib cage, found just the right spot, and plunged the long needle in.

"Hold the compressions."

He poked around, pulling back on the plunger until a sudden purple backwash announced that he had entered the heart itself. He pressed the plunger down, injecting a full milliliter of epinephrine solution. The drug would help Wallace's anaphylaxis, and it was also one of the first drugs of choice for cardiac arrest.

Provided Wallace was still alive.

Inverness pulled the needle out. "All right—go ahead."

The compressions and breaths resumed, a steady, rhythmic funeral march for hospital president Lionel Wallace.

Cy Kettering had snipped the end off of another syringe. He handed the plastic cylinder to Surfraire. "Here's your tracheostomy tube."

"Thanks." The surgeon nodded and slipped the tube into Wallace's neck. He clamped his fingers around the tube and breathed into it awkwardly.

"Here." Marta Oberlin knelt across from Surfraire. "You hold the tube. I'll give the breaths."

Patty Kidzek sat back from the body, hugging her knees to her chest and staring at the hospital president with dull disbelief. Cal slumped down beside her. She had finally caught her breath, but there was nothing for her to do.

Annie Nussbaum gently pushed Plato aside and continued the compressions. He nodded. It was the language of CPR—you might not realize you're tiring, but others can see it. Your compressions are shallower, or too deep, or your elbows are bent, or your back is twisted, and you aren't pumping efficiently. So someone helps you out, gives you a break.

"Millburn ran to get help," Patty explained.

Cal nodded. As the only nonmedical member of the team, it was a sensible job for him. Besides, with those long legs, Millburn could probably move pretty fast when he wanted to.

They kept it up for another twenty minutes, taking turns doing compressions or breathing into the tube or pausing every so often to check for the return of a pulse. But it had become a hopeless exercise long ago—probably even before Cal returned with the medical kit. They were all going through the motions, and they all knew it. But no one was willing to stop.

Even the paramedics kept up the compressions and the breaths, substituting an endotracheal tube and ambu bag for the clumsy syringe barrel. They kept it up all the way to the ambulance, all the way down the dusty dirt road, all the way to the hospital.

Until 9:45 that morning, when the emergency room physician at Geauga General Hospital finally pronounced Lionel Wallace dead.

Chapter 4

"This is a public relations nightmare."

Godfrey Millburn was standing near the back of the church, shaking his head and frowning at the casket before the altar.

"A total disaster," the administrative drone beside him echoed.

Plato and Cal Marley were standing just one row behind the two administrators, in the very last pew at St. John's Cathedral in Cleveland. The old church was filled to overflowing with mourners and hospital staff and reporters, all suffering through the endless funeral for Lionel Wallace.

The dramatic death of Riverside's chief executive officer had made the front pages of all the local papers and was a continuing saga on the television news. Even now, two days after it happened, reporters had flocked to the cathedral for more pictures and footage and interviews of Godfrey Millburn, David Inverness, and the other chiefs who had been present at Wallace's death. Even Plato and Cal had been accosted on the church steps by a reporter for Fox TV.

Not that Lionel Wallace's death was viewed as a particular tragedy by the city of Cleveland. But the *circumstances* of his demise had fascinated reporters and the public alike.

Standing before the ornately carved altar and crucifix, the priest nodded his head and circled the casket, waving a glittering gold censer. Wallace's remains disappeared in a cloud of incense. A dozen altar boys in cassocks and surplices rubbed their eyes and quaked with suppressed coughs.

"Though I walk in the valley of darkness," the priest intoned, "I fear no evil . . ."

"It's so goddamned embarrassing," Millburn griped. "Seven top doctors and the chief of nursing, and the guy *still* croaks."

Plato exchanged glances with Cal. They had heard it all before—on the news, in the papers. The *Cleveland Post* implied that the emergency had been mishandled, and tried to draw a connection between Wallace's death and the hospital's recent financial troubles. On a local television station, a doctor from the Cleveland Clinic claimed that any competent intern could have handled Wallace's anaphylactic reaction without breaking a sweat. And the *Plain Dealer* had run an op-ed piece criticizing Riverside for an alleged cover-up of the autopsy findings.

"Riverside General is the laughingstock of Cleveland," the acting CEO continued. "We're lucky we're still open at all."

The yes-man nodded sympathetically.

"You know what they asked me out there? They asked whether I would send my family to Riverside, whether I'd trust those doctors with my kid."

"What did you say?" the drone asked.

"What *could* I say?" Millburn replied. "I told them I *sent* my kid to Riverside."

"I didn't know you had a kid."

Millburn shrugged, muttering something in an undertone. Plato leaned closer, but he still didn't catch the remark.

Cal poked his arm and hissed, *"Plato!"*

"What?" He straightened up and frowned at his wife, a picture of wounded innocence. "What's wrong?"

"Stop eavesdropping," she scolded. "Pay attention to the service."

"I *can't* pay attention," he complained. "Millburn's talking too loud."

It was true. Sitting at the back of the church, several rows away from the rest of the crowd, the hospital's acting CEO seemed to think he was alone with his assistant. Apparently, he hadn't seen Plato and Cal slide in late behind him.

"Hummph." Cal folded her arms, then relented. Leaning closer to Plato, she whispered, "I didn't know Millburn had a kid."

"Neither did I," Plato confessed. "Kind of frightening, isn't it?"

He tried to picture Godfrey Millburn's offspring—a miniature undertaker, or a child extra from *Night of the Living Dead*.

"I didn't even know he was *married*." She giggled. "Now, *that's* a scary thought."

At the front of the church, the priest was spreading a brightly colored pall over the casket. He sprinkled holy water over the casket and pall, then gestured for the assembly to rise.

"Wallace was *such* an idiot," Millburn griped. "The hospital's finances are a mess. He couldn't even *die* without screwing things up."

The drone sighed and shook his head sympathetically.

Up at the lectern, the priest was reading from the New Testament. He finally raised his head and smiled sadly.

"In times of sorrow, the gathering of friends and family and the sharing of memories can help ease our pain." He extended a hand toward the mourners. "And so the family has asked Dr. Wallace's good friend, Godfrey Millburn, to deliver the eulogy."

The yes-man handed Millburn a folded sheet of paper. "Judy Randolph in PR finished it this morning."

Millburn took the paper and rose to his feet. "Did you check it?"

"Yeah." The administrator nodded. "She laid it on really thick."

"Good." Millburn gave a skeletal smile. "Maybe we can turn this thing around."

The acting CEO smoothed his jacket, took a deep breath, and molded his narrow face into the perfect blend of sadness and pain. His footsteps echoed in the sudden silence of the church. An altar boy coughed, and a mother shushed a little girl who was singing the Barney song. Millburn slowly ascended the altar like a reluctant chancellor announcing the death of his king. He moved to the podium and cleared his throat.

"My dear friend Lionel Wallace devoted his life to caring for others." Millburn took a deep, shaky breath and closed his eyes, seeming to compose himself with great effort. "Like all of us at Riverside General Hospital, Lionel never failed to put his patients first. . . ."

"I can't believe he's saying this," Plato grumbled.

"The poor man's *dead*," Cal replied. "Leave him alone."

"I'm not talking about Wallace—I'm talking about *Millburn*. He's turning this into an infomercial for Riverside General."

Cal listened, then nodded. The acting CEO was telling the story of Wallace's career, from the time he had joined the hospital staff, his years as chief of surgery, his great strides as an administrator and then as chief executive officer. With every sentence, he managed to make a pitch for the hospital itself, as though Lionel Wallace and Riverside were one and the same.

"You're right," Cal agreed. She gestured to the reporters in the assembly. "Free advertising."

In the pew ahead of them, Millburn's assistant was listening to the eulogy with pursed lips and a rapturous gaze. After each statement, he nodded his head firmly, tapping his fist into an open palm. He looked like an eager convert at a revival meeting.

"Caring, competence, and commitment," Millburn continued. "That was Lionel Wallace's legacy to Riverside General." He bowed his head humbly. "And that is Riverside General's legacy to our community."

Plato and Cal both shook their heads and sighed.

Ahead of them, the drone smacked his hand and leaned back, satisfied. *"Yesss!"*

"This isn't the way back to Cleveland," Plato said later.

"I know."

Cal was driving their used Acura back from the burial ceremony at All Souls Cemetery. She was having fun zipping along the back roads of Geauga County, diving through the swoops and turns like a driver in a car commercial. The Acura was their reward, celebrating their liberation from the first round of college loans, and Plato's promotion to chief of his division. It wasn't much extra money, but it covered the car payments.

Right now, Plato was missing their other car, an old Corisca, or better yet, the silver Chevette they once had. Cal's passion for speed was finally being satisfied with the zippy sports car, but Plato had left his stomach somewhere back in Chardon, on a sudden rise that had bounced his head against the ceiling. Now, she had taken a wrong turn and didn't seem to care.

Plato swallowed heavily and frowned at the map in his lap. "It says here that we should have taken I-90 back to Cleveland."

"We're not going back to Cleveland," she said.

"Oh." He grimaced as the Acura plunged down another steep hill and careened around another sharp curve, startling a flock of Canadian geese into frantic flight. "Do you mind telling me where we *are* going? Or is this another test drive?"

Cal had put over fifty miles on the little red Acura, test-driving it all over Cleveland with their green-faced car dealer a virtual hostage in the backseat. Finally, the salesman had begged the Marleys to name their price, *any* price, as long as they let him out.

They had gotten a very good deal.

"I'm driving to Godfrey Millburn's house, silly." She clicked her tongue impatiently. "I told you this morning—remember?"

"Oh." Plato sighed. Cal had indeed mentioned it at breakfast; Millburn had invited the chiefs to a gathering at his house after Wallace's burial at All Souls. It would be the first time the chiefs all met since the CEO's death—a chance to talk about what had happened last Saturday. And what would happen next.

"How long until we get there?" he asked hopefully.

"A couple more miles—he lives just inside Kirtland." She patted his arm and smiled. "But isn't this a *wonderful* ride?"

"Fantastic." Plato glanced out the window at the hills, the trees just beginning to bud, the puffy clouds in the sky, the winding strip of black asphalt. It *would* be a lovely drive, at anything under seventy miles an hour. He swallowed down another tide of nausea. "How about if I drive home?"

"Sure." Cal shrugged. "You can check the transmission for me—it's a little slow kicking into overdrive." She stomped on the accelerator, frowning as the car lurched over another dimple in the road. "There—did you hear that funny noise?"

"That was my stomach," Plato replied carefully. "It finally caught up with us."

She frowned at him, then turned back to the road, slowing down again and making a turn. "Here we are, I think."

"Thank God."

The Millburn house wasn't at all what Plato had expected. He'd heard that the acting CEO lived out in the country, but he had imagined the place as a sort of Bates Motel—a crumbling Victorian mansion perched on a hill, waiting to trap unsuspecting travelers.

But Millburn's house was surprisingly modern—a newer brick colonial just off Route 6, surrounded by white picket fences and a spreading lawn, rolling fields and meadows, a horse pasture and a quaint red barn. Even the mailbox was cute, a fat little sheep with a door for its mouth and a flag for a tail.

"This is the place." Cal gestured up the neat gravel driveway to where David Inverness and Marta Oberlin were getting out of their cars. Cal parked beside them, and a black Porsche 911 turned into the driveway just as they emerged from their car.

Plato whistled as the sleek sports car hummed up the driveway and eased to a stop with no more noise than a well-tuned kazoo.

"Nice wheels," he told Surfraire as the plump surgeon levered himself out of the car.

"I've had this little lady for years—she's still my favorite." He grinned. "Just don't tell my wife."

Surfraire guffawed at his little joke, nudging Plato with his elbow. He looked around, seeming to notice the farm and house for the first time.

"Quite a surprise, yes? Our new CEO spends his time with the cows and pigs."

"And horses." Godfrey Millburn had materialized

among them like a phantom. "I have a few racing horses, Andre—though I don't keep them *here*."

"Racing." Surfraire nodded his enormous head. He patted his car lovingly. "Now, *that* is a sport I understand."

Millburn turned to the others and explained. "Our chief of surgery races on the amateur circuit in his spare time."

"One or two races a year." Surfraire shrugged. "I don't *have* much spare time."

"That's just as well," Millburn observed. "You've been in a couple of accidents already."

"Not my fault," the surgeon grumbled into his shirt.

"I'm sure they weren't," Inverness said quickly.

Millburn shrugged and gestured back to his house. "Let's go inside; I have some refreshments laid out for you."

The other chiefs were already assembled in Millburn's dining room, clustered around a table of hors d'oeuvres like honeybees in a clover patch. Everyone was famished—the funeral had started at ten, and the last handful of dirt wasn't tossed onto Wallace's coffin until almost two o'clock.

"Welcome to my home," the acting CEO said. "Please, make yourselves comfortable."

The house was surprisingly cozy and quaint, just the opposite of what Plato had expected of Millburn. The dining and living rooms were packed with the familiar icons of country living—embroidery hanging on the walls, a patterned quilt tossed carelessly over the deep sofa, stone geese guarding the fireplace, and knotty pine furniture everywhere. A fan hung from the cathedral ceiling in the living room, and a warm log fire crackled in the hearth. An impressive rack of antlers hung from the chimney, and a huge stuffed bass stared glassily from the opposite wall.

Plato had heard that Godfrey Millburn ate, drank, and slept hospital administration. Apparently, the acting CEO had another dimension after all.

Over in the dining room, Patricia Kidzek smiled at the newcomers and gestured to the pine table, which was heaped with appetizers.

"Better get started," she warned, "before it all disappears."

"Don't worry," Millburn told them. "I've got plenty more in the refrigerator."

Surfraire waddled into the dining room, the others trailing in his wake. The chief of surgery loaded his plate and winked at Plato. "Godfrey is off to a promising start—he certainly *feeds* us better than Lionel ever did."

The table was piled high with shrimp, turkey, ham, vegetables and dip, a dozen different kinds of cheese, fruit salad, and three entire cakes. Plato began serving himself while Cal turned to their host.

"You must have an excellent caterer," she said.

"I did this all myself," Millburn replied proudly. "I just *love* to cook."

"That must make your wife very happy," Patricia Kidzek observed.

The room fell silent, and the acting CEO glanced away, suddenly uncomfortable.

David Inverness broke the silence. He gestured back to the living room and smiled. "I didn't know you were a hunter, Godfrey."

"Bow hunting, mostly." He shrugged. "I'm really a lousy shot; I just got lucky with that buck."

"I'll bet the *buck* didn't feel very lucky," Kettering observed dryly.

Once the conversation resumed, Patricia Kidzek sidled into a corner beside Plato and Cal. She shook her head, bewildered. "Was it something I said?"

David Inverness turned and smiled, touching the pediatrician's arm. "Not your fault. But I think Godfrey's wife is in a nursing home—I heard she had a stroke or something."

"Oh." Kidzek sucked in her breath. "I'm so sorry. I saw the house, and I just assumed—"

"It does seem to have a feminine touch, doesn't it?" Inverness nodded. "I think his daughter still lives with him, or at least she visits pretty regularly."

Her face cleared and she nodded. "I see. Thanks for straightening me out."

"No problem." The internist turned to Cal. "And maybe *you* could straighten us all out on something."

"What's that?" Cal asked, though she seemed to know what was coming.

"Lionel's death—did the Geauga coroner find anything more than anaphylaxis?"

The other doctors in the room seemed to edge closer, waiting for an answer.

"No." She shook her head. "He's ruled it an accidental death, of course. And both he and the emergency room physician agreed that we did everything we could—maybe even *more* than anyone should have expected."

She glanced meaningfully at the acting CEO, who shifted nervously beneath her gaze. Back at the church, he had finally noticed Plato and Cal sitting in the row behind him. He probably wondered how much they had heard.

"And yet they still don't know what *caused* his allergic reaction?" Marta Oberlin frowned into her Chardonnay. "A bee sting, perhaps? Or maybe something he ate?"

"Probably not a sting," Cal replied. "It's too early in the season, and he had no sign of any bites or stings." She shook her head, puzzled. "It could have been something he ate, but we hadn't had breakfast."

"Right," Inverness agreed. "It just doesn't make any sense."

"At least the coroner cleared *us* of any fault in his death," Oberlin said. "I can't *believe* some of the allegations that have been made. We did everything we could."

"I might have given a higher dose of epinephrine," Inverness mused aloud.

"I hardly think that would have mattered," Plato said. "By the time we got it, I think Wallace was already gone." He turned to Cal. "Even though you *did* get back to us in record time."

She nodded. "There's no point in second-guessing ourselves. We did the best we could."

"You certainly did," Millburn agreed heartily. He crossed his arms. "I'm backing you folks one hundred percent—it's obviously a smear campaign generated by our competition."

Marta Oberlin chuckled. "You're kidding, right?"

A glance at the acting CEO showed that he was completely serious.

"Have we gotten *that* competitive?" she asked softly.

"You don't know the half of it," Inverness whispered. "You should hear them down in Marketing."

"I'm sure this story will fade away soon enough," their host said. "Especially when the coroner makes his statement public."

They all nodded soberly.

Plato frowned at the acting CEO. He was having trouble squaring his host's warm, genial personality with the hard-nosed cynical administrator he had heard complaining at Wallace's funeral. Millburn even *looked* different. Dressed in a flannel shirt and khaki slacks, he looked less like a cadaver and more like a human being. And his narrow face actually had some color, in contrast to the deathly pallor he always seemed to have at work.

"I had *another* reason for inviting you to lunch today," Millburn continued, "aside from picking Cal's brains about the autopsy."

He took a deep breath and smiled paternally.

"Before Lionel's death, a number of unpleasant rumors were circulating around Riverside General." Millburn passed a bony hand across his mouth. "Most of the rumors focused on possible cutbacks in our educational mission."

"I understood they were more than just rumors," Inverness said bluntly.

"Perhaps they were," the acting CEO agreed. "Federal cutbacks in Medicare funding and reimbursement for education have created budget problems at virtually *all* teaching hospitals, and Riverside General is no exception." He frowned seriously. "I'll be honest with you. The fact is, the hospital is being sold to a for-profit health care conglomerate."

A collective gasp echoed around the room.

"It's our only chance for staying open," Millburn said. "Our budget problems are *that* bad. We had a seven-million-dollar loss last year, and that was an *improvement* from the year before."

"Did Lionel know about this?" Inverness asked. He was obviously shaken by the news.

Millburn nodded. "The sale was approved by the Board of Trustees just last week. We were planning to discuss it during our retreat."

"What will happen to the residencies?" Patricia Kidzek asked. "And our outreach clinic?"

The chief of pediatrics was also the director of the hospital's outreach program, a community health service that operated a pediatric clinic in one of the poorest parts of the city. The clinic was staffed by residents, and was heavily dependent on hospital funding.

"I hope the outreach clinic will stay open," Millburn soothed. "Charity work is fundamental to resident education. It won't be easy, but I'll do my best to keep every residency and fellowship program operating. I believe in medical education, and I know you all do, too."

Most of the chiefs sighed with relief.

But Plato wasn't so sure. He was thinking back to Millburn's false sincerity during the eulogy this morning. One glance at Cal showed that she was remembering, too.

And Cal was deeply committed to the pathology residency program. She loved teaching, at any level— medical school, residency, and fellowship. The prospect of sacrificing her pathology program because of budget problems always made her bristle. The hospital could afford hundreds of thousands of dollars for advertising and public relations, it could build multimillion-dollar wings and intensive care units, and it supported a top-heavy army of administrators. Why couldn't *they* cut back?

Listening to Millburn's promise while remembering his words at the funeral that morning, Cal didn't believe the acting CEO for a minute.

This one is even more dangerous than Wallace, she was thinking. At least Lionel was too stupid to hide his intentions—though he *had* kept the impending sale a secret until his death.

The party didn't last much longer; most of the chiefs still had a full day's work ahead of them. Riding back to Cleveland in the Acura, Cal slumped back in her seat and sighed.

"I thought that funeral would *never* end."

"At least Millburn gave us some lunch," Plato said, frowning out the windshield. It was starting to rain— the weatherman had predicted another ice storm. "He seemed like a completely different person today, you know?"

"*Two* different persons—Jekyll and Hyde." She glanced at him. "You didn't believe him about his 'commitment to education,' did you?"

"Not for a minute." Plato piloted the Acura down a winding hill and shook his head. "But Millburn was right about one thing—I think the uproar over Wallace's death is going to fade away soon."

"Right," Cal agreed. "At least we've put *that* behind us."

But for the Council of Chiefs, the trouble had only just begun.

Chapter 5

The world was frosted with a thick layer of glass, the product of a full-blown ice storm that made last Saturday's freeze seem insignificant. It happened at least once every spring in Ohio: cold drizzle turned to freezing rain and then to sleet, glazing houses and trees and streets like a mad craftsman's decoupage bomb. Drivers needed chisels or blowtorches to get their car doors open. Tree limbs and power lines cracked under the strain. Freeways turned into skating rinks. And if driving on glare ice wasn't hard enough, most of the city's streetlights and traffic signals were knocked out as well.

At least the traffic wasn't bad. These days, Plato and Cal never drove home during rush hour. With Cal's three half-time jobs and Plato's new responsibilities as chief of geriatrics, they rarely left work before eight o'clock.

Cal eased the Acura down their long driveway through the woods, pumping the brakes and skidding to a stop just inches from the carriage house door and thanking God the car had a new set of tires.

As expected, the ramshackle house was dark as a tomb; if power lines fell anywhere in northeastern Ohio, the Marley residence was always hit first.

Joyous barks and yelps split the night as Cal and

Plato walked through the front door. A furry tongue-tipped missile shot out of the darkness, squirming and whimpering and lapping their faces. Ghost, their new Australian shepherd, was his usual manic, ecstatic self. But tonight even Dante was glad to see them; the flame-colored tabby pranced and purred between Cal's ankles.

Plato fumbled with the dog and the leash in the pitch-dark. He finally stood and turned to Cal, his face a pale blur against the blackness of the living room doorway.

"How about getting some flashlights and scrounging up something to eat?" he suggested. His voice sounded tired. "I'll take Ghost for a walk. And then I'd better check the basement."

Cal nodded. The foundation of the old house leaked like a sieve; only the constant vigilance of a pair of sump pumps kept the Marleys from drowning in their sleep.

She watched Plato shuffle onto the porch with Ghost. The poor Aussie leaped onto the sidewalk, then fell flat on his stomach as all four legs splayed out on the ice. Plato gingerly lifted the dog onto the grass, then followed along behind with the careful, mincing steps of a novice skater.

Cal turned away and stumbled down the hall to the broom closet, dug out a pair of flashlights, found the hurricane lamp in the basement, scavenged a few candles from a cupboard in the kitchen, and spent the next fifteen minutes hunting down a pair of matches. She had just lit the candles when Plato returned with Ghost.

He marched into the kitchen, rubbing his hands eagerly.

"So—what's for supper?"

Cal glared at him. "Matches."

"Matches?" He cocked his head, squinting at her in the dim light.

"Where did you put all the matches?" Cal demanded. She waved her hands in the air. "Last time the power went out, I bought a whole box of blue-tips—one *thousand* matches—and put them in the closet." Her voice grew in force, surrounding Plato like a hurricane bearing down on a tropical island. "I just spent fifteen minutes tearing the house apart looking for matches, and all I could find was a pack from the—let's see . . ." She squinted at the pack. "The Winking Lizard Tavern."

"Oh—sorry. I must have left the blue-tips by the grill." He turned away. "I'll just go get—"

"That's not the point, Plato." She spoke with exaggerated care, like a teacher explaining the playground rules to a particularly slow pupil. "It's not enough that you leave your socks all over the bedroom, that you never do the dishes unless we run out, that you always leave the toilet seat up. No. You've got to—"

"What do dishes and toilet seats have to do with anything?" Plato asked, clearly bewildered. "I thought we were talking about matches."

"You never *think*; that's my point. You never put anything away where it belongs. If I've told you—"

"I'm not *supposed* to do the dishes, remember?" He raised his voice triumphantly. "I do the cooking."

"When's the last time you cooked anything, Plato? You never get home early enough anymore."

"Neither do you."

"Humph." Cal frowned at the matchbook in her hand. "We've never been to any Winking Lizard." She spat out the name with pained disgust, then glared at the matchbook cover. "Live entertainment," she read. "What *kind* of live entertainment?"

"Belly dancers, Cally." Plato moved closer, grinning.

"They did the dance of the seven veils on our table and plied us with demon rum."

He tickled her ribs, sanded his beard against her neck until she relented.

"The dance of the seven veils?" She giggled.

"Just kidding." He shook his head. "It was a rock band—the bass player was an old friend of Nathan's."

"Your wild weekend again, huh?" She sighed. "I'd better start bringing you along to my conferences."

Plato shrugged. "At least we'd get to spend some time together."

Cal pursed her lips. It was another sore point, one that had touched off several arguments in the past few months—and had almost led to another one tonight. Cal blamed Plato for accepting the position of chief when he was already so overextended, and Plato blamed Cal for working no fewer than three half-time jobs. More often than not, their dinner conversations degenerated into arguments over whose fault it was that they were eating so late. It was usually *both* of their faults, or neither; their work was like the stone of Sisyphus—every time they got the boulder up to the top of the hill, it rolled right back down again.

Plato moved behind Cal, pressing against her back and massaging her aching shoulders, sending tingles up and down her spine. She leaned back, letting her head loll and smiling into her shirt.

"I wish we could just go to bed," she sighed. "And call in sick tomorrow."

"Can't," Plato replied. "I've got three meetings, two lectures, and half an office day."

She slumped into a chair. "I'll see your three meetings and raise you two."

"You win." He moved away and picked up the flickering hurricane lamp. "Tell you what—you just rest there and I'll whip up some cold meat loaf sandwiches. You're right—I haven't made dinner in a long time."

"I'm sorry I laid into you like that," she sighed. "I'm awfully tired tonight."

"Zen juist relax," Plato advised in his awful French accent, "and let Chef Marley prepare for you a meal of zee highest order—a work of gastronomic *chef d'oeuvre*."

"Cold meat loaf?"

"*Mais oui, ma chérie*—you shall see."

Maybe it was the darkness, or the cold, or the horrible gnawing in the pit of her stomach, but the meat loaf sandwiches tasted better than she would have imagined. Plato lit a fire in the living room hearth while Cal snuggled under a blanket and snarfed up a second sandwich and half a bag of ranch-flavored chips.

Plato glanced at her and frowned. "You look like a tiger shark in a feeding frenzy."

"I *feel* like a tiger shark," Cal replied. She gazed down at her plate sadly. "I'm still hungry."

"Maybe you're pregnant," Plato teased.

"I *couldn't* be," she said with a sniff. "You know that."

The Hippocratic oath didn't include any vows of chastity, but it might as well have. Lately it seemed like they were always too busy, or too tired, or both.

"I know," He slumped down beside her on the sofa and studied his sandwich in the flickering firelight. "Maybe after supper, we could—"

"Maybe," Cal agreed. She leaned over to pillow her head in his lap. "Or maybe this weekend—"

"Yeah." Plato sighed. "Who knows—in a couple of weeks, we might have *lots* of extra time on our hands."

"What do you mean?"

"David Inverness got a little inside information today," Plato said. "He caught a glimpse of a memo while he was waiting to see Godfrey Millburn. The Big Man's secretary had it on her desk, and David sent her off for a cup of coffee."

"Pretty sly," Cal mused.

"The memo had a breakdown of all the teaching departments, along with how much money each department was costing the hospital." He took a deep breath. "Geriatrics was the biggest loser, and pediatrics was second. Too many poor patients."

"How about pathology?" she asked anxiously.

"I think you folks are in the black," he replied. "Even with your residency, you *still* generate a ton of money from all those lab tests. Surgery was a big money-maker, too."

She closed her eyes. "But it's not *fair*—your patients are older, and sicker. They need a lot of time."

"But we don't get *paid* any more for spending more time." He shrugged. "It doesn't necessarily mean anything now. David said the memo was addressed to Lionel Wallace. Millburn may not have had anything to do with it. After all, he *says* he's committed to education."

She met his gaze and saw the doubt in his eyes, the disappointment. With the graying of America, geriatrics had long been touted as the wave of the future. The only trouble was that the wave was pretty damned expensive. Plato and his fellow specialists were trained to care for the oldest, sickest, most complicated patients—the ones that most physicians dreaded and were only too eager to refer away. Geriatricians rush in where internists fear to tread, or so said the conventional wisdom.

It was a labor of love, one that would never pay for itself in the current profit-based system. But Plato believed in it, teaching the next generation of practitioners, keeping the fire alive until the health care pendulum swung back to emphasize quality care rather than profits.

Loss of the geriatrics fellowship—*any* of the teaching programs—would sacrifice quality care on the altar of profitability.

"Anyway, Wallace is dead, and we know what *he* was planning." Plato said dryly. He took a last bite of his sandwich and stoked the fire, then turned, his face ruddy in the flickering light. "No signs of foul play, huh?"

"What do you mean?" Cal rolled her eyes. "It was an *allergic* reaction, Plato—you can't plan something like that."

"I guess not." He shook his head. "It sure was convenient, Wallace dying off just as he was planning to phase out the teaching programs."

"Who would be *that* devoted to their residency program?" Cal challenged. Then she frowned. It sounded ridiculous, but she knew it wasn't that simple. Some of the residency directors had started their programs from scratch—Cy Kettering, for example. The endless rounds of accreditation and recruitment, practicing and lecturing and supervising, sometimes took their toll on the department chiefs. For some of the staff, patients and residents and fellow faculty took the place of family.

Like David Inverness. Cal shivered.

"I wouldn't put it past Marta Oberlin," Plato teased. "She's a complete fanatic."

Cal chuckled. "She was ready to kill *you* on Friday."
Plato grimaced. "Don't remind me."

This whole conversation was crazy, Cal knew. She couldn't imagine *anyone* killing somebody for the sake of a teaching program. Anyway, it was an allergic reaction—she was sure of that.

"I sat in on the autopsy," Cal said, half to herself.

"All the tox screens were negative, and they did a pretty thorough search. Wallace had all the classic symptoms of anaphylaxis—hives, bronchospasm, pulmonary edema. The microscopic exam showed eosinophils and mast cells *everywhere,* Plato. You can't fake an allergic reaction."

"I guess not," he agreed reluctantly.

"Why are you so hooked on the idea that somebody killed Wallace?" she asked.

"I'm not," he insisted. "I just sort of wish somebody had—I would have liked to shake his hand."

Cal chuckled. "Wallace wasn't *that* bad. Was he?"

"I didn't think so before," he answered. "Now, I'm not so sure."

"Millburn might be even worse," she reminded him.

He sidled closer and nuzzled her neck. "Let's stop talking about work, okay?"

"Sure." She slid down lower on the couch. "What do *you* want to talk about?"

"Another wild weekend—with *you* this time." He nibbled her ear and breathed on her neck. "We could head up to the Wyndham for one of those weekend specials."

"Mmm. That would be nice." She smirked. "Better than Camp *Success!* anyway."

He unbuttoned her shirt. "Maybe we should start practicing now."

"Aren't you forgetting something?"

"What? Don't tell me you're on call this weekend."

"Nope—I've got the next two weekends free." She frowned. "But I was wondering—how are we going to *pay* for this wild weekend? The Wyndham ain't cheap, you know. One-fifty a night."

"We can afford it," he said confidently. "With my raise, and some of those student loans off our back—"

"That's *right*!" she exclaimed. "I keep forgetting about that."

"And we'd better take advantage of it while we can," he added. "While we both have jobs."

Cal giggled. "You're on."

He moved down lower, and she sighed, running her hands through his hair, imagining they were both off at the Wyndham, in a private suite, with nothing to do for a whole weekend but eat and sleep and—

Just then, the telephone rang.

Plato groaned. "Never fails. Why doesn't the telephone line ever get knocked out?"

"Ohio Bell's just too darned reliable." Cal patted his arm and smiled. "Don't worry. Whoever it is, I'll get rid of them."

"We'll see," Plato replied doubtfully.

She picked up the phone on the fourth ring. "Hello?"

"Cal?" The voice on the other end of the line was breathless, urgent. "Thank goodness. I was about to hang up again."

"What's wrong?" She recognized the voice now. Patty Kidzek, the chief of pediatrics at Riverside.

"I tried calling before, but there wasn't any answer. David wanted me to talk to you, so you'd be ready—in case the papers called. I left a message on your machine, but I guess your power's out, huh?"

"Patty, what's *wrong*?" Cal was frantic now—had Riverside burned down? Was Plato's uncle in the hospital again?

Hearing the tension in her voice, Plato poked his head over the back of the couch. He frowned at her. Cal shrugged back.

"It's Dr. Surfraire," the pediatrician finally replied. "You haven't heard?"

"No," she said, frustrated. The power came on just then, with that background hum that you never notice until it's gone. The clocks and furnace whined to life, one of the living room lamps flicked on, and the pumps in the basement clattered and clanked.

Cal spied the blinking red light on the answering machine in the corner. It would probably be quicker just to hang up and listen to Patty's message. But the pediatrician finally gathered her thoughts and stammered on.

"He missed all his surgeries this afternoon," she said. "They were looking everywhere for him."

"He never came back from Millburn's house?" Cal asked, puzzled. Surfraire's sleek Porsche had pulled out of the driveway just before theirs. He had vanished down the road ahead, in the direction of Riverside General.

"No," Patty replied. "We were the last people to see him alive."

Cal gasped. "What do you mean?"

"They found his car a couple of hours ago. At the bottom of a cliff near his house. Someone noticed that the guardrail was down and called the police. Dr. Surfraire must have skidded off the road; he was going pretty fast."

"He's dead?" Cal asked, then frowned to herself. Stupid question.

"He was killed in the crash," Patty said. "They think he must have died instantly. But that's not the worst of it."

Cal closed her eyes. What could be worse than getting killed?

"He was dead drunk, Cal." Patty took a deep breath. "One empty bottle of vodka under the seat, and a half-full one shattered all over the dash."

"Drunk?" Cal was shocked. Surfraire had seemed stone-cold sober at Millburn's house. Where had he been all afternoon? "How do they know? Did they check blood levels?"

Another dumb question—they sure hadn't done a Breathalyzer test.

"Uh-huh," Patty agreed. "Five hundred milligrams percent."

"Five *hundred*?" Cal was stunned. One-fifty was the legal limit.

"Yeah." Patty sighed. "Enough to kill most people, or at least put them in a coma."

"He must have been an alcoholic," Cal concluded. Over a period of months or years, the liver of an alcoholic learned to metabolize ethanol more quickly, so that more alcohol was needed to produce a high. Alcoholics could walk, talk, or even drive with phenomenal levels of alcohol in their blood. Not that they drove *well*. "I had no idea."

"Neither did most people. But he was a recovering alcoholic, a member of AA—supposedly hadn't taken a drink in fifteen years. But I guess he had."

"God!" She shook her head, dazed. No wonder the pediatrician was so flustered. Cal frowned thoughtfully. "Patty—how do you know all this about Dr. Surfraire?"

"My power never went out," the pediatrician replied. "I got it off the evening news."

Chapter 6

Cleveland's Riverside General Hospital was front-page news again. The death of Lionel Wallace last weekend—Millburn's "public relations disaster"—was a mere cloudburst compared to the tornado of scandal whirling over the chief of surgery's messy demise.

Some enterprising rescue worker had shot and leaked an excellent photo of the wreck—a picture taken through the passenger-side window, showing Andre Surfraire's broken body slumped over the steering wheel, a spider-web of cracks marking the place where his head had smacked the windshield, a smashed bottle of Smirnoff's wedged between the dashboard and the windshield. The photo had made the front page of all the area newspapers; the *Daily Press* even featured a small white arrow pointing to the liquor bottle for feeble-eyed readers.

The stories about Surfraire's accident, about Riverside General's financial woes, and about the unsettled issues surrounding Wallace's death crowded out most of the other news on the front page. Godfrey Millburn had been quoted as saying that an internal review of Riverside General's surgery department was already in progress. Gabrielle Surfraire—the surgeon's widow—admitted that her husband was a recovering alcoholic, but insisted that he hadn't touched a drink in fifteen years. She had requested that the Cuyahoga County coroner perform the autopsy. Ralph Jensson—the coroner—had stated that he could offer no conclusions about Surfraire's accident until the autopsy results were in.

Several patients had already canceled elective surgeries at Riverside General; the Cleveland Clinic had run a full-page ad in several papers touting their record of success and quality care, and inviting Cleveland-area patients to "compare the difference." Other hospitals had taken out similar ads. The allegations and scandal swirling around Riverside General had already become personal. When interviewing the county coroner, one reporter had asked whether it would be a conflict of interest for Cal Marley to perform the autopsy. After all, he pointed out, Marley was also an employee of Riverside General.

Jensson had replied that he had every confidence in Dr. Marley, but that he would perform the autopsy personally. As an interested party, Dr. Marley could certainly attend if she wished. For that matter, so could the reporter.

And so Cal was just a spectator at Surfraire's autopsy Tuesday morning. She and Leonard Reiss, the *Daily Press* reporter, were gloved and gowned, standing across the autopsy table from the county coroner. Between them lay the mountainous remains of Andre Surfraire. The former chief of surgery was completely naked. His bruised and battered face was mottled deep purple with livor mortis, the settling of blood into dependent areas after death. A wide flap of Surfraire's forehead had been flayed away when his head hit the windscreen. A pair of dark lines curved across his chest. His vast abdomen rose from the table like the dome of some magnificent building.

"Observe the pattern of the steering wheel," Jensson began in his faint brogue. The coroner had come to

Cleveland from Banffshire decades ago, but he still rolled his R's and twanged his E's—especially after his annual visit to Scotland. Jensson traced the curved lines on the chest and continued his narrative. "The stamp is difficult to see, given the subject's pigmentation. But distinct enough—probably premortem."

"Premortem?" Leonard Reiss frowned behind his mask. The *Daily Press* reporter was constantly twitching, as though his gown were packed with fire ants. He was small and pudgy, with a pink complexion that was already tinged green.

"Before death," Cal translated.

"Oh." Reiss nodded, then swallowed heavily. Out in the hallway, he had been anxious for the autopsy to begin, gloating over the incredible story he would write about it, the "inside details" he would share with his readers.

Now he seemed slightly less eager.

Jensson waved a gloved hand, and the morgue's photographer moved in to shoot pictures of Surfraire's face and chest.

"We'll begin with the typical Y incision," the coroner said. He raised a huge surgical steel knife.

From the corner of her eye, Cal saw Leonard Reiss actually flinch.

She frowned, concerned. "Are you all right?"

"Just fine," Reiss gurgled. His face was more green than pink now.

"We'll need to check the stomach and small intestine for alcohol," Jensson explained. "That will be our first priority, once we enter the abdomen."

The huge knife descended, splitting the mountain in two perfect halves and carrying the incision up to the chest. Despite the length of the knife, two incisions were needed before Jensson finally reached the rectus abdominus muscles guarding the outer wall of the abdominal cavity.

"This promises to be quite a messy autopsy," the coroner complained. He frowned down at the incision and shook his head, then raised a pair of surgical scissors. He glanced at the clock on the wall. "Entering the abdominal cavity at, let's see, ten forty-two a.m."

Bentley, the lab assistant—or diener—scribbled the time on a chalkboard in the corner.

After a few snips, Jensson was inside. Cal was actually grateful to be only an observer at this postmortem. The corner was up to his elbows in the enormous walls of fat, and he still hadn't reached the stomach. Jensson moved the greater omentum and large intestine aside to reveal the abdominal organs—the dark hulk of the liver looming over the stomach and duodenum, the endless coils of small intestine packed into the center of the abdomen, the bright green gallbladder peeking out from the lower edge of the liver. Buried so deep within that mountainous abdomen, the organs themselves seemed ridiculously small.

Jensson carved two tiny slits in the walls of the stomach and the small intestine, then collected samples of the contents for analysis. He glanced up at the clock before passing the containers to Bentley, who received them with dignified solemnity. Bentley had been on the morgue staff almost as long as Jensson himself, working his way up from a clerical position to a part-time lab assistant and finally becoming the morgue's senior diener. With his bald head, paunchy build, and dignified air, Bentley looked far more like a proper English butler than a morgue technician.

He even *moved* like a butler, eyeing the vials of fluid critically before settling them in a rack. He might have been handling a tray of champagne glasses.

"Label these as 'stomach' and 'duodenum,' " Jensson told him. "Both collected at ten forty-six a.m."

"As you wish, sir." Bentley pulled a wax marker from his lab coat and labeled the specimens with a flourish.

The coroner glanced at Cal. "Of course, we'll also need a sample of blood and vitreous fluid, collected at about the same time."

"Vitreous fluid?" Reiss asked.

"The fluid inside the eyeball," Cal explained. "Alcohol levels in the vitreous lag behind those in the blood by about two hours. By checking the alcohol levels in the eye and the blood, we can get some ideas about the time of death relative to the drinking episode."

"Exactly," Jensson noted. He squinted at Reiss, then grunted. "I fear, Dr. Marley, that we may soon have *another* patient on our hands."

Cal glanced at the reporter. Like a chameleon, Reiss had faded to match the green tiles lining the lab. His eyes were dull and glazed. He bobbed and weaved like a punch-drunk boxer awaiting the final blow.

Jensson delivered it.

"We pull out the vitreous juice with a needle," the coroner explained helpfully. He grabbed a syringe from the tray beside the table and waved it beneath the reporter's nose. Then he lifted Surfraire's left eyelid and positioned the needle with exaggerated care. "A simple procedure, really—poking into the eyeball like *this,* pulling back on the syringe, and sucking the fluid out. Very neat, very tidy."

He held up the syringe with its teaspoonful of clear viscous fluid for Reiss to see. The reporter staggered backwards, swallowed two or three times, then clapped his gloved hands over his mask. Muttering incoherently, he lurched from the room.

"Third door on the right," Jensson called helpfully.

He waved the syringe and grinned at Cal. "Gets them every time."

"You sure know how to deal with reporters, Ralph." Cal shook her head in admiration.

"Years of practice, m'dear. I wanted him out of here." He gestured to the enormous body overlapping the edges of the table. "I'm afraid Dr. Surfraire is far too big for one decrepit coroner to handle—even with Bentley's assistance. Now, you can help me out."

Together they completed the autopsy. Jensson was right—Surfraire's enormous size made the procedure difficult; it was like dissecting a young sperm whale. But with Cal's and Bentley's help, the autopsy went far more quickly.

After an hour, only the head remained to be dissected. Bentley had already carved through the lid of the skull; the aristocratic diener had a fine touch with the bone saw. Jensson peeled the scalp forward and down over the face, then lifted the top of the calvarium away.

The cause of death was obvious: a baseball-sized clot filled the front of the brainpan, squashing the frontal lobes nearly flat.

"Massive subdural hematoma," Jensson said. He gestured for the photographer again, then vacuumed the clot away and studied the lid of the skull, checking for signs of a fracture. Finally, he lifted the brain up and out, setting it on a tray and squinting at the surface while Cal checked over the lower half of the skull.

Jensson whistled, pointing at a bruised area centered at the left occipital lobe, the back of the brain. He gestured for the photographer again and nodded to himself. "Cerebral contusion, presumably contrecoup." He clucked, frowning. "Though it's quite rare to see contrecoup fractures in the occipital area."

Contrecoup contusions were common in falls, Cal knew; the bruises appeared on the *opposite* side of the brain from the point of impact. Contrecoup injuries resulted from the brain literally bouncing inside the skull, moving away from the bone at the primary site and smacking into the skull on the opposite side. Confronted with two different brain injuries, a careless pathologist might conclude that an accident really resulted from foul play—a blow to the skull followed by a fall.

On the other hand, as Jensson had said, contrecoup contusions of the *occipital* area were quite rare. Cal took another close look at the victim's skull in the corresponding area—the back of the skull—and gasped.

"It's not a contrecoup injury," she announced.

Jensson nodded, seemingly not surprised. "You've found a fracture?"

Cal nodded, tracing a small hairline break at the back of the skull, just below the point where Bentley had used his bone saw. They had checked the skull before making the cut, but none of them had noticed the tiny fracture.

"Excellent, Cal—your eyes are far sharper than mine." He gestured for another photo, then nodded. "We'll have the skull X-rayed for good measure."

"You don't seem very surprised," Cal said.

"I'm not." Jensson was silent and thoughtful as they completed the autopsy, sectioning the brain, noting a fracture in one of the facial bones, and checking the neck for possible breaks or other injuries.

Finally, the coroner peeled off his gloves and gown and tossed them into the trash, then turned to Bentley. "You'll reassemble the good doctor for me, I trust?"

"Certainly, sir." He glanced at the enormous body and nodded thoughtfully, just a flicker of a frown crossing his face. "This may take some time."

"It may take all *day,*" Jensson agreed. He shrugged.

"Take your time; I'll pull Delaney out of the file room to help with the other posts."

"Thank you, sir." Bentley hurried off to gather suture materials and sponges.

The coroner led Cal upstairs to his office, poured her a cup of coffee, lit his pipe, and settled back in his deep leather wing chair. Jensson's inner sanctum was more like a library than an office—deep pile carpet, a quartet of club chairs, and walls of dark walnut bookcases crammed with pathology texts, forensics journals, and books on Scottish and American history. The coroner spent much of his free time researching the American civil war; several of his articles on medical treatments available during the conflict had been published in prominent historic journals.

Heavy curtains shut out the bustle and noise emanating from University Hospital across the street. A print showing the battle of Culloden—from another and much older civil war—hung from one paneled wall, and a chart mapping the various types of craniocerebral injuries hung from another.

"A fascinating postmortem, no?" The coroner's eyes glittered like obsidian through the haze of pipe smoke.

"There *were* some inconsistencies," Cal agreed cautiously. She sipped her coffee and considered. With over forty years' experience as a pathologist, Jensson was a founding member of the American College of Forensic Pathology and a regular lecturer at several medical schools. Ralph was always teaching, always testing—even with his own staff. He could turn even the most mundane, routine autopsies into learning exercises, and that was one of the main reasons Cal loved working with him.

Of course, this wasn't a mundane autopsy. Far from it.

"I'll be very interested in seeing those alcohol levels," she continued.

"Quaite." Jensson puffed until the bowl glowed bright red in the dim light. "You think the results will be, hmm, *illuminating*?"

"I hope so." She frowned thoughtfully. "I *suppose* Surfraire could have simply relapsed, like the papers said."

"With a blood alcohol level of five hundred?" He chuckled. "I imagine he would have been comatose long before he reached three hundred."

"Unless he was a chronic drinker after all," Cal said. She sighed. "Which he obviously wasn't."

"Aye." Jensson nodded slowly. "And there's the rub."

Cal took another sip of coffee and threw her mind back over the autopsy. If Surfraire *was* a chronic drinker, capable of staying conscious despite a blood alcohol level of five hundred, he should have shown some signs of his drinking. But the liver appeared perfectly, vibrantly healthy, with none of the fatty degeneration or cirrhotic scarring you might expect in an end-stage alcoholic. Bentley had even mounted a quick slide for microscopic examination, and the cell structure and organization appeared completely normal. The chief of surgery showed none of the other side effects of alcoholism, either—signs like swollen veins in the digestive tract or ruptured blood vessels in the skin. Aside from his phenomenal obesity, Andre Surfraire appeared to have been remarkably healthy.

In the face of marked liver disease, the other inconsistencies in the autopsy could have been explained away. Even the fracture at the back of is skull might have happened during the crash—a freak impact against the driver's-side window as the car tumbled down the cliff. But the healthy liver suggested another, far more ominous explanation. One that was really quite bizarre.

"I've never heard of such a thing before," Cal confessed.

"Indeed." Ralph cocked his head and squinted at his pipe. "It *is* quite unusual." He leaned back in his chair. "But not unprecedented. I remember a case, back in 'sixty-four or 'sixty-five, I think it was. A nurse, who did her husband in by—"

Just then, a knock sounded at the door. Bentley poked his head in discreetly.

"Very sorry to disturb you, sir . . ."

"Please come in, Bentley." The coroner leaned forward eagerly. "I see you have the lab results for us. Hand them to Dr. Marley, if you please."

"Most unusual, ma'am." The diener frowned at the lab slips and handed them to Cal. "I really can't imagine—"

"Quaite," Jensson said curtly. "We were just discussing the possibilities."

He glanced meaningfully at the door until Bentley took the hint and departed.

"An excellent diener," Ralph said. "One of the best, but sometimes just a bit too free with our information, I suspect."

Cal almost replied '*Quaite*' before she caught herself. Instead, she glanced down at the lab slips. The results were exactly as she and Jensson had expected. No wonder Bentley was confused.

"The repeat blood alcohol is almost identical," Cal said. "Five hundred and twenty. But the samples of gastric and duodenal contents are negative for alcohol or other drugs."

"Mmm-*hmm*." Jensson puffed his pipe to life again. "Very much like that other case. We never *did* get a conviction." He glanced up sharply. "And the vitreous fluid?"

"Only one hundred milligrams percent," she replied.

"Indeed." The coroner nodded, satisfied. "Your interpretation?"

"The vitreous alcohol concentration lags behind blood levels by about two hours," Cal began. "And at equilibrium, the alcohol level in the eye should be about twenty percent higher than that in the blood—which would add up to about six hundred, in this case."

"Precisely." Puff, puff.

"Because the vitreous level is *lower* than the blood level, we can assume that the level in the eye was rising, rather than falling."

"Quaite." The dark eyes glittered with anticipation.

"And the large difference between the vitreous level and the blood level gives us an idea about the slope of the rise—the speed with which the alcohol was given."

"*Given,* eh?" He chuckled wryly. "A very apt term."

"With such a huge difference, the alcohol must have been given very quickly."

"And?"

"And it was given shortly before death," she concluded. "*Very* shortly—perhaps half an hour, maybe even less."

"Excellent reasoning." He clamped his pipe in his teeth and grinned. "And of course the most obvious point is how the alcohol was administered."

"Intravenously." She shrugged. "If he had drunk all that alcohol just half an hour before the crash—assuming anyone *could* drink that much without tossing it right back up—he should still have had plenty in his digestive tract. And he didn't."

"Poor Mr. Reiss," Jensson clucked. "He missed such a *fascinating* story." The coroner shook his head. "And so, given the evidence of the blow to the back of the head, the lack of liver disease, the apparently rapid intravenous administration of alcohol, and the carefully staged accident scene, we can—as dear Mr. Holmes was so fond of saying—reach only one conclusion, however improbable."

Cal nodded. "Andre Surfraire was murdered."

"Your administration will be most relieved. And so will Gabrielle Surfraire, the poor widow." Jensson sighed, then chuckled as he refilled his pipe bowl. "Which newspaper should I call first?"

Chapter 7

Plato's first meeting of the afternoon was a big disappointment. When he had been assigned to the hospital's Strategic Planning Commission last week, Plato had assumed that he would be helping plot Riverside General's strategy for improving patient care, streamlining the interaction between doctors, nurses, and other hospital personnel, and determining which improvements the facility might need in the future. The commission included members from administration, the medical staff, nursing, and other departments.

Plato was surprised and pleased when he heard about the appointment. In accordance with the unwritten rules of hospital medicine, he already belonged to over a dozen committees and spent at least a quarter of his time attending worthless meetings where absolutely nothing significant took place. His only worthwhile achievement as a committee member in the past three years had occurred on the cafeteria safety panel: he and three other doctors had certified tuna salad as a health risk after an outbreak of food poisoning.

But the Strategic Planning Commission sounded different, promising. Perhaps it would actually be worth his time, maybe provide him with an opportunity to really make a difference.

It didn't.

The meeting was held in the hospital's administrative annex, a huge multimillion-dollar monstrosity of glass and chrome that had been completed just the year before. Standing beside the moldering brick and granite of the hospital proper, the glitzy administrative wing was as out of place as a diamond necklace on a warthog.

Finding his way to the meeting was harder than Plato had expected. The administrative building was connected to the hospital on the ground floor only, through a small, unmarked portal just behind the cafeteria. The new wing was built for comfort: a fountain and lush tropical greenery in the sunlit atrium, hammered metal sculptures lounging in the corners, dulcimer music floating through the air, and abstract paintings hanging from the fake stone walls. A private bridge led to the staff parking lot so that administrators never had to set foot in the hospital proper unless absolutely necessary.

Aside from the discreet dulcimer music, the atrium was as still and hushed as an empty church. A receptionist examined Plato's name tag, nodded, and guided him to the elevators with the dignified solemnity of an acolyte. Even the elevator's bell was subdued.

Godfrey Millburn glanced meaningfully at his watch after Plato walked through the door of the conference room. "Dr. Marley—glad you could join us."

Plato glanced up at the clock. He was ten minutes late.

"Sorry. My last office patient had an MI—I had to admit her."

"Maybe you should plan your office days better," Millburn advised. But he shrugged it away. "Regardless, you're here, so we can finally get started."

Plato slumped into a chair. He was bone-tired and wolfishly hungry, and the day wasn't even half over. He was also disgusted with Millburn's comment. Beatrice Evans hadn't planned on having a heart attack in

Plato's office; it was hardly something you could *schedule* for.

Across the table, Anne Nussbaum caught his eye and smiled sympathetically. Plato was relieved that the director of nursing was on the committee, too. And David Inverness—the chief of staff and medical director— was sitting at the other end of the table, hunched back in his chair with his eyes closed. As always, Inverness looked tired.

Plato recognized the other two committee members as well—one was the director of marketing and the other was Millburn's assistant—the administrative drone who had sat beside the acting CEO at Wallace's funeral yesterday. The drone was tapping away on a notebook computer.

At some unspoken cue from his boss, he stopped typing and dutifully closed the lid.

Godfrey Millburn stood and folded his arms. His cadaverous face looked even more solemn and mournful than usual. He glanced around the table.

"Some of you are probably wondering why I created this committee," he began. "It's quite simple, really. Riverside General is about to undergo a series of sweeping changes aimed at improving patient care and profitability, to ensure that we keep our doors open well into the twenty-first century."

"What sort of changes?" Inverness asked. But his voice was resigned, hopeless, as though he already knew the answer.

"As you know, David, the hospital is experiencing some serious financial difficulties," Millburn replied. He turned to look at each member of the group in turn. "But I think we can get through this—*together*. We've created a plan to streamline our operations through team-building, overhead reduction, aggressive pursuit of new business through partnerships with local industry, and application of an exciting new marketing strategy."

He gestured to his right. "But before we go into the details, I want to announce the appointment of our new vice president and chief operating officer—Quentin Young."

Millburn paused while the administrative drone smiled modestly.

The director of marketing stood and shook Young's hand. "Congratulations, Quentin—you really deserve it."

Young shook his hand unenthusiastically, like a victorious king reluctantly accepting homage after a bloody war.

"Thanks, Frank." He smiled broadly. "And I'd rather you didn't call me Quentin. Understand?"

"Sure, Mr. Young." The marketing director's smile froze, and he sat down again.

Millburn watched the exchange approvingly. "Mr. Young will explain the details of our new strategy—and your role in implementing it."

The new vice president stood and carried his notebook computer to a projector at the back of the room. He flicked a remote and a screen lowered while the projector came to life. The lights dimmed automatically, and the curtains drew closed.

The whole operation reminded Plato of the S.P.E.C.T.R.E meetings in the old James Bond films. If anyone disagreed with Mr. Young, a trapdoor would slide open and the unlucky victim would fall into a pool of piranhas.

"This is our first presentation of the new strategic plan," Young began. "Please do not discuss this information outside this room; some of the details involve sensitive restructuring issues."

Annie Nussbaum's ears perked up. She obviously smelled layoffs. "What sort of restructuring?"

"Please." Young held up a hand and smiled patiently. "That will become clear as I explain the plan." He pressed a button on the computer and a phrase flashed onto the screen.

" 'Client-centered care,' " the new vice president read. "I imagine the concept is quite new to you, but it will soon become a watchword here at Riverside General."

Young explained that part of the problem with medical care today was the rigid hierarchical relationship between patients, nurses and other care providers, and doctors. Patients visiting hospitals tended to see themselves as helpless cogs in an impersonal system. But when patients learned to see themselves as *clients,* the entire relationship changed. Doctors, nurses, and other health care providers became *allies* in the health care system.

Doctors and nurses were partners with each other, and more importantly with the client. Patients were empowered and encouraged to take an active role in the healing process, and the allies—doctors and nurses and staff—became part of a team, open to suggestions and improvements from any hospital employee, from Godfrey Millburn himself all the way down to housekeeping.

"We're all part of the same team," Young concluded. "A team with just one simple goal: making our clients healthy and happy, as quickly and cost-effectively as possible."

"That's why we're having this meeting," Millburn said. He spread his hands on the table. "Lionel Wallace and I shared the view that administrators, doctors, nurses, and other hospital staff should learn to work together, to share decisions and improve communication. In future meetings, this committee will be composed of representatives from several communities within the hospital, a model for *teamwork*."

Plato swallowed heavily. The presentation sounded ominously similar to the teachings at Camp *Success!*

Annie Nussbaum frowned critically at the fine print on the last slide. She turned to Young and shook her head. "This sounds an awful lot like the client-centered care model I've heard about at other hospitals."

"With some slight modifications," the vice president agreed. He smiled at her quickness, and seemed tempted to pat her on the head.

She turned away before he could, glancing at the screen again. "I see that you're planning to train the housekeeping staff to perform 'certain aspects of patient care.'" She swung her eyes back to Young. "Would that include nursing duties?"

"Under supervision only," the vice president explained. "Simple procedures—taking temperatures and checking vital signs. Routine things that a child could do."

"And could a child interpret those findings?" Nussbaum challenged. "Would a child know when to call a doctor, when it's worthwhile to check orthostatic changes, when a patient's mental status is abnormal?"

The administrator shook his head patronizingly. "I hardly think that those issues will apply. We're simply talking about a limited shift in duties." He smiled again. "You've said yourself that the floors are short-staffed."

"Because you've *laid off* two dozen nurses in the past two months," she retorted. "I've heard about reorganizations like this. You'll train the housekeeping and dietary staff to perform routine nursing, replace the college-trained registered nurses with practical nurses, and save the hospital a bundle." She glared at Young.

"But what happens when a floor sweeper screws up and a patient crashes? Have you thought about that?"

"Liability is hardly an issue." he tugged at his tie, the patina of coolheadedness beginning to dissolve. "Several hospitals have already implemented—"

But Nussbaum wasn't finished. "I'm not talking about *liability*. I'm talking about *lives*. Would you want to be monitored after heart surgery by someone who hadn't graduated from high school?"

"We don't have any plans to use those personnel on the postoperative floor."

Plato rolled his eyes. "Where *are* you planning to use them, then? Labor and delivery?"

The administrator smiled. "As a matter of fact, yes. Since the patients there are generally healthy—"

"Oh, dear God." Annie Nussbaum closed her eyes and took a deep breath. She opened them again and glanced at David Inverness. The hospital's meek medical director was sitting with his forehead in his hand, watching the fracas with obvious discomfort. He had cleared his throat to speak several times, but never managed to get a word out.

"The *obstetrics* floor," Nussbaum repeated. "What do you think of that, David?"

"I've been against the new plan from the start," Inverness replied finally. "I've made that clear in several memos, but I have yet to receive any replies." He turned to Young. "And your idea of starting the program on the obstetrics floor is foolhardy. Labor and delivery is a minefield of potential patient risk and litigation. I thought you would realize that."

Plato was pleasantly surprised at Inverness's firmness. The medical director generally preferred compromise to confrontation, but he could fight when he had to.

Unfortunately, this seemed to be a losing battle.

Quentin Young merely shifted his smile to Inverness and continued his explanation.

"I assure you, my team has conducted a cost-benefit analysis that shows minimal risk in the obstetrics division. As long as patients' potential complications are adequately sorted out beforehand—"

"*Beforehand?*" Nussbaum challenged. "We can't predict who will have an uncomplicated delivery and who'll need a crash section!" She took a deep breath and stared at a point above the vice president's head. "Just how much clinical experience do you have?"

"Mr. Young received his M.B.A. from Harvard," Millburn replied quickly.

"And I've worked here at Riverside for two years," Young piped. He seemed to be having trouble with his vocal cords.

"Two years in this glass greenhouse," Nussbaum spat, waving a hand around the opulent conference room. "Have you ever seen a real, live *patient*, Mr. Young?"

The administrator reddened, but didn't answer.

"There's no need to get personal here." Millburn stood, his cadaverous skin flushing faintly. "The purpose of this meeting is to iron out differences. You've raised some very good points, Annie, and I'd like to discuss these issues further at our next meeting. Would that satisfy you?"

"I suppose." She nodded grudgingly. "Provided the changes aren't implemented before our discussion."

"Then let's move on." The CEO smiled sympathetically at his assistant—the same smile a hunter might give a bloodhound when calling off the chase. *Next time, boy.* He gesture to Young's right. "I'd like you all to hear from the marketing department. Frank Evans has some exciting news for us."

Reluctantly, Quentin Young sat down and glared at Annie Nussbaum. The nursing chief ignored him.

Frank Evans had maintained a diplomatic silence during the battle. But he bounded to his feet at Millburn's cue.

"*Exciting* isn't the word!" Evans said breathlessly. "I'm *absolutely thrilled*, and when you hear our plans for Riverside, I know you will be, too!"

From his tone of voice, Plato could tell that Frank Evans was the kind of guy who even sprinkled exclamation points throughout his interoffice memos.

The marketing director moved to the head of the table and stood beside Millburn. Even standing, Evans was hardly taller than the skeletal CEO in his chair. His pale reddish blond hair was loosely crimped to hide the thinness on top, but it couldn't disguise the age lines beside his nose and eyes, the product of decades of vacant smiles. With his boundless energy and high-pitched voice, the marketing director reminded Plato of a red-haired Richard Simmons.

He loaded a carousel of slides onto a projector and switched it on, grinning as he waved the remote.

"I feel like a kid on Christmas morning—I just can't wait to show off what we've done!" He flicked the switch, and the first slide flashed up on the screen. "The old Riverside General is history, people. A part of the past. Today we look forward, to the twenty-first century. A new name, a new logo, a new beginning." He paused, seemingly tempted to put his hand over his heart. "For a new health partnership."

RiversEdge Wellness Center, the slide proclaimed in huge script letters. *A new vision for the twenty-first century, and beyond . . .*

"Wellness Center." David Inverness frowned, puzzled. "What's that—another satellite clinic? Some kind of ambulatory care facility?"

"You'll see," Evans replied mysteriously. "The name change is only the beginning."

He clicked the remote, and another slide flashed up. The photograph showed a current aerial view of Riverside General Hospital, complete with the bizarre administrative wing sprouting from its northern face like Darth Vader's battle cruiser come to earth.

He clicked the remote again. The slide showed another photograph, an architectural model of the same scene. The administrative wing was unchanged, but the hospital had disappeared. The ancient brick-and-granite building was replaced by another of approximately the same shape and size. But this building was covered with glass and chrome to match the administrative wing. A mock ambulance was parked in the foreground, beneath some spreading shade tress. To the south, the old nurses' dorm had been replaced by an enormous parking deck, plastered with chrome and glass to match its sister buildings.

A ponderous granite sculpture rose from the courtyard in front of the hospital entrance. Fully two stories tall, the abstract carving might have represented a half-melted snowman, or a giant termite giving birth. Looking more closely, Plato guessed it was a liberal interpretation of a mother holding a small child.

At the foot of the statue, huge block letters announced the facility's new name: RIVERSEDGE WELLNESS CENTER.

"This photo is a window to the future," Evans proclaimed. "*Our* future."

"I still don't get it," Inverness said. "What's a Wellness Center?"

"We're changing the hospital's name," Millburn replied flatly. "From Riverside General Hospital to RiversEdge Wellness Center."

"I think it's a brilliant stroke," the vice president added.

"We've been testing various names for *months*," Evans explained. "We finally settled on three possibilities and mall-tested them."

"Mall-tested?" Plato asked.

"A survey method," the marketing director replied. "*Very* effective and efficient. Many local malls have survey firms who'll test your product or your packaging for you. RiversEdge had the top score in *every single* survey we ran! It's an absolute winner!"

"That's the new name of the *hospital*?" Inverness finally asked. He grimaced. "You're joking, right?"

Evans hardly seemed to hear him. "Wellness Centers are the wave of the future—emphasizing health rather than sickness. A more positive image. Nobody calls hospitals 'hospitals' anymore. Even 'medical center' is passé." He waved his hands like Richard Simmons warming up for a round of jumping jacks. "And RiversEdge carries the name recognition of Riverside General while giving a more modern feel." He clapped his hands together. "Seven out of ten survey respondents felt that RiversEdge reminded them of the phrase 'cutting edge.' That's a *very* good image for the hospital!"

"RiversEdge Wellness Center, huh?" Inverness tapped his pencil against the lacquered rosewood tabletop. "Sounds more like a day care than a hospital."

"I assure you," Evans protested, "the mall-testing results were uniformly—"

Millburn lifted a hand, and the marketing guru stopped speaking as though the CEO had flipped a switch.

"Maybe we can just get on with the presentation, Frank."

Evans nodded, relieved. He lifted the remote and the next slide flashed onto the screen. The granite sculpture from the previous screen was outlined in bas-relief on a field of blue. To Plato, it looked more like a pregnant termite than ever.

Beneath the logo was the hospital's new slogan: RIVERSEDGE CARES.

"Our core mission statement," Evans explained. "All the other aspects of our mission flow from that central commitment—RiversEdge Cares. The statement will be part of all our television, radio, and print advertising, as well as appearing on all hospital literature and letterheads."

"Simple, direct, and to the point," the vice president said. "I think it will sell well."

"Mr. Young thought up the slogan himself," Evans told them. Clearly, the marketing director believed in giving credit where credit was due.

"It'll save on ink, anyway," Inverness commented dryly.

Before Young could reply, Evans flipped to the next slide and lowered his voice reverently. "And here is our new mission statement."

The policy was printed in gothic script on a scrollwork background. *We, the staff of RiversEdge Wellness Center, pledge to deliver economical, cost-effective medical care and strive to the best of our abilities to satisfy our clients, embodying in our work and our lives the commitment, service, and dedication that have earned our institution the reputation it deserves: RiversEdge Cares.*

"The mission statement will be printed on laminated badges, along with our new logo," Evans said proudly. "The entire staff will be required to wear the badges at all times, and to recite the statement by rote. Copies of the mission statement will be posted in all hospital corridors, lounges, meeting areas, and patient rooms."

"Who wrote it?" Annie Nussbaum asked.

"Judy Randolph," Evans replied. "One of my top staff members—an outstanding writer. I'll tell her you liked it."

"I don't," the nursing director said. "It sounds more like an advertisement than a mission statement. And forcing people to memorize it is demeaning."

Inverness nodded. "I think it sounds like something from a used-car dealership."

"That's quite enough," Millburn flared. It was the first time Plato had seen the CEO demonstrate any emotion at all. He glared at Inverness. "The point behind inviting you to this meeting was to facilitate cooperation, to work together—not to tear each other apart."

"We're not being asked to work on this," the medical director replied quietly. "We're simply being told what the administration's plans are for doing a two-bit face-lift on Riverside."

"I hardly need to remind you that if it weren't for the medical staff, the hospital wouldn't be in such dire need of a face-lift."

"What's *that* supposed to mean?" Plato asked.

Annie Nussbaum spoke up. "I think he's referring to Dr. Surfraire."

"And the way Lionel Wallace's accident was handled," the CEO added. "This whole mess is a public relations nightmare—and it's the fault of your medical staff, Dr. Inverness. Mr. Young and Mr. Evans are just trying to clean up your mess."

The medical director slapped the table. "If you're implying that we were at fault in Lionel Wallace's death—"

"I'm not implying *anything*," Millburn answered. "The damage is done. Now we need to figure out how to handle it." He turned to Young and Evans. "This marketing campaign couldn't have come at a better time. If we can distance Riverside from Dr. Surfraire—"

Plato's pager went off just then. He flipped the switch, relieved. As a newcomer to the higher levels of administration, he was reluctant to join the argument. Unlike Inverness and Nussbaum, Plato lacked the seniority and political power to stand up to the new CEO.

He stepped into the hallway and answered the page. It was Cal.

She filled him in on the results of Surfraire's autopsy. He listened for a full minute, stunned at the news. He didn't even remember hanging up; he just drifted back into the conference room.

Inverness was standing now, still arguing. "You're going to claim Surfraire was on *probation*? That's an outright lie. Just because Andre had a drinking problem—"

"He didn't have a drinking problem," Plato said quietly.

All eyes swiveled to him. Quentin Young's brows fluttered, as though he had forgotten Plato was a member of the committee.

"That was Cal—Dr. Marley," Plato explained. "She sat in on Surfraire's autopsy. The crash wasn't an accident."

"He was sloshed to the gills," Young said with a sneer. But the new vice president seemed nervous, edgy. He shook his head. "Don't tell me they found out he wasn't drunk—what about that bottle of Smirnoff's?"

"He *was* drunk," Plato agreed. "But he didn't *drink* that vodka. Someone hit him over the head, then gave it to him intravenously." He paused. "Andre Surfraire was murdered."

Silence reigned in the room.

Finally, Frank Evans spoke. "That's just *fantastic*! It'll be like a shot in the arm for RiversEdge Wellness Center!"

Chapter 8

The Deeble sisters were holding Plato's office under siege.

"Tell him about your *foot*, Eustacia!" one sister shouted.

Eustacia Deeble, who was moderately demented as well as hard of hearing, turned to her sister, Annabelle. "What? What's that?"

Annabelle, who actually *was* a sister—a retired nun—pounded the floor with her white cane. Although she was far sharper than her older sister, poor Annabelle had lost her sight to diabetes. She had lost most of her patience along with her sight. Not that she had much patience left to lose anyway; she had dedicated her career to hammering sense into grade-school students, before finally retiring last year.

Eustacia, a former flapper and rumrunner's moll who had outlived three husbands, two sons, and a live-in "gentleman friend," seemed determined to drive her prim, teetotalling sister into a life of drinking and gambling and licentiousness. She still dyed her hair platinum-blond, wore high heels and halter tops in the summer, and had a wicked Bingo habit.

Together, the Deeble sisters made a formidable pair.

"What's that?" Eustacia repeated.

Annabelle hammered the floor over and over again.

"Your *foot*! Remember how your foot was paining you?"

Annabelle's cane came down hard on her sister's left foot. Eustacia squealed.

"Ouch! What'd you have to do that for, missy?" She turned to Plato. "Dr. Marley, my foot's been paining me *ever* so much."

Plato sighed. Visits with the Deeble sisters always took at least an hour, and usually more. But his new receptionist had scheduled them into two ten-minute slots. When he had protested that it was far too little time, the receptionist had smiled sweetly and pointed out the bright side—Plato could stay as long as he wanted, since the Deebles were his last patients of the day.

A very long day. To help make the residencies and fellowships more cost-effective, most of the teaching practices were holding evening office hours. Wednesday was Plato's turn. So here he was, at eight-thirty in the evening, trying to get rid of the Deeble sisters.

The daytime receptionist had left at five.

"Let me take a look," Plato muttered.

"What's that?" Eustacia tweaked her hearing aid. Most of the time, she kept it turned down low so she couldn't hear her sister's well-intentioned rantings. Which made Annabelle even angrier. "You'll have to speak up, doctor. My hearing isn't so good."

She smiled sweetly at him, then turned to her sister. "He sure is a looker, ain't he?"

"Eustacia!" Annabelle bristled, scandalized.

"Well, he *is*," Eustacia insisted as she watched him remove her shoe. "Too bad you can't see him. Reminds me of Marvin."

"Your first husband," Annabelle noted. "The only one I liked."

"Marvin was my second," Eustacia corrected. "You forgot about Sweet Jimmy."

"You didn't really marry *him*. Not in a church, anyway." She curled her lip. "Plus, Sweet Jimmy ended up in jail."

Eustacia sighed. "But he *was* sweet."

Plato tuned out their conversation while he examined the foot. Like her sister, Eustacia had diabetes, and her pain could be a warning sign of severe circulation problems. But the diagnosis was far more mundane, highlighted by a lumpy knob on the inside of the foot, which was tender to the touch.

"It's your bunions again, Eustacia."

"Oh." The woman's face fell. She had apparently been hoping for something more dramatic.

Plato held the shoe up and eyed it critically: a pointy-toed model with spike heels. At eighty-five years of age, it was a wonder Eustacia didn't fall and break a hip.

"Why aren't you wearing those shoes I prescribed?" he asked.

"I keep telling her," Annabelle interjected, rolling her eyes and sighing with a martyr's patience. "But she won't listen to me, not on your life."

Eustacia licked her lips and smiled slyly. "I lost them."

"Eustacia Madeline Deeble!" Annabelle hammered her cane on the floor again. "You tell this nice doctor the truth girl!" She turned to Plato. "Don't listen to her. She's lied morning, noon, and night since the day she was born."

"You shut your *mouth*," Eustacia sputtered in a rare show of anger. But she was more embarrassed than mad; she turtled her head down between her knobby shoulders and stared defiantly at Plato. "I just don't *want* to wear those clodhoppers. They make me look like a two-legged cow."

"That's not the *shoes*," Annabelle muttered softly.

Eustacia eyed her sister suspiciously. "What'd you say?"

"Who's going to see you, anyway? We never get any callers, and *I* sure can't tell the difference."

"You *have* to wear the shoes, Eustacia." Plato patted her knee. "Otherwise, that pain will just keep getting worse and you're going to need surgery."

"Oh, *Lord!*" Her lower lip quivered. "Not another operation."

"That's telling her." Annabelle cackled approvingly.

"If you wear the shoes, you won't need surgery," Plato promised. That wasn't necessarily true, but he couldn't think of any other way to ensure that she would actually wear them. "And they'll make your feet feel a lot better. Try it, for me. Okay?"

"Do I have to wear them to Bingo?" she asked sadly. "It's just one night a week."

"No," Plato replied. "As long as you sit most of the time."

"Then you've got a deal." She nodded, then turned her hearing aid back down again.

As Plato helped her get the shoes back on, Annabelle leaned over and murmured, "I heard about that surgeon getting killed."

Plato looked up. "Dr. Surfraire?"

Eustacia's hearing aid squealed like a trapped mouse. She fiddled with it and frowned. "What're you two whispering about?"

"That doctor that got himself killed—Surfer, I think his name was." Annabelle turned to her sister. "He operated on you, remember?"

"Oh, Lord!" Eustacia rubbed her stomach where

Plato knew a huge scar lurked. "Don't talk to me about operations!"

"She doesn't remember," Annabelle said quietly. "But *I* do. He said he'd take her gallbladder out, simple as pie. Except it wasn't simple at all—poor Eustacia almost *died*. Father McHenry even gave her the last rites."

"I did *too* remember it," Eustacia insisted. She rubbed her stomach again. "Never wore a two-piece bathing suit after that."

"Good thing, too—you were about seventy years old by then." Annabelle leaned closer to Plato. "Surfer said it wasn't his fault, but I knew better. I'd swear on a stack of Bibles that he was drunk as sin that day." She sniffed, then jerked her head toward her sister. "Believe me, I can *tell*."

"You quit your whispering!" Eustacia complained.

"Good riddance, I say—even though it's a sin to think so." She nodded firmly. "The Lord works in mysterious ways."

Plato nodded. "He certainly does."

After finally showing the Deeble sisters the door and dictating their charts, Plato went down to Medical Records and asked to see Eustacia Deeble's hospital file. The clerk took his order and disappeared through the swing doors that hid Riverside's tons of charts in a mysterious warren of elevators and pulleys and sliding aisles. She reappeared five minutes later, pushing a heavy steel cart. Atop the cart was a stack of medical records. Plato expected her to hand him one of the charts.

"Here you go," she announced.

"Which one is it?"

"All of them," she replied simply, then disappeared into her chamber again.

Plato stared at the stack, stunned. And Eustacia was the *healthy* one.

He fingered the top chart on the stack, wondering why he was bothering. What possible difference did it make if Andre Surfraire had screwed up Eustacia's gallbladder operation?

But somehow he had to know, had to find out whether the allegations about Surfraire's drinking problems were true. *Had* the surgeon allowed his addiction to affect his performance?

Plato pulled the cart over to a desk, selected a chart at random, and loosened his tie. Winter or summer, the dictation room was always hot as a furnace. Literally— the room was flanked on either side by the heating plant and the power generators.

Based on his office records, Plato knew that Eustacia had her gallbladder operation about twenty years ago. Finding the chart didn't take long—it was the thickest one in the pile. A sixty-day hospitalization, eighteen years ago. Plato thought it odd that the chart hadn't been reduced to microfilm, until he realized that Eustacia had never stayed out of the hospital for more than a year or so. The hospital only microfilmed patient records that were inactive for a period of several years.

Plato pulled his tie off and unbuttoned his shirt, feeling the sweat roll down his neck and chest. With a few rocks and some redwood paneling, the dictation room could do a nice business as a sauna.

Eustacia's chart was like a time capsule from the past—antibiotics and drugs that had been off the formulary for the past decade, lab results written by hand, unfamiliar routines and styles. But the biggest difference was the lack of concern with time and money. Eighteen years ago, the government and insurance providers were just learning the ropes of medical care restrictions, just beginning to impose limits on lengths of stay and reimbursements for procedures. Eustacia Deeble was well insured (thanks to husband number three), and so she had been admitted two days before the operation for testing and "preoperative observation." From what Plato could see, the surgery itself had gone well, although there had been extensive bleeding which required a transfusion.

Plato recognized one of the names on the list of participants: the chief O.R. scrub nurse on the operation was an A. Nussbaum.

Interesting—he hadn't realized that Annie had started out as a surgical nurse. On the other hand, she had to start somewhere. And her participation in a surgery with Surfraire certainly didn't make her a murderer. Did it?

Two days after Eustacia's operation, infection had set in. The wound had broken apart, requiring the sutures to be removed. Because it had to stay open for the infection to drain, the incision had healed by "primary intention," a slow and clumsy process leading to the formation of the massive scar that Eustacia bore to this day.

But Plato could certainly find no evidence that Surfraire had been drunk, or indeed had made any obvious mistakes. On the other hand, medical records were notoriously cautious in reporting problems, always trying to avoid pointing the finger of blame.

The infection *had* been investigated, by a representative of the peer review committee. The physician—another surgeon whose name Plato didn't recognize—had cleared the team of blame, stating that the infection was simply "an unfortunate and random consequence that might follow any surgery." The chief of surgery himself had reviewed the results and cosigned the report.

Plato *did* recognize that name. It was quite familiar.

Eighteen years ago, the chief of surgery had been Lionel Wallace.

"*There* you are!"

Cal was standing in the doorway to the chart room, hands on her hips, exasperation in her eyes.

Plato closed the chart and flipped it onto the pile. He smiled at Cal. "You finally ready to leave?"

"I've *been* ready." She stalked over, folded her arms, and glared down at him. "I called your office half an hour ago, no answer. I've paged you five times since then. How long does it take you to answer a page?"

"I didn't get any pages. Maybe the battery—" Plato patted his pocket. "*Damn!* I must've left it across the street." He shrugged apologetically. "Sorry."

"It's okay. I got a whole ton of paperwork done tonight." She smiled. "I'm just glad I'm not one of your patients."

Plato shuddered, thinking of Eustacia and Annabelle Deeble. "Believe me, *I'm* glad you're not one of them, too." He squeezed her hand, then stood and wheeled the cart back to the counter.

Cal frowned at the pile of charts. "Behind on your dictations again?"

"Nope. I was just checking something out."

They followed the maze of corridors toward the tunnel leading back to the outpatient building. As they walked, Plato told her about his visit with the Deeble sisters, Annabelle's reaction to Surfraire's death, and her claims about the surgeon's incompetence and drunkenness.

"Did the chart show anything?" Cal asked.

"Not really—just the infection." They had reached the basement of the office building. Plato punched the elevator button and waited. "They even did a peer review of the case, but they didn't blame anyone. I *did* find out a few interesting things, though."

"Like what?"

He followed her onto the elevator and grinned. "Guess who was the head scrub nurse on the case?"

"Annie Nussbaum," Cal replied instantly.

Plato's face fell. "How did you know?"

"I didn't—it was just a guess." She shrugged. "But I've heard Annie did a stint in the O.R. before she got her Ph.D."

"You're no fun."

"What else did you find out?" she asked as they stepped off the elevator. "You said a *couple* of interesting things."

"You probably already know," he replied glumly. "Guess who was the chief of surgery eighteen years ago."

"Lionel Wallace," she replied confidently.

Plato sighed. "Is there anything about Riverside you *don't* know?"

"Yeah." She waited while he unlocked the office door. "I don't know which residency is going to get cut first."

They walked through the slightly seedy waiting room, past the dusty fake potted plants, and down the long, dark corridor that led to Plato's office. He flicked on the light. Sure enough, the black Motorola pager was sitting on his desk.

"Thank goodness," Cal sighed. "I was afraid we'd spend another night hunting all over the hospital for it."

"Last time, it was *your* pager that got lost," he pointed out. They had spent two hours stalking the hospital for Cal's pager, dialing its number and over and over again, then listening in hushed silence like a pair of hunting dogs for the telltale *peep-peep-peep* of their prey. Cal had finally found it in the cold room of the morgue downstairs; it had slipped out during an autopsy. "Remember?"

"I know, I know." She leaned against the doorjamb. "I'm just hungry, that's all. How about if we head down to John Q's for a steak?"

"You're *that* hungry?" he asked, surprised. John Q's Steak House on Public Square was famous for serving brontosaurus-sized slabs of beef. "Maybe you *are* pregnant."

"Impossible, remember?" She patted her stomach. "I just skipped lunch, that's all."

"John Q's is fine with me—at least we can afford it. For now." He picked up the pager and glanced at the display. "Just let me flip through these numbers and make sure nobody else paged me."

Sure enough, Cal's office number showed up five times on the display. But the pager held a sixth message: an outside number with a Shaker Heights exchange.

"Funny," Plato said. "I don't recognize this one."

Usually, the paging service screened his calls. But a few people had the direct number for his pager—Cal, and Plato's cousin Homer, a few friends and colleagues, and a couple of terminally ill patients. He worried that one of those patients was paging him directly—a true emergency.

Cal cleared some debris from one of his chairs and slumped into it with a sigh. "You'd better check it out."

Plato dialed the number. To his surprise, Cy Kettering's raspy voice answered.

"This is Plato Marley, Cy. Did you page me?"

"Yes." The chief of psychiatry took a deep breath. "Yes, I did."

Plato waited for him to explain. The silence on the other end of the line stretched on and on. Finally, Kettering spoke.

"I'm not sure if I'm doing the right thing." His voice

was tired, and edgy. "I suppose it all depends on whether my guess is on target."

Across the room, Cal was frowning a question. Plato shrugged back.

"What's this about, Cy?"

Again, the psychiatrist seemed to need time to gather his thoughts. He cleared his throat twice, then finally replied.

"It's about Andre Surfraire." Kettering's reserve seemed to fall away, like a dam bursting. "I think I might know something about the case. That is, if what I heard was true. Did they really find out he was murdered?"

"Yes," Plato confirmed. "Cal was at the autopsy— she told me herself."

"Then I need to talk to you," he said. "To *both* of you, but especially to Cal. I need to know what she found out."

"Have you said anything to the police?" he asked, though he could guess the answer.

"*No!*" Cy almost shouted, then lowered his voice again. "I'm not even sure I should be talking to you folks—not sure whether it's right, ethical. But I have to tell *someone*—other doctors, anyway. Just in case."

"In case *what*, Cy?"

"Can you two come over to my place?" he asked suddenly. "Now, tonight?"

"Come over?" Plato echoed. "We're just leaving work—we haven't—"

He broke off when he saw Cal nodding her head vigorously.

"I guess we can drop by," he amended. "How about giving me directions?"

Plato jotted down the street and address. It would be easy to find—a side street off Fairmont, out in Shaker Heights.

"We'll be there as soon as we can," he promised Kettering.

"Just be careful," the psychiatrist warned. "If I'm right about what happened to Andre—and Lionel—someone else might get killed before this is over. Maybe all of us."

"What do you—" Plato asked frantically. But the phone was dead. The psychiatrist had hung up.

He turned to Cal. "Let's go. I'll explain on the way."

Chapter 9

"He said *what*?"

Plato ignored Cal's remark and concentrated on the road. He'd taken a shortcut near Case Western, lost his bearings among the winding, tortuous streets around Severance Hall, and finally ended up in Little Italy. Which wasn't surprising—some sort of psychic force seemed to draw all the lost travelers of Cleveland to that tight-knit neighborhood of posh Italian restaurants and bars and bakeries and delicatessens.

And at the heart of the enclave, Mayfield Road tapered down to a cramped two lanes, with a stoplight that seemed to change only every ten minutes or so. The strategy was to keep you there until you surrendered to temptation and dove headfirst into one of those mouth-watering restaurants on Murray Hill or Mayfield, and admitted that life was made for living and that a little stop for a bite to eat wouldn't hurt, since you were already late anyway. To get you into that easygoing Mediterranean state of mind.

Which was fine, unless you really *had* to get somewhere fast. Like now.

Plato crawled past Holy Rosary Church, saying a silent prayer to the flock of saints on the roof that he was going in the right direction. Finally, he turned to Cal.

"Cy said something about how more people might

get killed before all this is over." He licked his lips.
"And then he said something like 'maybe all of us.' "

"All of *who*?"

"I don't know." Plato shrugged, exasperated. "He
hung up before I could ask."

"Maybe all of us," Cal repeated quietly. "Why was
he calling *us,* anyway?"

"Because we're doctors," he answered, suddenly remembering. The light finally changed, and he gunned
the Acura up the steep stone-walled road and into the
Heights. "It's some kind of ethical problem—something
he didn't want to talk to the police about."

"I don't like the sound of this, Plato." She shivered,
then put a hand on his arm. "You'd better hurry."

"I *know*." Nearly an hour had passed since Cy's call;
they had gathered up their coats and rushed to the
physicians' parking lot near the river, only to realize
that the Acura was almost out of gas. And at this time
of night, finding an open gas station downtown was as
likely as bumping into a Baltimore Ravens fan.

But they were almost there. Plato turned onto Fair-
mount, racing east and pausing every block to read the
signs. Finally, he spotted the cross street that led to
Kettering's home, a winding road lined with ancient
mansions of brick and granite, ivy-covered and slate-
roofed, relics of Cleveland's grand old days. Despite
their age, most of the homes were well kept, with
neatly manicured lawns and hedges, stately oaks and
maples, and a Lexus or Audi in every other drive.

Luckily, Cy Kettering's home had an illuminated address sign near the street. Plato pulled into the driveway and parked, suddenly realizing that he knew
almost nothing about the old psychiatrist; he didn't
even know whether Kettering was married or had children. The chief of psychiatry had been at Riverside
since long before Plato began his training, but he never

attended hospital functions or social gatherings. He rarely even made it to the medical staff meetings.

So it was especially impressive that Wallace had successfully cajoled Kettering into joining the Camp *Success!* venture. Plato wondered what sort of threat the late CEO had made to convince his chief of psychiatry to attend.

Kettering's home was more modest than most on his street, a tidy brick villa with mullioned windows and marble trim. A broad stone walkway wound through a small garden toward the sheltered front porch. Wrought-iron benches and marble lawn statues were scattered randomly through the garden; the statues were worn and chipped, like markers in an old cemetery.

The doorbell looked like it had been installed by Thomas Edison himself. Cal pressed it dubiously, and Plato tried the huge brass knocker. They waited a few minutes, then tried again. No answer.

"Maybe he went out," Cal suggested.

Plato shook his head. "He wouldn't do that—not after asking us to come over." He gestured to the window. "Anyway, most of the lights are on."

She shrugged. "This is a pretty big house—knock a little harder."

Plato slammed the knocker until old paint shivered down from the doorframe overhead. They waited a few more minutes. Cal frowned.

"You're *sure* you got the address right?"

"Come on, Cal," he began. "I wrote it down—you want to see?"

"Shh!" She tilted her head, listening.

Plato leaned out to peer through the front window. Nothing—the foyer was empty except for an antique mahogany lamp table and a matching chair. A flight of carpeted stairs led up into the darkness of the second floor.

"Is he coming?" Plato asked.

"No." She tugged his arm. "Follow me."

Cal led him back down the walk to the driveway, then paused. "Hear that?"

"Hear *what*?" Plato asked, exasperated. Cal's hearing had always been better than his—too many rock concerts, he supposed. "What's going on?"

She didn't answer, just motioned for him to follow her up the driveway. Frustrated, he complied. And as they moved past the back of the house, he finally heard it. A muted *thrum,* like a well-tuned machine. An engine, maybe—

Cal was running now, and Plato finally understood why. He followed her to the garage, an old one-car building in the back corner of the lot. The dull throb of a car's motor was obvious now, coming from behind the closed swing doors of the garage. They ran to the doors and tugged the handles, only to hear the rattle of chains.

The huge doors were padlocked shut. Plato ran around to the side of the garage, but that entry door was also closed and locked. It was sturdy, too—newly installed, unlike the swing doors at the front.

He ran back to the double doors, where Cal was wrestling with the padlocks. She turned to him, her voice breaking. "They're too *strong*. I'd better run to the neighbors' house and call the police."

"Go!" he urged. "I'll keep trying to get in."

He turned to the doors again. By the time the police came, it would be too late. It probably was already. Summoning all of his strength, Plato backed up from the doors, took a running start, and crashed his shoulder into the old wood.

And nearly broke his collarbone. It always worked in the movies, but this time the doors had barely budged. The chains glinted in the moonlight, mocking his efforts.

Wincing with pain, Plato turned around and saw the pretty red Acura parked at the end of the driveway. He ran back, hopped in, and started the car.

After edging the front bumper against the doors, he slowly stepped on the gas. The swing doors buckled and creaked, shuddered, and finally tore loose from their hinges, crashing down on the hood of the Acura like a wooden avalanche, rocking the car and shattering the front windshield.

Plato wrestled the car door open and stepped out, nearly retching from the sudden rush of hot exhaust fumes. He climbed over the wreckage of the swing doors, slipping and falling onto the back fender of Kettering's Audi. Finally, he made it to his feet and stumbled to the driver's-side door.

Cy Kettering was inside, with the windows rolled down. The old psychiatrist was slumped against the steering wheel, his leathery face slack and lifeless in the dim light.

Trying to hold his breath, to stay alert, Plato yanked the door open and dragged Kettering onto the dirt floor of the garage before remembering to reach in and switch the motor off. Cautiously, he took a slow, shuddering breath. The air had already improved, no doubt because of the massive opening left by the shattered double doors.

Plato leaned down to grab the old psychiatrist's hands. Kettering had always seemed like a parched and shriveled mummy of himself, a sun-dried raisin of a man. Talking to him, you got the feeling that a sneeze or a harsh word might send him spiraling into the air. He probably didn't weigh much over a hundred pounds.

But as Plato tried to move him, Cy Kettering suddenly seemed even heavier than Andre Surfraire, the late chief of surgery. He wrestled the body along the garage floor, panting and wheezing with effort. His head was starting to pound, and his vision was growing dim. Every step, he paused to cough and gasp for air, waiting for his sight to clear again. With each pause, the darkness seemed to take longer to wash away.

And finally Plato was stumbling blind, yanking on someone's hand and trudging along a few inches at a time, not knowing why but remembering that it was somebody important, that there was some reason he had to keep walking, keep dragging this heavy *thing* behind him, and then he lost even that, stumbling forward and lurching into something solid. He fell, vaguely hearing a sound like jangling bells or broken glass, remembering that shattered kitchen window from when he was just four years old, how his mother had kept the secret, paid to have it fixed before Dad came home. Remembering her smile, a face that somehow merged into Cal's.

And then, nothing.

"Plato? Plato?"

Cal stared down at her husband. Despite the ambulance's oxygen mask, his breaths were coming in quick, ratchety gasps. His lips were a bright cherry red, and his face was flushed as though he had just run a marathon. And yet his tissues were starving for oxygen. His flushed color was a sure sign of carbon monoxide poisoning; the gas tied up oxygen in a victim's red blood cells, latching on to it so that it couldn't get to the rest of the body. Each red blood cell was like an ice cream truck that kept touring the neighborhood, ringing its bell and showing off its treats, but never unlocking its doors to let the customers buy.

With their flushed, healthy color, carbon monoxide victims always made their embalmers look good.

"Stupid man." She felt hot tears brimming over. Stupid, stupid stupid. Why couldn't he have waited for her?

Damn it, Plato—wake up.

She must have said it aloud, for his eyelids flickered open. Plato's green eyes stared blankly at the dome lights overhead, then swiveled to fix on her face. The plastic mask misted over with a word.

"Mom?"

Cal leaned over and kissed his forehead. The ambulance lurched around a curve, and Cal almost fell into her husband's cot.

To her surprise and relief, Plato smiled and squeezed her hand. "Better wait till we get home, dear."

He glanced over at the paramedic sitting in the other seat. The ambulance attendant smiled, then leaned over and adjusted the oxygen flow.

"Looks like he'll be okay," he told Cal in a soft undertone. "Not like—"

She nodded. Not like Cy Kettering. Despite Plato's heroic efforts, the old psychiatrist had been long past hope. After asking the neighbors to call for an ambulance, Cal had dragged Plato out through the doorway and rushed back inside for Kettering. But the psychiatrist had no spontaneous breathing or pulse, and judging from his stone-cold skin, he was long past resuscitation.

Still, she had been about to try when the ambulance arrived.

Even the paramedics had seemed to see how hopeless it was; they had carried on their work mechanically, going through the motions of attempting resuscitation as they packed him into an ambulance.

The vehicle had drifted away silently, with no lights or flashers. More like a hearse than a rescue vehicle.

But Cal had discovered one important piece of evidence as she had prepared to resuscitate the psychiatrist: a damp, sticky lump on the back of the head. On the left—the exact same place where Surfraire's skull had been fractured.

She doubted the lump had come from Plato's attempt to drag Kettering out; the psychiatrist was probably dead long before they arrived. Still, while the paramedics were loading Plato into another ambulance, Cal had stolen back inside the garage. Sure enough, she found a deep red stain on the driver's headrest.

If only they had answered Kettering's page sooner, if only they hadn't stopped for gas or gotten lost in Little Italy, they might have caught the killer.

She glanced down at Plato. His eyes were closed again, and he was still breathing with obvious effort.

She shuddered. Maybe it was just as well that they *hadn't* arrived earlier.

The trip back to Riverside General took substantially less time than their drive to Kettering's house had. The ambulance had charted a course for the Cleveland Clinic, but Plato had insisted on Riverside.

They could use the business, he had joked, then had another coughing fit.

Luckily, Plato was stable enough to be admitted to the regular floor—just for observation, the ER doctor had told her reassuringly. But as a physician, Cal knew the dangers of carbon monoxide poisoning well enough. Victims could return to consciousness and seem perfectly stable, then crash days later when delayed brain damage set in. Some of the worst long-term effects of carbon monoxide poisoning were dementia, blindness, and psychosis.

So Cal waited beside her husband's bed, held his

hand, read him to sleep, and waited to learn about Plato's carbon monoxide levels.

And while she was waiting, a familiar face appeared in the doorway. Jeremy Ames—friend, poker buddy, and manic homicide lieutenant with the county sheriff's office. It was past midnight, and Plato was asleep—along with most of the city of Cleveland—but Jeremy Ames's thyroid condition limited him to about three hours of sleep a night. The rest of the time, he annoyed criminals and fellow cops, taught Tai Chi, and earned enough money to pay alimony to his three ex-wives.

Ames poked his snout into the doorway and squinted into the darkness like a lost puppy looking for its master.

"Cal?"

She jumped to her feet and hurried to the door. "*Shh. He's sleeping.*"

"How's he doing?" Jeremy whispered anxiously. He edged into the room and peered at the patient. Plato was still tied to the oxygen mask as well as an IV pole, and his eyes were black circles in the faint light.

"I think he'll be all right," she said cautiously. "We're still waiting for some test results."

"God, he looks *awful*." The detective frowned at Cal. "That *stiff* downstairs looks better than Plato—I saw him just as they were wheeling him out." He squinted at Plato again. "I think they pronounced the wrong guy."

"Very funny, Jeremy." Cal flashed a tired smile. "Dr. Kettering died from carbon monoxide poisoning—that's why his skin looks so flushed."

"Sorry. Hey, Plato doesn't look so bad." He peered at the bed again. "He looked lots worse on St. Patty's weekend—when you were out of town. Spent the whole day in bed after that party. Had to skip our poker match."

Cal huffed impatiently. "Are you here for a reason, Jeremy?"

The detective's face fell. "I just came to see how Plato was, to make sure he's okay."

"Uh-huh," she replied dubiously. "And what else?"

He shrugged. "And maybe ask a few questions, see what's going on here. I'm worried about you two kids."

His concern seemed genuine enough. He spread his hands innocently. "Listen—I ain't even assigned to the case. *Nobody* is, yet. But when I heard that call on the radio, about Plato being down at the scene, I had to come and check it out."

"I'm sorry, Jeremy. Really." She reached out and touched his arm. "That's awfully sweet of you."

"Kettering wasn't a friend of yours, was he?"

"No." She glanced back at Plato. He was sleeping like a baby.

"I've been reading about this stuff in the paper, Cal." He shrugged. "Takeovers and layoffs and shake-ups in the administration, and now three of your top people are dead. It all sounds crazy to me."

She took one last glance at Plato, then grabbed Jeremy's arm. "Come on."

"Where we going?"

"You can buy me a cup of coffee, and I'll tell you all about it."

Twenty minutes later, Jeremy Ames had heard the whole story, including the part about Cal's finding the bloodstained headrest in Kettering's car. He whistled.

"You're sure there's no way this Wallace guy might've been murdered?"

She shook her head. "None that I know of. Not unless the Geauga County coroner himself was involved—and he's as straight as they come.

"Yeah, I know." He frowned into his coffee—black as charcoal and thick as hot fudge at this hour. He tipped the Styrofoam cup back and drained it to the dregs, then smacked his lips. "Good stuff." He shook his head. "We'd better get back upstairs."

Cal felt a sudden chill. "Why?"

He stood and shrugged. "Well, look at it this way. Ten people went on that trip last weekend—ten high-ranking members of this hospital staff." He held up both hands, then dropped one thumb and two fingers. "Three of them are already dead. Who's left?"

"That's *crazy*, Jeremy." Cal stabbed the elevator button, willing it to hurry. "Why would anyone want to kill off the Council of Chiefs?"

"Disgruntled employees, some crazy ex-patient?" He shrugged. "Maybe it has something to do with this takeover business. How should I know?"

"But we don't have anything in common—it's not like we all worked on the same patient. And most of us have hardly any power in the hospital." She shook her head, then dashed into the elevator. "Anyway, Lionel Wallace's death was an accident."

Her calm words belied her sudden feeling of dread. Jeremy was an old friend—a smart cop with an instinct for danger. It had gotten him through Vietnam and Lebanon, and now it served him just as well on the sheriff's staff.

"And Surfraire's death would have been an accident, too," he pointed out, "if it hadn't been for some sharp forensic work." He waited calmly for the elevator doors to slide open at Plato's floor. "And the shrink's death would have been a suicide, right?"

Cal was jogging now, with the detective matching her stride for stride. An intern glanced up from a nursing station, then automatically followed, assuming a

code blue was in progress. Two medical students joined
the procession, then a nurse.

Running down Plato's corridor, she saw the truth of
Jeremy's warning. Maybe there *was* a connection between the victims, and they just hadn't found it yet. Or
maybe the killer was just targeting the Council of
Chiefs. It didn't *have* to make sense, not if they were
dealing with a psychotic killer.

Regardless, the hospital was an ideal killing
ground—the easiest place to make a murder seem like
a natural death.

Cal finally stopped, panting, at Plato's door. The
procession of medical personnel lurched to a halt behind her. She turned to explain that it wasn't a code after all when a senior resident hustled past her, calling
over his shoulder for a heart cart, *stat*.

Cal rushed inside, nearly colliding with the senior
resident as he turned back toward the door. He eyed her
with a puzzled frown.

"Must be the wrong room," he said, pointing over
his shoulder.

Cal smiled, relieved. She shook her head. "This is
my husband's room; there's no code blue. I was just—"

She followed the resident's gesture, and gasped.

The bed was empty. Plato was gone.

Chapter 10

The bathroom door opened. A haggard figure, clad in a hospital-issue bathrobe and flimsy gown, emerged.

"Jeremy! What arc *you* doing here?"

"Plato!" Cal rushed to his side. "Don't *ever* do that again!"

He glanced back at the bathroom and shook his head, puzzled. "Now, how can I make a promise like that?"

"You scared me half to death," she continued. Hefting his arm over her shoulders, she dragged him back to bed and strapped the oxygen mask over his face. "You stay right here until I say you can get up. Understand? *Stay.*"

Cal always used the same firm, shrill tone with Ghost at home when they left for work in the morning. Plato nodded dumbly, still confused.

"You're supposed to be on bed rest," she reminded him.

"I had to go to the bathroom," he mumbled into his mask.

"Bedpans, Plato. Ever heard of them?" She scrabbled under his bed and brandished the plastic seat like a lethal weapon. "You ring for the nurse and use this."

"I *can't*," he grumbled. "I tried. It's unnatural—it's like trying to breathe underwater."

"Well, you'd better learn, and fast." She perched on

the edge of the bed and glared at him. "I'm staying here tonight, to make sure you do."

"That's crazy," he huffed. "What are you so worried about?" He nodded at Jeremy. "And what's *he* doing here?"

"I came to see how you're doing, buddy." Jeremy slumped into a bedside chair. "I wanted to make sure you're all right."

"That's really sweet of you," Plato muttered dubiously. He frowned at his friend.

"And maybe to ask a few questions," he added.

"Uh-huh."

"I'm glad he's here," Cal said. "I'm worried about you—about *all* of us."

"All of who?"

"Cy Kettering was murdered," she finally said. Watching his face fall, Cal realized that Plato hadn't known Kettering was dead. "I'm sorry—you did the best you could. But Cy was probably already dead when we got there."

"You're sure it was murder?" he asked, then shook his head slowly. "I guess that's a dumb question. It couldn't be suicide—not after he asked us to come over."

"It could have been a suicide *gesture*," Cal admitted. Suicide attempts were sometimes made just before a person expected help to arrive. But sometimes a gesture became reality when that help arrived a little too late.

Except it wasn't a gesture, not this time. Kettering would hardly have locked both garage doors if he had hoped for a rescue. And after Surfraire's carefully staged death, a suicide by Kettering would have been quite a coincidence. Not to mention the strongest evidence of all.

"It could have been a gesture," Cal repeated, "except for one thing. I found clear signs that he was murdered."

She told him about the bloody lump on the back of Kettering's head, and the dark stains on the car's headrest.

"The killer *must* have known Kettering's death would be seen as murder," Jeremy observed.

Cal shrugged. "He—or she—may not have intended it to turn out that way. Maybe Cy struggled, or maybe the killer just hit him too hard. We almost missed Andre Surfraire's head injury."

"A blunt instrument." Jeremy nodded. "He or she knocks the victim out with a rubber cudgel or something, then stages a plausible death. For Surfraire, it was alcohol and a car wreck. And for Kettering, it was suicide." He sniffed. "Kind of ironic, that—a psychiatrist committing suicide."

"It happens," Plato said. "Anyway, I still don't see what this had to do with *us*. Why is Cal so worried? I barely knew Kettering or Surfraire. I never referred any patients to either of them."

Cal told him about her conversation with Jeremy, the detective's concern that a killer could be targeting Riverside's Council of Chiefs.

"That's ridiculous." He waved a hand. "We've got nothing in common—nothing at all, other than our positions here at Riverside. No sane person would—"

"The killer doesn't *have* to be sane," Jeremy pointed out.

Plato rolled his eyes. "Let's not get melodramatic, here. Besides, Lionel Wallace's death was an accident, right?"

Cal nodded, then shot a glance at the detective. "Jeremy was just asking me about that. I told him you can't *fake* an allergic reaction."

"Exactly." Plato folded his arms. "I still think this is

all a coincidence. We're not even sure that Kettering and Surfraire were killed by the same person."

"We're pretty damned close to sure," the detective interrupted. He glanced at Cal. "Two doctors, hit on the head, both in the same spot, right?"

Cal nodded.

"But even so, Wallace's death doesn't fit the pattern." Plato adjusted the oxygen mask, then grinned at Cal. "Is that why you looked so scared just now? You thought someone came in and kidnapped me?"

"We didn't know *what* to think," Cal confessed. "You had just disappeared."

"If this killer is as clever as you think, he wouldn't bother kidnapping me." Plato chuckled, his breath clouding the plastic mask. "He'd just slip some cyanide into my IV line, or smother me with a pillow. Easy as pie."

"That does it." Cal hitched closer and squared her shoulders—a lioness protecting her helpless cub. "I'm staying here tonight."

"Suit yourself," Jeremy told her. He glanced at the clock on the wall. It was past two a.m. "I'm heading back home and to bed. If I don't get at least three hours of sleep a night, I'm a wreck the next day."

After Jeremy left, Cal built herself a nest of chairs and blankets and pillows, then settled in. Plato tried to coax her into the hospital bed, but she stood firm. Riverside General already had enough gossip floating around. Besides, she would have probably strangled herself on the intravenous tubing or the oxygen line.

Their fitful sleep was interrupted by the usual hospital routine: nurses checking vital signs and drawing blood, overhead pages blaring from the hallway, and a delirious patient who wandered into their room looking for the main entrance to Halle's department store.

Not long after that, Cal heard a furtive rustling. She glanced up to see Plato slipping off his oxygen mask and creeping out of bed. She reached out and yanked him down again.

"Going somewhere, big boy?"

"Just a little pit stop." He smiled hopefully.

"Nuh-uh." She strapped the oxygen mask back on and paged the nurse. "You're on strict bed rest, remember?"

He slumped back down again, defeated.

The nurse who responded to the call was young and slim and gorgeous. She looked like a television nurse. Her dark blue uniform identified her as a nursing student; it fit her so snugly that it might have been professionally altered. Perhaps it was.

She saw Plato and smiled. "What is it, Dr. Marley?"

"I—uh—er," Plato stammered.

"My husband needs to use the bedpan," Cal replied, standing. "And don't let him talk you into helping him to the bathroom. He's on strict bed rest, and he's kind of a smooth talker."

The nursing student giggled. She couldn't have been more than twenty years old. "I know—about how he's a smooth talker."

Heading out of the room, Cal frowned. "You *do?*"

"Yeah." The student giggled again. "I met him at the St. Patrick's Day party last week." She turned to Plato. "Remember, Dr. Marley?"

He frowned. "I—uh—er—"

"What a *character,*" she continued. "Well, when he and Dr. Simmons talked us into dunking poor Dr. Wallace, I had no idea—"

Plato interrupted her reminiscence. "Could I have that bedpan now?"

"Oh, sure." The nursing student scurried over. "Right away."

Cal moved back to Plato's side and patted his shoulder, grinning wickedly. "I think I'll go for a little walk. I know I'm leaving you in *very* good hands."

Nathan Simmons arrived at the crack of dawn. The Marleys' family doctor was an old medical school buddy of Plato's. Tremendously compulsive, but equally dedicated to his patients, Nathan was a good friend as well as a good doctor. He also understood Plato and tolerated his cantankerous behavior as a patient with the even-tempered resignation of a mother soothing a cranky child.

Nathan had paraded in with the hospital chart, tossed good-mornings left and right, and flipped through Plato's lab results while he stood at the foot of the bed, grunting and muttering to himself and finally eyeing Plato with ill-concealed disapproval.

"You're going to have to change your lifestyle, Plato." He snapped the chart shut and clucked. "Pneumonia last year, then someone tried to knock your block off with a crowbar, and now this."

He wrinkled his forehead, waggling his ill-fitting toupee disdainfully. "Blue Cross isn't going to thank you for this."

"Is he going to be all right?" Cal asked suddenly. "Nobody told us how the labs turned out."

"They didn't?" Nathan shook his head. "I'm sorry— I asked the intern to let you know when they came in. The labs look just fine." He squinted at Plato. "Your carbon monoxide level was just below the danger point, so your brain won't be any more damaged than it was to start with."

"Thanks, Nathan." Plato pulled the oxygen mask down and grinned. "Your sympathy is overwhelming."

"You didn't hire me for my bedside manner," he

replied. "You hired me for my skill, and expertise, and encyclopedic clinical knowledge."

"But most of all, because you're cheap."

Cal giggled. Like most physicians treating their peers, Nathan saw them for free, as a professional courtesy. Plato treated Nathan's mother the same way. Of course, they would still have to pay the *hospital's* charges.

Plato unclipped the mask and reached over to turn the oxygen valve off. "So I can go to work today, right?"

Nathan gave a mournful sigh. "I had hoped to keep you here one more day for observation. Carbon monoxide is a serious thing—brain cells are mighty precious, especially yours."

The patient grinned and tapped his head. "Because they're so powerful?"

"Because they're so *scarce*." He turned to Cal. "Can I trust you to get this guy home and *keep* him there? Make sure he doesn't exert himself?"

"He'll behave himself," she promised. "If I have to tie him down, he'll behave."

"Don't talk dirty in front of Nathan," Plato warned. "You know how sensitive he is."

"Yeah," she agreed. "Wouldn't want to spoil his lily-white reputation."

"Speaking of reputations, Cal—*you're* beginning to get one over in the medical education department." Nathan frowned. "You're two months behind with your new curriculum outline."

Nathan Simmons chaired the hospital's curriculum committee, which oversaw the various residencies at Riverside.

"I need another month, Nathan." Cal shrugged. "I just haven't had time. Besides, we may not *have* a residency next year."

"That's not the point." Nathan was a stickler for detail. "If you don't get it in by tomorrow, we'll have to report it to David Inverness."

"Another month," Cal pleaded. Not only would it be embarrassing to be reported to the chief of staff, but Inverness had the power to dock her pay until her department complied. *"Please?"*

"Tomorrow," he threatened. "Or else."

Cal sighed, then edged closer to Nathan with a menacing gleam in her eye. "You know, I've been meaning to ask you about something."

"What's that?" he asked, scribbling in his chart.

"About a certain St. Patrick's Day party last week." She smiled slowly. "I understand you and Plato had a pretty good time."

"Oh, yeah." He glanced up at her and froze. "You wouldn't say anything to Leah, would you?"

Nathan's wife, Leah, was a dermatologist, a health-food nut, a runner, and a strict Puritan when it came to alcohol. Like Cal, she had been away at a conference the weekend of the St. Patrick's Day party.

"That's up to you, Nathan." She folded her arms. "I'm *sure* she'd be interested."

"Come to think of it," he replied, "we *do* have a pretty full meeting planned tomorrow. Maybe you'd better take another month to polish up that curriculum plan. Okay?"

"Fine." She patted his shoulder fondly. "I was sure you'd see things my way."

Nathan glanced at her hand as though a tarantula had landed on his coat. He edged away and scurried out the door with a quick farewell.

Cal watched him vanish, then flashed a quizzical smile at Plato. "He sure was in a big hurry."

Plato grimaced. "You wouldn't *really* say anything to Leah, would you?"

"Of course not." She shrugged. "But he doesn't have to know that."

"I'm glad you're on my side." He shivered, then sat up. "Let's get out of here before Nathan changes his mind."

He dressed quickly, and they hurried down the hall toward the elevators. But Plato paused as they passed the nursing station.

"What is it?" Cal asked.

"I want to take a look at my chart." He sidled around the counter and flipped through the rack. "I'm curious to see how my other labs turned out."

"Well, hurry up." She wriggled her shoulders. "I want to get home and take a shower."

"Me, too." He found his chart and carried it over to a desk. "I feel like a snake that's ready to molt."

Together they leafed through the paramedics' notes, the emergency room report, the admitting intern's history and physical, and the laboratory workup. Plato glanced at the first carbon monoxide blood level and whistled. "Thirty percent. It's a good thing you pulled me out of there in time."

"No kidding." Cal grimaced. "Too bad we couldn't help Cy Kettering. I heard his blood level was almost eighty."

"Wow." Plato turned to the last page of the lab section. With oxygen therapy to push the deadly chemical out of his red blood cells, the carbon monoxide in his system had quickly dropped to nearly undetectable levels. "Looks like I'm okay now."

"Not quite." She pointed to the bottom half of the page, which had a printout from Plato's standard blood chemistry panel.

"Look at that cholesterol," she scolded. "And your triglycerides are way up, too."

"That's the sign of a healthy diet."

"That's the sign of a *diet,* period." She patted his stomach. "Diet and exercise. You're starting to look like the Pillsbury doughboy with a beard."

"I don't have *time* to exercise anymore," he complained. "Not with the fellowship, and these new office hours. Neither do you."

He was right, Cal knew. Between the long hours, working nights and weekends, and the added responsibilities of chiefhood, they never had time for anything but work. The long walks they used to take through the woods behind their house were a thing of the past. So were the home-cooked dinners, the trips to the metroparks, and their weekly "dates." Their workloads had grown and spread, consuming their lives and crowding everything else out like some kind of cancer.

How had it happened so quickly?

Plato had turned back to the original history and physical, the required workup that was standard for all hospital admissions. He grunted, then frowned at Cal.

"What?"

"The intern forgot about my allergy to sulfa drugs," he replied.

Sure enough, the intern had written "NKA," for "no known allergies."

"Big deal," Cal said. "It was late by the time you got up here. He messed up—so what?"

"I was just thinking—if he *had* written it down, anyone who read my chart would know about it. Right?"

"Yeah." She shrugged. "So what?"

"So—what if I went on a camping trip, and somebody had checked my chart and knew I was allergic to sulfa?" He lowered his voice. "And what if they slipped a big dose of Septra into my food? I might die of an allergic reaction, right?"

"Maybe," Cal agreed grudgingly. Now she understood Plato's thinking. "But there are just a few problems. Like, how would the killer have gotten Wallace to eat a sulfa antibiotic? You can't just put it in somebody's food—it tastes pretty awful."

Plato's face fell. "That's right."

"And besides, we didn't have breakfast that morning, remember?"

"What about dinner—the night before?"

"That was an *immediate* hypersensitivity reaction," she pointed out. "The substance entered Wallace's system within an hour or so before he died."

"Oh, yeah." He slumped in the chair. "Dumb idea, I guess."

"That's okay." She patted his head fondly. "You've probably still got some carbon monoxide floating around up here."

"I guess so," he agreed glumly.

But as they walked down the hall to the elevators, Plato was quiet and pensive. Apparently, he wasn't ready to discard his theory just yet. Cal led him down the elevator and through the lobby, leaving him alone with his thoughts. It was a nice idea, but totally impractical. Wallace's death didn't seem to fit with the others. It probably *was* just a coincidence.

"I'll go and call us a taxi," Cal said.

Plato didn't seem to hear. He was frowning at the window of the hospital gift shop.

"Plato? Are you all right?"

He whirled and grabbed her arm. "Forget the taxi. We've got to check Lionel Wallace's hospital chart."

"Why?" Cal followed him as he turned away and scurried into the gift shop.

He stopped and pointed to a display beside the cash register. An elderly pink-coated, blue-haired hospital volunteer beamed at them. "Can I help you?"

"The pill dispenser!" he cried.

"Wonderful things," the volunteer said. She un-hooked a plastic case from the rack. The dispenser had seven compartments, each labeled with a day of the week. "I don't know what I'd do without mine. It's so hard to keep all my medications straight these days."

"Plato?" Cal hissed. "What's going *on*?"

He turned to her and explained. "Lionel Wallace had a seven-day pill dispenser. Just like this one. I knocked it off his chair when I came out to the living room last Friday night."

Cal nodded slowly. "You think somebody might have switched—"

"Easily." He flapped his arms. "The killer could have emptied a capsule and refilled it with powdered sulfa, or penicillin, or whatever Wallace was allergic to. He might have even substituted the pill itself, if he could find one that looked similar enough to Wallace's regular medicine."

"That's *assuming* Wallace had a drug allergy," Cal noted cautiously.

He nodded. "That's why we've got to check his hospital chart."

"Would you like a pill dispenser?" the volunteer asked hopefully. "Only two dollars, plus tax. And all of the profits go to the Children's Outreach Center."

Plato dug into his pocket and paid for the dispenser. Then he and Cal rushed for the elevator down to the chart room.

Once the attendant handed them Lionel Wallace's records, Plato and Cal pored over the latest hospitalization. The former CEO had been admitted just last year, for bronchopneumonia. Unfortunately, the admission history and physical bore the same cryptic notation as Plato's: NKA—no known allergies.

Cal shook her head, disappointed. "It was a good idea. An *awfully* good idea. I thought for sure—"

"Wait!" He flipped through the chart until he reached the discharge summary at the end. The final record of the hospitalization bore two principal diagnoses: bronchopneumonia, and a severe hypersensitivity reaction.

Wallace's pneumonia had been responsive to a very simple treatment—plain old penicillin. But on the second day of treatment, the CEO had developed watery eyes, hives, and mild wheezing which progressed to full-blown respiratory arrest. He had been placed on a ventilator and treated in the intensive care unit. Skin testing had later confirmed a severe allergy to penicillin.

"I take it all back," Cal said quietly. "Maybe *I'm* the one with carbon monoxide in my brain."

"You didn't see the pill dispenser that night," he replied. "*I* did. That's what made me so sure—"

He broke off, staring at the bottom of the page. Cal saw it at the same time.

The discharge summary was signed by Lionel Wallace's attending physician. The chief of staff and chief of internal medicine—David Inverness.

Chapter 11

They bumped into him on their way out the door. David Inverness looked even more harried and frazzled and tired than usual. His eyes were red and raw, and his shoulders slumped. His suit was rumpled, and his tie was askew. His thick gray hair poked up like the crest of some exotic bird.

He looked like an internist who had spent the night in a tumble dryer.

But Inverness brightened when he saw Plato and Cal. "Thank goodness you two are all right." He squinted at Plato critically. "*Are* you all right?"

"Never better." He shrugged. "I'm just heading home to change and get ready for work."

"He's heading home to *rest*, and take the day off," Cal corrected sternly. "Nathan Simmons almost kept him here another day."

"You two made the evening news, you know." Inverness moved closer and lowered his voice. "Is it true about Cy? That he killed himself?"

Plato started to answer, but Cal gave him a gentle nudge. "We don't know. I won't be involved in *this* autopsy."

"They called it an apparent suicide on the news." He closed his eyes and sighed. "Cy was pretty depressed—his wife died of cancer last fall. It really tore him up."

Cal shook her head. "I didn't know."

"We didn't know Cy very well," Plato added. "He kept to himself quite a bit."

Inverness frowned. "That's what surprised me."

"What do you mean?" Cal asked.

The internist combed his hand through his hair until the crest stood even taller. He glanced around the bustling waiting area, packed with patients and families and scurrying volunteers, then gestured toward the door of the physicians' lounge. "Maybe we'd better go someplace private."

Luckily, the lounge was empty; most of the doctors were upstairs making rounds. David Inverness poured himself a cup of black coffee while Cal fetched juice for herself and Plato. She didn't trust the coffee; chances were it had been simmering all night and was as thick and strong as coal tar—even worse than the deadly cafeteria brew. But that was how many of the doctors liked it, David Inverness included.

They sat at a small table near the window and waited for the internist to collect his thoughts. Glancing outside, Cal could see that the latest cold snap was finally over. Night-shift nurses were hurrying out to their cars in light overcoats, and smokers were clustered outside the employee entrance like the first robins of spring. A few brave green shoots poked up from the planters outside the window.

Spring was finally coming, and the days were getting longer. Maybe someday soon she'd make it home before dark.

Inverness sipped his coffee and perked up visibly.

"I've been Riverside's medical director and chief of staff for almost ten years now." he began. His voice was quiet and thoughtful, as though he were speaking to himself. "I've seen three department chairmen come and go, helped overhaul our residency programs, and appointed half a dozen department chiefs, including the two of you."

He stared out the window and shook his head. "But I've *never* seen anything like this. One accidental death, okay. An allergic reaction and a phony car accident, maybe." He set his Styrofoam cup on the table and grimaced. "But this suicide, coming so soon after the other deaths, is too much to believe. Especially—"

He broke off, frowning at his hands, then asked softly, "Why did you go to Cy's house last night?"

Cal glanced at Plato. He shrugged. She turned to Inverness reluctantly.

"We haven't been formally questioned by the police yet."

The medical director's shoulders slumped even further. "Then there *is* something more to this. Isn't there?"

Why is he so interested? Cal wondered. *Was he involved somehow?* She started to stand. "After we talk to the police, maybe we—"

"No, wait," Inverness touched her arm gently. "If you don't want to say anything, let me tell *you* what I think happened." He took another sip of coffee. "Cy Kettering called you last night. He said he wanted to talk about something—a suspicion, a concern, we'll never know. But it had something to do with Andre Surfraire."

He read the surprised looks on their faces and smiled sadly.

"You see, he called me last night, too. But I was too busy to talk; I was writing up the latest quarterly report for our *dear* administration." He spread his hands helplessly. "So Cy settled for meeting with me this morning, instead."

"Did he say anything more?" Plato asked.

"No. He *tried* to, but I cut him off." Inverness

drummed his fingers on the tabletop and looked away. "The truth is, I was trying to get out of here because I had an appointment." His voice trailed off. "But *that* didn't work out, either."

Cal shifted in her chair. "When did Cy call you?"

"He paged me—around seven o'clock." Inverness looked at Plato, then at Cal. "So you can see why I wanted to know what he told you last night. Apparently, he called you for the same reason."

Plato nodded slowly. "Yes, he did."

"Was there any chance—did you see any sign that he might have been *killed*?" The coffee cup quivered in his grip.

Cal stared at her hands, as though Kettering's blood might still be there. She didn't see much point in hiding the truth from Inverness. The autopsy would be performed today, and it would undoubtedly show that Riverside's chief of psychiatry had been murdered. The findings would probably become public late today or tomorrow morning.

"He'd been hit on the head," she finally replied. "Just like Andre Surfraire."

Inverness breathed a slow, resigned sigh. "I thought as much. And I think I might know what Cy was planning to tell us."

Cal frowned curiously.

"Like I said, I know a lot more about Riverside's politics and problems than most people—except maybe Cy Kettering." He smiled up at them. "Did you know he was once our medical director?"

Plato grunted. "You're kidding."

Cal understood his surprise. It had nothing to do with Kettering's intelligence or competence. But the gruff chief of psychiatry had seemed utterly devoid of political ambition. Ironically for a man in his field, he was famously antisocial, and his blunt manner had often sparked bitter conflicts at interdepartmental meetings. Having Cy Kettering as Riverside's medical director was like putting Saddam Hussein in charge of a Middle East peacekeeping mission.

"He was better than you might think," Inverness continued. "Back then, he was a real go-getter—politically savvy, a forceful negotiator, and tremendously ambitious." He grinned at the memory. "Not that people necessarily *liked* him; two department chiefs left during his tenure. But he was effective—at keeping the clinical staff in line and balancing power between the administration and the doctors." He shrugged sadly. "Unlike me."

"Things are a little different, now," Plato temporized. "The whole system has changed."

"It was already changing *then*—back in the eighties." He ran his hand through his hair again. "Cy saw the writing on the wall. He got sick of it, the workload and the headaches and the pressure for profits. His wife even threatened to leave him. So he just quit—probably the smartest thing he ever did. And *I* took his place."

Cal could hear the envy in his tone, the disappointment.

He waved it away. "But that's beside the point. What I'm trying to say is, Cy always knew how things worked, even after he stepped down. He still followed the game even though he wasn't a major player anymore. He had a gift for reading people, for knowing what they were thinking and planning. Sometimes he'd drop by my office and chat, slipping me some good advice, but pretending *he* was asking for help." Inverness shook his head. "But when Cy needed *my* help, I turned him away."

Plato shook his head. "You couldn't have known—"

"I *should* have—I should have seen it. The same way Cy did." He took a deep breath. "You may not believe this, but Riverside is doing extremely well. Better than some of our competitors, and certainly well enough to hold our own."

"But Millburn told us just the opposite," Cal protested.

"He's playing with numbers," Inverness replied. "The fact is, our administration has been very effective at drumming up contracts and cutting costs. *And* at slipping the profits into capital improvements, so our bottom line looks a lot different than it should." He smiled wryly. "We were doing well *despite* having Lionel Wallace as our CEO. Millburn and Young were always the power behind the throne anyway, even before Lionel was appointed. I doubt whether our late CEO knew the difference between a quarterly financial report and a checking account statement."

"Then why did Millburn tell us otherwise?" Plato asked. "Why pretend that the hospital is about to go under?"

"For a lot of reasons." Inverness spread his hands. "To justify more layoffs, and to rationalize killing services like our outreach clinic. And probably to squelch any protests over closing the residency programs."

"They're really thinking about that?"

The internist sighed. "It's going to happen, and very soon."

"But *why*?" Cal asked, bewildered. "Medical education is one of the biggest strengths of Riverside General—we have better clinicians because most of them are teachers, and we have residents on-site round-the-clock."

"Our affiliation with Siegel Medical College has to help, too," Plato added. "They always mention it in the advertisements. Surely the administration sees the value of our programs."

"I'm certain they do." He grimaced. "That's exactly why they want to get rid of them."

Cal frowned. "That doesn't make sense."

"It does if you're planning to sell the hospital," Plato replied quickly. He glanced at the internist. "Is that what this is all about?"

"I think so." He leaned closer and lowered his voice—as though even in this physicians' sanctuary the walls might have ears. "I think *that's* what Cy was trying to tell me."

"I still don't get it," Cal complained. "They want to make the hospital *less* valuable before it's sold?"

"Exactly." Inverness nodded. "By allowing the sale to go through, and fostering a low price, our top administrators stand to make a *lot* of money."

"Vista Health Management is notorious for playing hardball," Plato continued.

"Vista Health Management?" she asked.

"Our prospective buyers," Plato explained. "They own a string of hospitals and clinics throughout the midwest, and they have controlling interests in two or three big HMOs. That way, they can work both sides of the system and make sure all the money goes in *their* pockets."

Cal nodded. The practice was becoming more common—insurers or HMOs buying up hospitals and clinics, gaining direct control over the delivery of health care. With a big enough market share, they could start squeezing services down, wringing every penny from their patients while cutting back on care in the clinics and hospitals.

"And Vista is planning to buy Riverside," the internist concluded.

She frowned. "I still don't see how our administrators end up ahead."

"Because that's how Vista works," he replied.

"Nearly every time Vista purchases a hospital, they hire the top administrators at exorbitant salaries and pay huge signing bonuses. Often, the administrators don't stay for more than a few months. But with a couple of million dollars in their pockets, they can afford to retire."

"A couple of *million*?" Cal was stunned.

"Supposedly." He shrugged. "Most of their deals are kept pretty quiet, as you can imagine. But a few of my friends went through Vista takeovers in Illinois and Minnesota, and they saw what happened."

"The administrators are *bribed* to reduce the selling price of their hospitals?"

"Nothing quite so blatant—that would be illegal." Inverness swigged the last of his coffee. "But a hospital might suffer serious setbacks during the year before its sale, reducing the price by ten or fifteen percent. That can be tens of millions of dollars." He flipped the Styrofoam cup into the trash. "And so some of that money is passed on after the sale—as consultation fees, or signing bonuses, or whatever."

"What about the hospital's trustees?"

"They buy them off, too," Plato replied.

"Everybody wins," the internist observed dryly, "except the patients. And the doctors and nurses."

"Vista has already bought our big competitor on this side of the river," Plato pointed out. "Erie Shores Hospital. What do they need us for?"

"I heard they want to buy Riverside and close us down, and they don't care how they do it." He glanced at Cal. "That could explain a lot of things."

"The murders?" she asked, shaking her head skeptically. But then she thought about millions of dollars in bonuses, and the idea didn't seem nearly so implausible. Last week, she had autopsied a seventy-year-old man whose son had killed him and buried him in the backyard just after he cashed his social security check. The victim still had the stub in his pocket: one hundred sixty-seven dollars.

No, the explanation Inverness proposed didn't seem far-fetched at all.

But Plato still didn't see it that way. "I can't imagine anyone bumping off half our medical staff just to get a payoff."

"I know, it sounds crazy," the internist agreed. "But I think that's why Cy wanted to talk to me. He knew that Lionel and Andre were opposed to Riverside's sale; Andre sat on the Board of Trustees. Cy thought there might have been a connection with Lionel's death." He glanced meaningfully at Cal. "Of course, that *was* just an accident, wasn't it?"

Cal fidgeted under his gaze. "There are some other possibilities."

He sat up quickly. "Such as?"

"Allergic reactions can be induced." She shrugged. "It wasn't worth considering before. But now, after two other deaths, the coroner may want to take another look." She eyed him innocently. "What would you suggest?"

Inverness didn't hesitate. "I assume you knew I was Lionel's physician?"

"We didn't, until this morning." Plato sighed. "We took a look at his hospital chart."

"Then you know he was allergic to penicillin." He shifted in his chair. "*Terribly* allergic. Did you test for penicillin during the autopsy?"

"I didn't perform Lionel's autopsy," Cal reminded him. "That was done in Geauga County. But no, they didn't test for penicillin."

The internist frowned critically, until Cal explained that a special test would be required to check for the presence of penicillin in Wallace's blood. Routine toxicology screens had been performed to check for common poisons and narcotics, but identification of other drugs required far more specific tests.

"But you're planning to check?" Inverness asked finally.

"I'll talk to the Geauga coroner." She nodded. "I know he saved some blood samples, and I'm sure he'll be glad to run the test. He seemed puzzled by the autopsy, too."

"I should have mentioned Lionel's allergy earlier, I guess." He rubbed his eyes. "But it didn't seem important. Not then."

"How firmly did Wallace oppose the sale?" Plato asked.

"He was dead-set against it—I knew that for a fact." He grunted. "Last month, his blood pressure was sky-high. That's when he told me about the Vista offer. Apparently, Millburn and Young were all for it, but Lionel hated the idea. He thought it would be selling out."

Cal frowned. "I wonder if Vista approached him with an offer."

"He didn't say." Inverness shrugged. "Lionel probably didn't even *know* Vista worked that way."

Cal nodded. Wallace really was just a figurehead at Riverside; Vista didn't need to pay him off.

"Have you told the police about this?" she asked.

"What police?" he countered. "We've had three deaths in three different counties. I don't know who I would tell."

"We've got a friend in the Cuyahoga County sheriff's office." She told him about Jeremy Ames, and jotted down the detective's officer number. "Give him a call; I think he'll be very interested in talking with you."

"I will." Inverness pocketed the slip of paper and glanced at his watch. "I've got to run; I've got a full day ahead." He stood, then frowned down at Cal. "I understand that Plato won't make it to the medical staff meeting tonight, but I hope you can come."

Cal glanced at Plato; she had completely forgotten about the meeting. He shrugged back helplessly.

"I'll try," she promised. With all the extra work, they both had missed more evening staff meetings than she cared to think about. And as department chiefs, they were required to attend every single one.

"I really hope you can," he urged. "We'll be discussing the hospital's makeover—Plato has already heard about *that*." He rolled his eyes and sighed. "Plus, I'll be making an important announcement. I'd like as many chiefs as possible to be there."

Oddly enough, he sounded suddenly defeated, desperate. The medical director almost seemed to be pleading with them.

Cal found herself nodding in sympathy. "You can count on me—I'll be there."

After Inverness had left, Plato raised his eyebrows at Cal. "What do you suppose that was all about?"

"I don't know, but I think I'd better not miss this meeting." She shook her head. "Something tells me it's more bad news."

He nodded, and they walked to the door. "Maybe David wants us all to be pink-slipped *together*—for moral support, you know?"

"I don't think so." She grimaced. "Somehow, I'm thinking it's something even worse."

"What could be worse than getting fired?"

"I don't know." Cal shivered. "But I have a feeling we'll find out tonight."

Chapter 12

"I don't think you should stay home by yourself," Cal said later that morning.

"You want me to hire a babysitter?" Plato asked.

Cal had paid the taxi and walked Plato into the house—and now that they were finally home, she was fussing and fretting about leaving him behind. Plato felt perfectly fine, well enough to work and certainly fit enough to sit home by himself. If Cal hadn't already called Plato's partner to reschedule his appointments, he would have insisted on staying at Riverside.

She had taken her shower—alone, insisting that Plato needed his rest—then dove into a clean pair of slacks and a blouse and headed for the door. But on her way outside, she had paused and flashed a worried frown at him, like a first-time mother leaving her baby at a day care center.

"I wish I could stay here, but I've got to give a lecture at noon." She glanced at her watch and frowned up at him. "I really don't like leaving you here alone."

"No problem," Plato replied agreeably. "I'll just come back to work. I've got a ton of paperwork to finish up before the fellowship gets site-reviewed." He grinned. "Hilda can take my pulse and blood pressure every hour."

Hilda was Plato's nurse. Surely Cal would trust her

to keep an eye on him. He only wished he had thought of the idea earlier, back at Riverside.

"I'm not worried about your pulse and blood pressure, Plato." She turned away to stare out the storm door.

Standing behind her, Plato followed her gaze. The shattered Acura was parked in the driveway. Jeremy Ames had pulled some strings to get the vehicle towed home for them, but the windshield was still a jumble of cracks and splinters. They wouldn't be driving *that* car for a while.

"I'm worried about you," Cal said quietly. "About us."

"What's there to worry about?" he asked innocently. As though he didn't know.

She turned around and slid into his arms. Plato stroked her hair, touched and surprised by her sudden concern. Usually Cal was the fearless, reckless one, unafraid of anything.

"Three people have gotten killed," she muttered into his shirt. "So far."

"We don't know Wallace was murdered," he pointed out, blithely ignoring the fact that he had come up with the penicillin theory. "Anyway, why would anyone want to kill *us*? We're certainly not obstacles to the Vista takeover. We'll be lucky if we have jobs next week."

She leaned back to glance up at him. "I don't think David is right about that Vista business."

"Why not?"

"Because I don't believe the killer is thinking that clearly." She shrugged. "I'm wondering if it might be one of Cy's patients."

"Why do you say that?"

"Why else would the killer do these crazy things?" Cal shook her head. "He couldn't have hoped to make last night look like suicide. Surfraire's murder was already announced; the game was up." She stared at her hands again; she'd been doing that all morning. "Anyway, Cy's head bled quite a bit—the police found blood on the living room carpet and a trail of drops leading out to the garage."

Plato grimaced. "Maybe he just hit him too hard."

"But why bother dragging Cy out to the car?" she asked. "He was half-dead from the head injury; why waste time staging an obviously fake suicide?"

Plato stroked his beard thoughtfully. "So what do *you* think it's all about?"

She stared at the Acura again, as though the answer might be hidden in the shattered window glass, like a Magic Eye picture. "I wonder whether the *cause* of death might be more important than covering it up."

"The *cause* of death?" Plato frowned. Cal wasn't making any sense today. He thought David's theory about Vista was perfectly reasonable. So the killer screwed up last night—everyone makes mistakes.

"Assuming Lionel Wallace *was* murdered, we have three wildly different causes of death." She counted them on her finger. "Anaphylactic shock, a staged but quite fatal car accident, and a staged suicide. Doesn't that suggest something?"

"Three different killers?"

Cal rolled her eyes.

"What?" He folded his arms. "I thought murderers always used the same M.O."

"M.O.?"

"Method of operation," he said offhandedly. "Police lingo."

"Maybe they always use the same M.O. on television," she conceded. "But in real life, a killer can do whatever he wants."

"So the same guy—or girl—used three different techniques." Plato shrugged "I still don't see why that means he's crazy."

"It doesn't—it just reminds me of a case I read about." She closed her eyes. "Way back during my fellowship. This lady saw her husband get killed with a shotgun. She went off the deep end and started killing people with shotguns."

"Not many folks get killed with penicillin, Cal." He chuckled. "Unless they're germs."

"Very funny." She shrugged. "It's just an idea. But I wonder if somebody's acting something out through the murders. Something that's happened before . . ."

She shivered and moved close again. "Do you see why I'm worried?"

"I guess so." He squeezed her shoulders sympathetically. He didn't really see it, didn't understand why she had to assume some nut out there was trying to kill off all the chiefs at Riverside.

What method would they pick for Plato? Suffocation under a mountain of medical charts?

Cal pulled his head down to give him a long, intense kiss. Finally, she moved away and eyed him suspiciously. "You'll really stay home and rest?"

"Of course." He smiled reassuringly and gestured at the Acura. "It's not like I'm going anywhere in *that*."

She nodded, satisfied. "I'll call around six, just before the meeting. To make sure you're okay."

To make sure I'm still home, Plato thought.

He smiled again. "I'll be fine. If anyone comes by, I'll just sic Ghost and Dante on them."

But staying at home was easier said than done. After an early lunch of cold lasagna and Cap'n Crunch cereal, Plato settled down on the couch with three novels and couldn't get past the first chapter of any of them. The television was running nothing but daytime talk shows and informercials.

After catching himself getting excited about Martha

Stewart's idea for creating colorful window planters from old coffee cans and yarn, he flipped over to the Weather Channel. The steady drone of the meteor-evangelist lulled him into a dazed torpor.

Plato woke with a start and glanced at his watch. One-fifteen. He had slept for all of twelve minutes.

Five hours until dinnertime, he thought. Seven hours until Cal got home.

He moved over to the window and studied the Acura once again.

Stranded. But even if the car was okay, he wasn't supposed to drive. Plato had promised Cal that he would stay at home and rest. And a promise was a promise.

Still, it wouldn't hurt just to have the windshield fixed, he realized. As long as he was home, he might as well get something done. After all, what if their other car broke down?

Once his conscience was satisfied, Plato ambled into the kitchen and flipped through the telephone directory. The Windshield Doctors advertised that they made house calls. Plato dialed the number. Luckily, they weren't busy; after taking down his make and model, they promised to send a crew in just half an hour.

Plato hung up the phone and noticed the blinking light on the answering machine. Just one message. He pressed PLAY, expecting yet another AT&T solicitation.

But it wasn't. The gravelly voice was quite familiar; Plato had heard it just last night. For the last time, he had thought.

"Plato? This is Cy Kettering."

Plato shuddered. He felt like he was hearing a voice from the grave. Actually, he *was* hearing a voice from the grave.

"I guess you folks are on your way already, but I just wanted to warn you. I think I know why Andre died—I

realized it when I checked the location of the crash." He paused for a long moment. *"If I'm right, Lionel Wallace was murdered, too. It all fits togeth—"*BEEP!

"Damn it all!" Plato pounded the countertop.

Sprawled on the floor beside him, Ghost glanced up with sudden concern.

"It's okay, boy." He patted the dog's head, then waited for the tape to continue. Sure enough, the next message was an old one—the daily AT&T solicitation. He played Cy's message three more times, but couldn't glean any more information. Finally, he popped the tape out to save and pass on to Jeremy.

He moved into the living room and sifted through the stack of old newspapers. Tuesday's *Plain Dealer* gave the precise location of Surfraire's accident. A sharp curve out in Waite Hill, an exclusive part of Lake County on the east side of Cleveland. Near the Chagrin River.

Plato was familiar with the spot; he had once lived in Willoughby, just across the river from Waite Hill. He studied the article more carefully. Apparently, Surfraire's car had plummeted down the hill at high speed, crashed through the guardrail, and continued down the side of a cliff. The Porsche had been discovered nose-down in the mud of the river valley, crumpled beyond repair.

But what was so important about the location?

At the time, the police had offered no opinions about the cause of the accident; one officer simply stated that Surfraire probably traveled that stretch of road quite often, since his home was just up the street.

Why had Surfraire gone home after Millburn's gathering, rather than returning straight to the hospital?

Had he gone home, or had the killer simply staged the accident there? If the latter, why choose that particular spot?

Still carrying the newspaper, Plato crossed the living room and glanced longingly at the Acura. His conscience rumbled a warning, but he ignored it. Out near the street, the Windshield Doctors had just turned into the driveway. They were cautiously navigating an ancient converted ambulance through the pits and potholes of spring. The driver announced their arrival with a short blast from his siren.

Plato walked outside and met them in the driveway. The Windshield Doctors were both wearing white lab coats embroidered with their names. The driver was tall and grizzled and massively built, with a beer belly and a cheekful of chewing tobacco. The assistant was clearly his son—aside from the family resemblance, their lab coats were labeled BOB and BOB, JR.

"Where's our patient?" Bob asked with a grin.

"Over there." Plato gestured to the Acura nosed up against the carriage house door like a shy little girl hiding her face in her mother's skirt. "You brought along a replacement?"

"Sure," Bob answered as he sauntered over to the car. "But you might not need one—not if it's just a leak or a little crack." He spat into the grass and chuckled. "She might just need a little CPR, you know?"

"I think she's way beyond that," Plato replied.

Bob moved to the front of the Acura and gawked in amazement. He scratched his head and frowned at the intact hood and bumper, the immaculate roof. The damage was strictly limited to the windshield. Even the front bumper was barely dented from its impact with Cy Kettering's garage door.

"You're right," Bob said finally. "She's *way* beyond CPR."

Bob, Jr. sauntered up behind his father and whistled. "What'd you run into? An airplane?"

"Maybe a UFO," Bob answered with a chuckle. He

shook his head and sobered. "Pranksters, huh? Lots of kids hanging out on the freeway overpasses think it's funny to take somebody's head off with a rock."

"It wasn't a prank," Plato replied. He sighed. "It's kind of a long story."

"Say no more—we see a lot of those, too." Bob shot a knowing glance at his son. "Like I told you before, boy—don't *ever* get married."

Bob, Jr. nodded.

Plato just shrugged. He didn't see any point in trying to straighten them out; they wouldn't believe the truth if they heard it.

Bob jerked his head back to the ambulance, and Bob, Jr., scrambled to retrieve a new windshield. They did their work quickly and efficiently, pulling the ruined glass away and fitting a new windshield in its place. While Bob, Jr., sealed the edges to the frame, Bob, Sr., tallied up the bill. He took Plato's check and frowned.

"Plato Marley—now where did I hear that name before?" He folded the check into his pocket and squinted at his customer, sizing up his height and frowning at his midriff. "You didn't used to play for the Browns, did you?"

"Afraid not," he replied, sucking his gut in. "I work up at Riverside."

"Riverside?" Bob slapped his forehead. "*That's* it! You were on the news last night—you and your wife. Right?"

"That's what I heard," he admitted. "I didn't see it myself."

"I *knew* I recognized that name. You don't see many Platos around these days. 'Cept out in Youngstown." He thumbed another wad of tobacco into his cheek. "Too bad you couldn't save that guy. Damn brave thing you did, crashing the door and pulling him out."

Plato shrugged again, suddenly embarrassed.

"Tell you what I'll do." He reached into his pocket and tore the check in half. "Let's call this one on the house."

"I can't let you do that," Plato protested. He finally talked Bob into taking another check to cover the wholesale cost of the windshield itself, an absurdly small amount, and promised to call the Windshield Doctors if he ever needed another replacement.

Climbing into the ambulance again, Bob frowned at Plato. "Too bad about that hospital of yours. All sorts of bad things going on."

Plato nodded glumly.

"Course, you can't convince me that car crash wasn't an accident." Bob continued.

Plato looked up sharply. "What do you mean?"

"That surgeon folla that slipped off the road." He shrugged. "My brother's a collision specialist—body work. He gets a couple of customers every year from that stretch of road. They must get a crash a month there in the wintertime—it's a wonder they don't just shut it down."

After they left, Plato glanced back at the car. Bob had assured him that the seal would dry and the car would be perfectly safe to drive in just half an hour.

It wouldn't hurt to take if for a spin, to make sure that the windshield was secure and everything was still running properly. And while he was out, Plato just might happen to drive by the place where Andre Sufraire had suffered his last crash. After all, sitting in the car wasn't that much different from sitting around the house.

And besides, Cal would never know.

Plato's conscience grumbled once more, then finally surrendered.

Chapter 13

"That was an outstanding lecture," Marta Oberlin told Cal. "One of the best we've had this year."

"I bet you say that to all your guest faculty," Cal replied with a grin.

But she was pleased at the compliment. Oberlin was supposedly a tough person to satisfy, a firm hand at the tiller of the obstetrics and gynecology residency who had turned the failing program around in the two years since she had taken over as chief.

The two of them were siting in the "cockpit" of the obstetrics ward, eating the Chinese food that Marta had ordered after Cal's noon conference. The residents had eaten their lunches during the lecture, but Cal had had no opportunity. By the time the last question had finally been answered and the obstetrics residents had filed out of the conference room, Cal had been ravenously hungry. With everything that had happened last night and this morning, she hadn't eaten a normal meal since breakfast yesterday.

And the cafeteria was closed by the time her lecture was over.

Luckily, Marta treated her guest faculty well. Steaming cartons of Szechuan pork, fried rice, General Tso's chicken, and vegetable stir-fry were waiting for them after the conference. The chief of obstetrics had led her down to the cockpit of the labor and delivery ward, explaining that her office was being recarpeted and smelled like a petroleum refinery.

"Anyway," Marta had confessed, "I usually eat my lunch here. It's peaceful, and I can keep my eye on things."

Cal saw what she meant. The cockpit was warm and dim, lit by the faint blue glow of a dozen uterine and fetal monitors stacked against the wall. The little glass-walled station was empty; the chief resident was performing a delivery on a house patient, and the two junior residents were assisting on a Cesarean section.

"I'm serious—about your lecture." Marta continued. "You really have a good teaching style. Pathology can be pretty tough to understand, but you made it sound simple."

Cal had been covering the staging and treatment protocols for various types of uterine and ovarian cancers—a bewildering array of diagnostic plans, prognoses, and therapies. CT scans, MRI, and surgical staging. Chemotherapy, radiation, and hormonal treatment. Medical advances were wonderful, but the changing recommendations were sometimes hard to keep straight. She had worked hard preparing the lecture and slides, and she was relieved it had paid off.

"I like teaching," she said simply. "And I remember how hard it was for *me* to understand this stuff."

"We *all* like teaching, or we wouldn't be here."

Cal nodded. Someone like Marta Oberlin could probably double her annual income on the outside. More and more these days, hospital faculty were expected to earn their own salaries through patient billing, in addition to teaching residents and fellows. And since teaching took up half of their time or more, teachers' salaries were generally lower than those of private doctors.

Marta shrugged and speared a turnip absently. She lowered her voice. "Not that we're likely to be teaching *here* much longer."

"I know." Cal stared at the bank of monitors. The little blue lines swimming across the screen were almost hypnotic—tracing slow waves of uterine contractions and gentle fluctuations in fetal heart rates. "We just talked to David Inverness this morning. It doesn't sound good."

"So I hear." She shook her head. "Somebody told me Vista has already made a bid on the hospital."

Cal nodded, then sketched their conversation with David Inverness and his comments about the impending Vista takeover. As it turned out, Marta already knew most of it; she and David were apparently very close friends. Cal didn't mention the part about Cy Kettering's telephone calls last night, but she described David's theory about a possible connection between the Vista deal and the two chiefs' deaths.

"Then it's true?" Marta asked. "About Cy and Andre?"

"They were murdered; that's pretty clear," Cal admitted. "But I don't know about David's idea—it sounds pretty far-fetched."

"I know. He's mentioned it to me already." She sighed. "Poor dear—he's very upset. He doesn't show it, but the whole thing is tearing him apart. It's taken him *years* to get Riverside's academic programs on a firm footing, and it's all ready to go down the tubes." She shrugged. "I think David might just be looking for someone to blame."

"Like Godfrey Millburn?"

The obstetrician chuckled. "Wouldn't *that* be great? But it doesn't fit—I just heard Millburn is stepping down soon, to take a job in St. Louis. With Vista's main competitor."

"You're kidding."

"That's the rumor, anyway."

"Has David heard the rumor?"

"He's the one who told *me*—he heard it this morning, from a friend of his in Administration." Marta dumped some more Szechuan pork onto her plate and sighed. "Anyway, David's much more hung up on our vice president—he thinks Quentin Young is really behind all these changes."

"Millburn's assistant?"

"Yeah. He'll take over as CEO when Godfrey leaves." She shrugged. "Lucky us—out of the frying pan and into the fire."

Cal cocked her head. "Then Quentin Young might get a big bonus if the deal goes through?"

Marta sighed and touched Cal's arm. She lowered her voice even further. "Don't put too much stock in David's theories. Like I said, he's *very* upset about all of this."

Cal frowned questioningly.

The obstetrics chief set her dish aside and patted her stomach. "I've got to watch that stuff—it's ruining my girlish figure." She chuckled with just a tinge of bitterness. "Not that anyone really cares."

She sat up and turned to Cal. "David and I are close friends—*very* close." She read Cal's expression and shook her head. "No, not *that* close, though I've tried. But he tells me everything."

Marta's voice was wistful, almost maternal. She tossed her plate into the trash and sipped a cup of coffee.

"David has sacrificed an awful lot to get this place on its feet." She turned to look at the fetal monitors. "You know his wife and kids left him."

It wasn't a question; the whole hospital knew about it. Cal nodded dumbly.

"It was his job as medical director, and his damned commitment to his patients. Compulsive idiot." She smiled sadly. "He kept telling Cynthia that he'd change, that he just needed another few months, another few weeks to set things straight. Another few days. But after a few years, she finally gave up." She leaned back in her chair and stared up at the ceiling. "It was a very rough divorce, and she ended up with full custody. He sees his kids once a month—if he has time."

An intern ducked into the cockpit to scribble an update on the whiteboard. The huge chart on the far wall displayed patients' names, conditions, and the time of the latest cervical measurement. Beside Room 12's name, the intern changed the cervical measurement from "3 cm" to "3+".

Cal grimaced. According to the whiteboard, the poor woman had been admitted almost six hours ago for induced labor, but she had made little progress. The cervix—the neck of the uterus—had to stretch to ten centimeters before the woman could give birth. She had a long way to go.

The intern frowned at his notation, then asked Marta for permission to increase Room 12's oxytocin drip, the medication used to strengthen contractions. Marta glanced at the corresponding monitor screen and nodded slowly, giving the order to increase the flow rate. She waited until he had disappeared again before resuming her story.

"David learned to live with the divorce," she continued. "He buried himself in his work here, and tried to put the whole disaster behind him. Over the past year or so, he had finally seemed content, if not happy." She shook her head. "But then Godfrey Millburn pulled the rug out from under him. After everything he's done to keep this place going."

Marta Oberlin was genuinely angry. She slapped the arm of her chair with her hand. "It's just not *fair*. Not to any of us—but least of all to David."

"I know," Cal said quietly.

The obstetrician started, as though she had forgotten Cal was there.

"I'm really going on about all this, aren't I?" She chuckled, the bitterness suddenly submerged again. "I'm sorry. But like I said, David and I are really good—*friends*."

"He's a great guy," Cal agreed carefully.

"Don't I know it." She shrugged. "He's still *very* attached to his wife."

"Oh." Now Cal understood Marta's hesitation, her ambiguity about David.

"That may be the one silver lining to all this," the obstetrician noted quietly. "David has finally come to his senses. He's trying to get back together with Cynthia."

She smiled crookedly.

"Do you think he will?" Cal asked.

"I honestly don't know." She shook her head. "He was supposed to have dinner with her last night—to make some plans—but I saw him here at nine o'clock."

"Wow."

"Yeah." Marta shrugged. "But who knows? Maybe it wasn't his fault this time. Maybe *she* got busy and canceled for once."

From her tone, Marta obviously doubted it.

"He's a pathological physician," she continued. "You know the type."

Cal nodded. She certainly did. People who couldn't say no to their patients, who couldn't leave anything undone, who couldn't bear to be anything less than perfect physicians. The only trouble was, perfection never came; it was always just around the corner. And sometimes the ones who tried the hardest ended up losing everything.

Like David Inverness.

"He's still fighting, still trying to keep the teaching programs alive." Marta shrugged. "But he can't hold out much longer." She eyed Cal curiously. "Do you have any prospects in sight—if it really happens?"

"I have three jobs already," Cal reminded her. "The coroner's office, the medical school, and here."

"Oh, yeah—I forgot." Marta shook her head. "Talk about workaholics."

"Not at all," she protested. "I just kind of fell into it."

"Admit it," Marta teased. "You're an addict."

Cal laughed uncomfortably, realizing that Marta might have a point. Back when she was single, Cal had actually enjoyed juggling the part-time deputy coroner's post with her half-time job here at Riverside. But then she had been promoted to chief of pathology; even though she was still nominally half-time here, she was working full-time hours. And last fall she had accepted a part-time teaching appointment at the medical school.

She really didn't *want* to do all these things. Did she?

That was the funny thing about working too much— you never had enough time to catch your breath, to look around and see what you were missing.

"I *had* been thinking about cutting back somewhere," Cal insisted. She watched the monitor from Room 12. The contractions had grown taller and steeper, jagged mountains of pain. The intern must have turned up the oxytocin. Cal's voice grew quiet. "I *need* to cut back, sometime soon."

Marta shot her a sharp glance. "That old biological clock, huh?"

"Biological *alarm* clock," Cal replied. She shrugged. "Only trouble is, I keep hitting the snooze button."

"Don't we all." Marta sipped her coffee and sighed.

Down the hall, a low groan rose in a slow crescendo, like the first notes of a police siren.

"Now *there's* someone who put it off a little too long," the obstetrician said. She tapped Room 12's monitor with her finger. "Forty-two years old, and this is her first. Two weeks late, so we're inducing her."

The blue line tracing Room 12's contraction slowly dipped, but began another sharp rise almost immediately. The awful keening began again. A nurse darted into the room and closed the door.

Cal shuddered.

"Didn't want any anesthesia, no narcotics, not even Tylenol," Marta was saying. "But induced labor can be pretty rough, especially at this level of oxytocin." She shrugged. "Poor lady's so tired out, she won't be able to push even if we *do* get her dilated enough."

"Maybe I'll just turn my alarm clock *off*," Cal muttered.

Over the years, she had all but forgotten her obstetrics rotations from medical school and internship. The siren cry from Room 12 had brought it all rushing back—her patients' waves of pain, the frantic *lub-dub* of tiny heartbeats heard through the ultrasonic monitors, the quick snips of episiotomies and Cesarean deliveries. The joy of new life, and the stark tragedy when things went wrong.

Other people *enjoyed* their obstetrics rotations—the new babies, the hopeful expectation of pregnancy, the delight of each new arrival. But Cal had seemed to feel every contraction, every incision, every tragedy. She had grown physically ill during almost every on-call night.

That was part of the reason she had decided to become a pathologist. The only patients she ever saw were already dead, long past the pain and the heartache.

"Don't tell me you're *afraid* to have kids," Marta said with a smile.

Cal was staring at the monitors. More jagged mountains, more crescendos of pain.

"Of course not," she lied.

The poor woman's keening even penetrated the closed door. Cal shuddered again.

"Believe me, most of my patients are a *lot* more comfortable than this," Marta assured her. She glanced at Room 12's tracing and nodded, satisfied. "Much better contractions, much stronger. We may just have a normal delivery after all."

Down the hall, a nurse opened the door and gave a thumbs-up sign to Oberlin. The obstetrician stood and grinned at Cal.

"Time for me to give my pep talk—and maybe convince her to take a *little* medication." She patted Cal's shoulder. "Thanks again for lecturing. I hope you can do it again sometime."

Cal smiled. "I'd like that."

She watched Oberlin rush down the hall. A minute or two later, a nurse hurried out to the medicine locker and grabbed a vial of Demerol. Before Cal had finished her coffee, Room 12's bed flew past at a brisk clip, centered in a flurry of white coats and nurses. The haggard father-to-be held the woman's hand like a drowning man clutching a life preserver. Marta Oberlin grinned at Cal through the window. Cal nodded back.

She stood to go, but felt a strange reluctance—as though she were leaving a theater just before the end of the movie. She finally decided to stick around, pouring herself another cup of coffee and slumping back into her chair.

And mulling over her conversation with Marta.

The obstetrician was obviously in love with David Inverness; she saw everything else in relation to her feelings for him—even the murders. Just as obviously, David felt little more for Marta than a very close—and very convenient—friendship. His attempts to reconcile with his wife weren't surprising; David had always worn his feelings like a badge. But Cal *was* surprised that Marta had told her about the situation.

Was it just her friendship with Cal, or a wish to vent her frustration with David? Or was she perhaps trying to tell Cal something? Trying to protect David?

Inverness had known about Cy Kettering's theories regarding the murders, his urgent desire to communicate his ideas to someone else. Yet he had turned down Cy's frantic plea, and apparently missed an important date with his wife. Neither seemed consistent with David's personality—he might have sacrificed the dinner with his wife, but he was unlikely to refuse a call for help.

Had David really been that busy last night? Or had he shown up at Cy's house just minutes before Plato and Cal?

Was Marta's story just a clumsy attempt to provide David Inverness with an alibi? She certainly had the timing right; Cal and Plato had reached Cy's house just minutes after nine o'clock; the murder was probably committed between eight-thirty and nine. If Inverness had really been at the hospital then, he was definitely not the murderer.

But David *was* Wallace's physician, and he also knew about Andre Surfraire's drinking problem. He certainly had the expertise to pull off the murders.

But why? Cal kept returning to that same question. Three completely unrelated deaths, three physicians who seemed to have little or nothing in common, other than being chiefs at Riverside General. None of it made any sense.

Was it the work of a mentally unbalanced killer after all? Could she or Plato be the next targets?

The delivery room doors swung open again. The mother was propped up in bed, pale and wan, her forehead still beaded with sweat. But she smiled beatifically at the tiny blanketed bundle in her arms. Walking beside her toward the recovery room, the father strutted like a man on the moon, his feet only touching the floor every three or four paces.

Marta Oberlin trotted back to the cockpit and pulled her patient's chart, then noticed Cal.

"I *thought* you might still be here," she said with a grin.

"I wanted to know how it turned out."

"Uncomplicated vaginal delivery," Marta replied. "Boy—eight pounds, six ounces. Dad fainted dead away when I asked him to cut the cord." She shrugged. "But Mom came through it like a trooper—really surprised me. One push and he was out. Practically fired him into the wall."

Cal laughed. "I'm glad."

The obstetrician waved her pen at Cal. "You know, if you ever decide to quit hitting that snooze button, just give me a call. I'd be glad to catch one for you."

"We'll see," she replied, then shrugged. "First we've got to find out whether we've still got jobs."

"No kidding." Marta frowned. "You coming to the meeting tonight?"

"I'm not sure." She shook her head, wondering about Plato. Maybe it was time to give him a call, to make sure he was still okay. "It depends on how Plato's doing. I was thinking about giving him a call, checking up on him."

"Good idea," Marta said. She gave that shrewd, feline smile. "Knowing him, he's probably out prowling the town."

Cal laughed hollowly, wondering if maybe her friend was right.

Chapter 14

As it turned out, Plato was quite familiar with the scene of Andre Surfraire's accident. He had spent his teenage years in a small house in Willoughby, moving there from Cleveland's east side when his father had finally joined the exodus to the suburbs. He knew Waite Hill particularly well.

The area had been a favorite bike route for Plato—zipping down into the Chagrin Valley on his ten-speed, cutting over on Waite Hill Road and panting up the steep and winding asphalt ribbon on the east bank of the river. He and his cousin Homer had been stopped at the village limits countless times by town cops who meant to keep Waite Hill as exclusive as possible, but they had never heeded the warnings. It was too beautiful an area—sharp hills, winding roads canopied by deep woods, duck ponds and cattails, and fairy-tale estates sprawled over scores of acres.

Plato crossed the river in his Acura and parked at the bottom of the hill, beside the softball field at Daniel's Park. He stepped out and began the long walk up Waite Hill Road, plucking up lost memories as he climbed.

The area hadn't changed much, really. But the story of the crash was carved out in the mangled guardrail and broken trees, a narrow corridor of flattened saplings and gouged cliffside where the car had bounded down the hill. The low-slung Porsche had even blasted through the stone curb lining the roadway.

Plato stood at the edge of the broken guardrail for a long moment, looking down the hill to where a small crater marked Andre Surfraire's demise. The car had obviously been hauled away by some kind of excavating equipment; caterpillar tracks wound through the underbrush from the base of the hill to the lip of the crater.

He turned back to the road itself—a narrow two-lane strip of asphalt that hugged the side of the hill like a lover's arm. Certainly if Surfraire had lived nearby, this was a very plausible site for an accident. Plato vaguely remembered hearing about a few other crashes here, back when he was growing up in Willoughby. The road came partway down the hill before making a sharp right turn and plunging into the valley. On an icy day like last Tuesday, even a sober driver might have missed the turn and slid through the guardrail.

In fact, the accident scene seemed so plausible that Plato wondered why the killer had bothered injecting his victim with alcohol. The vodka wasn't needed to make Surfraire unconscious—the blow to the head had taken care of that. If the surgeon's blood alcohol levels hadn't been so high, the killer would probably have gotten away with it.

So why risk exposure by getting fancy?

Cal was right—it almost seemed as though the killer was more interested in using certain *methods* for the various murders than in covering them up.

Glancing back up the road, Plato glimpsed a figure from the corner of his eye and realized he wasn't alone. A woman was standing just across the street, hugging herself and huddling against the wind. Her chin was tucked into the front of a heavy wool overcoat, and her features were hidden by a wide-brimmed black hat.

Only her eyes were visible—dark and glistening as they stared unblinking down the hill past Plato.

He turned away, puzzled and curious but reluctant to disturb the woman's privacy. Instead, he started walking down the hill again, studying the car's path through the trees and wondering once more why the killer had chosen such an unusual murder method.

He hadn't taken five paces before a police car sidled up across the road, lights flashing. The driver's-side window slid open, and the officer poked his head out. "You have some business here, mister?"

It was high school all over again. No matter that Plato was now an adult, on a public road, perfectly entitled to look down the hill at the scene of his coworker's fatal crash. He was fifteen years old, his heart jumping in his throat as the awful majesty of the law came crashing down on his head.

"I—uhh—I—" Plato stammered. "I was just looking—"

"Then I suggest you move along," the officer replied brusquely. He lowered his head and squinted at Plato over the tops of his mirrored sunglasses. His eyes were tiny and close-set, like a nearsighted hamster's. His hooked nose and prominent teeth accentuated the resemblance. "We don't appreciate lollygaggin' sightseers around here."

Lollygaggin' sightseers, Plato mused. The phrase was eerily familiar. So was the voice—a high-pitched squeak, nothing like what you'd expect from a cop. Plato looked closer at the driver. Incredibly enough, it was Officer Gerbali, the Terror of Waite Hill. Gerbali had chased Plato and Homer out of the exclusive little village far more times than all the other officers combined.

Plato smiled to himself, remembering. Gerbali—the Italian gerbil.

The officer's face puckered even more than usual. "What're you grinning at, mister?"

"Gerbali!" Plato chuckled. "You're still a patrolman?"

Clearly it was the wrong thing to say. Gerbali opened his door and stepped out.

"I've got half a mind to haul you in for loitering and disturbing the peace." The thin nose twitched menacingly.

"You've got half a mind?" Plato couldn't help asking. Yes, it was juvenile and disrespectful and not even very funny. But he and Homer had always said it before; the response was practically a reflex.

"What's your name?" Gerbali finally asked. "You look familiar—maybe I'd better just take you down to the station."

"His name is Plato Marley," a voice said.

Plato glanced up the road. It was the woman—the same one who had materialized so silently at the crash scene. She looked even more familiar, but with half her face hidden, he couldn't quite place her.

"You know this guy?" Gerbali asked in a pitying tone, as though the woman had just admitted she had a terminal disease.

"Yes. He's with me." She moved closer and hooked her arm in Plato's, glancing up at him with those dark, glittering eyes. "Aren't you, Dr. Marley?"

"Umm—err, yes." Plato smiled weakly at the patrolman, trying not to betray his astonishment.

"I see." Gerbali squinted at the woman, gave a suspicious twitch of his nose, then reluctantly sidled back toward his car. "Awfully sorry about that, Mrs. Surfraire, ma'am. Just trying to keep our little town safe."

"That's quite all right, Rudolf." She shrugged and smiled briefly. "I *do* appreciate it."

"*Rudolf?*" Plato asked wonderingly.

Gerbali scowled at him, but turned to Mrs. Surfraire and nodded. "Good day, ma'am."

He eased over to his car without turning his back, like a timorous servant leaving a royal presence. He drove down the road, turned around in the softball parking lot, and sped by again with a respectful wave for Mrs. Surfraire.

The woman watched him disappear around the bend, then slowly turned and squeezed Plato's arm.

"And now, Dr. Marley, perhaps you can tell me just what you're doing here."

Gabrielle Surfraire was at least twenty years younger than her late husband. It had been a second marriage for both of them; she had been widowed once before in France, and Surfraire had summarily divorced his first wife when he met Gabrielle.

At least that's how the gossip went. And seeing Gabrielle Surfraire made the stories quite believable. The surgeon's widow was an astonishing contrast to her troll-like husband: she was tall and sleek and elegant, with stunning chiseled features and a model's delicate figure.

In fact, she had been a model once, crossing the Atlantic to grace the pages of magazines like *Vogue* and *Cosmopolitan* before coming to Cleveland on a fashion designer's tour and meeting Surfraire. Her marriage to the wealthy surgeon had ended any need for her to work, but she still dressed and moved with the flawless, untouchable, and slightly plastic grace of a model, as though each step, each gesture were a calculated pose on a fashion show runway.

She had led Plato uphill to her car, another Porsche parked just around the bend, then invited him back to her house for tea. Minutes later, they were sitting in the glass-walled conservatory of one of Waite Hill's finest old homes.

Andre Surfraire had done quite well for himself. The estate had been one of Plato's favorites in his biking days—a sprawling castle of rough-hewn granite lording over acres of arbors and orchards and horse pastures and stables.

The perfect hostess, Gabrielle Surfraire filled the minutes with small talk while Plato finished his tea. He now remembered having met her, at last year's medical staff dinner dance. Surfraire had introduced her with ill-concealed pride; they had been married just the year before.

But how she had remembered Plato's name, from among all the doctors she had met that evening, was a mystery.

"I saw you on the news last evening." Gabrielle said, seeming to read his thoughts. "Your brave attempt to rescue Dr. Kettering."

Her English was nearly flawless, with just the slightest hesitation over the harsher consonants, as though she *could* pronounce the English sounds correctly but found them slightly distasteful.

"Maybe more stupid than brave," Plato replied. Now he knew how she had remembered his name. "Anyway, it didn't work."

"Ahh, but you couldn't know that, could you?" She set her cup down with a soft click, then turned to Plato. "And today, perhaps, you are trying to discover a connection with the tragedy last night?"

He fidgeted under her stare. Those deep brown eyes were disquieting, seeming to guess his thoughts before he could read them himself.

"I'm not sure," he answered softly. "There are some things about your husband's death—about *all* the deaths—that don't make sense."

"That is hardly surprising," she replied, giving a quick European shrug. "Murder is a nonsensical act. But perhaps you mean something more?"

Before Plato could answer, she leaned back on the sofa and stared at the ceiling. "The coroner called me yesterday, to tell me about the autopsy. As though it would make me feel better." She shook her head. "And perhaps it did—I *knew* Andre had stopped his drinking, long before he met me." The brown eyes swiveled to Plato's again. "But it makes no sense. Who would want to kill my husband? And why?"

She paused, as though waiting for an answer.

"I don't know," he finally replied.

"*That* was why I went there today," she explained. "To see where it happened again. To try to understand."

The telephone rang. Gabrielle turned away to lift the receiver. She listened for a moment, wincing as though the instrument were conducting raw electricity directly to her brain.

"No, I have told you already." Her voice grew more strident, less controlled. "*Quelle betise! Fichez-moi la paix!* Stop calling, or I will tell the police."

Plato could faintly hear the voice on the other end of the line—a raw, venomous shriek, speaking in what might have been French, though he couldn't be sure. Gabrielle took the receiver away from her ear and gently rested it on the cradle, as though she were snuffing out a candle. The shrieking stopped.

"I'm sorry." She smiled bitterly. "Andre's first wife saw the news reports this morning. She claims that I—" Gabrielle broke off and shook her head. "The woman is *tout folle,* a lunatic. Andre knew that when he divorced her."

Plato frowned sympathetically.

"So now you see another reason why I am so curious." She shrugged, but shot an angry glare at the telephone. "Perhaps it was that crazy woman herself, though she has always seemed harmless before. A former nurse, you see."

"Have the police talked to you about this?" he asked.

"Yes. They came this morning." Gabrielle stared at the floor. "I was *tres peur*—not for me, of course. But for Andre's memory—things best left unsaid. But they kept at me, digging up rumors and probing into Andre's past. Even asking about poor Consuela." She gestured to the phone and grimaced. "*Le bon Dieu* only knows what that woman will say about *me*."

"The police will be able to see past that," Plato assured her, hoping that it was true.

"Do they have any theories?" she asked hopefully. "Any suspects?"

Plato shrugged. "I honestly don't know."

It was true. Because Surfraire's death had occurred in Lake County, even Jeremy Ames could offer few insights—other than a suspicion that Surfraire's and Kettering's murders were linked. The Lake County sheriff's office was looking into it, and supposedly collaborating with Jeremy Ames and the Cuyahoga office. But so far the only theory was that the same killer had committed both crimes. Big deal.

"You spoke of inconsistencies," she said. Her high, smooth forehead furrowed. "Things that didn't make sense."

He paused. Why was Gabrielle Surfraire so curious? To protect herself?

The model's careful poise was dissolving, he saw. Surfraire's widow was twining her fingers in her lap and chewing her lower lip as she stared out the windows of the conservatory. If anything, her tension made her even more appealing, and far less artificial.

She swiveled her gaze to Plato, seeming to understand his hesitation.

"You must understand," she insisted. Her accent was richer now, a slurring of words reminiscent of Catherine Deneuve. "Andre and I were deeply in love—*au premier coup d'oeil*." She shook her head. "Some people found it difficult to believe—that I didn't marry Andre for his money."

Plato had been one of them. Surfraire had seemed like the typical discontented middle-ager, trading his first wife in for a younger, more attractive model, much like he might have done with a worn-out Porsche. And Plato supposed he had written Gabrielle off as a fortune hunter, though he had never really given it much thought.

That Surfraire had been quickly smitten with Gabrielle was hardly surprising. But the converse—the prospect of someone like Gabrielle falling in love at first sight with Andre—was the stuff of fairy tales. The Beast taking Beauty away to his enchanted castle in Waite Hill. Except in the fairy tale, the Beast didn't have a first wife.

"He had his faults," Gabrielle acknowledged. "The revolution in Haiti left its scars on him." She swept her arms around. "This house, the cars, his wealth—he hoarded his pleasures as though he was still a refugee. But he was a generous man, a *kind* man." Her eyes brimmed with tears. "And I loved him dearly."

Plato was reluctantly convinced. Hesitantly at first, he told her about Wallace's death, and Kettering's, and how her husband's crash seemed to fit the pattern. As he recounted the story, he began to trust Gabrielle Surfraire more. She was quick to understand, following his reasoning and making insightful observations of her own.

"But he didn't come home that afternoon," she said. "I *know* that—I was here all day." She shook her head. "Why did the killer choose *that* place?"

"That's exactly what I was wondering," Plato agreed. Andre clearly hadn't been en route *to* his home; the Porsche had been heading in the other direction. And though Waite Hill was partway between Millburn's house and the hospital, the freeway would have been much quicker.

"Did Andre have any friends in the neighborhood?" he asked. "Anyone he might have been visiting?"

Gabrielle shook her head. "We knew very few of the other people here—he had little time outside of work." She smiled sadly. "And most of that time, he spent alone, with *me*."

She cocked her head, thinking. "It's very strange, about that hill. If the killer had really known Andre, he wouldn't have chosen that spot at all."

Plato frowned. "Why not?"

"Andre was very nervous about that road," she replied. "Once in a while, we would take that route; it was the quickest way back to the city." Lost in memories, she stared out the window at the lush rolling lawns, the budding trees in the orchards. "But Andre would get very anxious on that hill, crawling around that corner slow enough to walk. I teased him about it once, and he snapped at me." She turned back to Plato, tears brimming in her eyes again. "It was our only fight. After that, he always took another road."

"Did he ever say *why* he was so nervous?" Plato was puzzled; Andre Surfraire was a risk-taker, an amateur racer, regardless of his dismal record. The curve on Waite Hill Road was dangerous at high speeds, but it certainly didn't warrant *that* kind of caution. Especially for a driver like Surfraire.

"No. I asked him about it once, but he wouldn't say." She frowned. "We didn't have many secrets from each other."

"I see." Plato's mind was racing. He wanted to leave,

to think. "Did you say anything about that to the police?"

"No—it didn't seem important." She flipped her silky black hair over her shoulder and squinted at Plato. "You have been honest with me, now I will be honest with you." She sighed. "Andre was afraid—for himself and for me."

"Afraid of what?"

"Consuela's family," she replied. "His first wife. You must know that Andre fought against Duvalier many years ago."

Plato nodded. Surfraire had told the story at every medical staff party since he could remember. Each year, his role in the fight had grown; in his latest renditions, he had been sort of Papa Doc Enemy Number One.

"He escaped through the hills to Puerto Rico, along with Consuela's family." She shuddered. "Consuela has several brothers—violent men, not like Andre."

"Had they ever threatened him?"

"Not exactly—but he was always afraid to divorce her." Gabrielle stared at her hands, still twisting in her lap. "Until he met me." She shrugged. "I've told the police; they didn't think it was important."

"I see." Plato was inclined to agree with the police; her theory sounded like an echo of Andre Surfraire's inflated ramblings. Besides, he couldn't see any possible connection between Consuela Surfraire's angry brothers and the deaths of Lionel Wallace or Cy Kettering.

But he listened patiently to Gabrielle's stories about Surfraire's first wife, her obvious fear of Consuela's family, and her conviction that the woman was patently crazy. Having heard her shrieks firsthand from the telephone receiver, Plato supposed Gabrielle had good reason to doubt Consuela's sanity. And judging by the way she poured her heart out to him, he guessed that

Gabrielle Surfraire had few relatives or friends to lean on in her grief.

She drove him back down to the softball field where his car was parked, then touched his arm as he stepped out. "You've been very kind, Plato. *Merci*." She paused. "You *are* coming to Andre's funeral tomorrow?"

"Of course." Plato nodded firmly, though he hadn't originally planned on attending. He and Surfraire hadn't been very close, but he couldn't refuse Gabrielle's request.

Climbing into the repaired Acura, Plato watched the widow spin back up the hill in her Porsche. *She* hadn't hesitated on the curve.

He glanced at his watch and gasped. Five-thirty. Cal was due to call the house at six o'clock. He was thirty-five minutes from home.

If Cal found out where he had been, what he had done this afternoon, she'd pitch a fit that would make Consuela Surfraire seem positively tame.

Plato stomped on the gas pedal and headed for home.

Chapter 15

"Where have you *been*?"

Tearing home along I-271, Plato had been expecting the worst. He had plotted out his strategy for answering Cal's phone call, armed himself with a battery of half-truths and white lies, and crossed his fingers. He pulled into the driveway at five fifty-six, congratulating himself on making excellent time despite the rush-hour traffic.

But all his confidence and carefully laid plans had melted away when he spotted the Corsica parked beside the house. He was stunned, nonplussed by the sudden assault. All his carefully honed husbanding skills deserted him. He could think of nothing, no excuse, no possible reason why he would be pulling into the driveway at this house when he had promised to stay at home all day and rest.

So he activated the Plan of Last Resort, the only strategy left to husbands who are caught red-handed without a single plausible excuse on their lips. He walked into the house, tail between his legs, and apologized.

Not that it helped much. The apology had about as much effect on Cal's wrath as a stray raindrop hitting a river of molten lava. She rolled through the kitchen and living room, scattering insults and searing anything that stood in her path. Even the animals stood clear as blistering words and scorching glares boiled into the air.

"Taking the car for a *test drive*?" she asked in disbelief. "To make sure the *windshield* worked? Come on, Plato—even *you* can't be that stupid."

She was right; even he wasn't quite that stupid. He watched his wife's fury with a sort of dazed awe, like a natural disaster victim watching his world collapse around his ears. His conscience chuckled evilly as he realized how flimsy his excuse really was.

It was time to activate the second half of the Plan, the most desperate measure a husband can take. He decided to tell her the truth.

Amazingly enough, Cal's anger began to dissipate as he confessed to driving to Waite Hill, visiting the crash scene, and meeting Gabrielle Surfraire. A smile even played about her lips as she heard about his visit to Surfraire's mansion.

"Then Gabrielle Surfraire isn't quite the fortune hunter everyone thinks she is, huh?"

"Maybe not," Plato agreed. "She also mentioned something interesting about the crash site itself."

He told her about Andre Surfraire's apparent dread of that particular curve, his odd reluctance to even travel on that stretch of road, which was all the more surprising in light of his driving experience.

Cal nodded. "That *is* strange."

"The killer must have known him quite well, to be familiar with his fear of that piece of road."

"Or not at all," she replied, frowning thoughtfully. "After all, if he usually avoided that route, it made the accident far *less* plausible, didn't it?"

Plato stroked his beard, considering. Did the scene of the crash really mean anything? Maybe not. But it *was* awfully coincidental that he was afraid of the particular stretch of road where he ultimately died. If Plato were superstitious, he might wonder if Surfraire some-how *knew* he would die there.

Or perhaps there was another reason, far more earthly and practical. After all, why would he be so frightened?

"Maybe he was in a crash there once before," Plato mused aloud.

Cal shot him a sharp glance. "That's just what I was thinking. Accident victims sometimes become terribly phobic about the spot where a crash occurred. Some-times they get so paranoid that they cause *another* acci-dent, by driving too cautiously."

"Or they may avoid the area altogether," he pointed out. "Like Surfraire."

She nodded. "I'll ask Jeremy to check it out—he's been working with the cops in Lake County."

"Even so, does it mean anything?" Plato challenged. "Even if he was in an accident there once, what does it have to do with Wallace and Kettering?"

"I don't know." Cal shrugged, then brightened. "But speaking of Lionel Wallace, I've got some interesting news." She walked back to the front hallway and turned, a half smile on her lips. "The Geauga County coroner checked Wallace's blood for penicillin today."

"And?"

"And you were right—positive. A very high level." Her lips pouted. "I tried calling earlier this afternoon, to tell you, but you weren't here. That's why I came home—I was *worried*."

"High enough to kill him?" Plato asked, trying to head her off from revisiting the broken-promise motif.

"Probably." She sighed. "We may never know for sure—there isn't a lethal dose for allergic reactions."

He nodded. "But it certainly looks like we have three murders, instead of two."

"Right." She shrugged her coat on and stepped onto the porch, then glanced back at him. "Come on, let's go."

"Go where?" he asked innocently.

"To the medical staff meeting." She flashed a wicked grin. "You're obviously well enough to attend."

"But—but—" A dozen excuses flashed through his head, each one more implausible than the last. Plato spotted the lava still brewing behind Cal's copper-brown eyes, and his husbandly survival instincts told him he'd better shut his mouth and give in. He sighed, fetched his coat, and followed her out to the car.

Plato hated medical staff meetings even more than any of the dozens of other meetings he was required to attend. Not that medical staff meetings were any more of a waste of time than the others—actually, he had to admit that the sessions were occasionally productive and useful. The only trouble was, the monthly gatherings were always held in the evenings, at six-thirty—too early for most physicians to have eaten dinner beforehand, but so late that the attendees resembled a pack of growling bears by the time the meetings were adjourned.

To alleviate the problem, the cafeteria staff always sent up a tableful of appetizers, if you could call them that. Fruit salad left over from the lunch buffet, over-ripe, stickly sweet and brown around the edges. Pumice-hard biscuits that might have traveled over on the Mayflower. Assorted vegetables and Heart-Smart dip—a pale green concoction of dubious origins that, to Plato's knowledge had never been tasted; they probably just trotted the same bowl out every week, year after year. And the pièce de résistance—Chinese vegetable rolls—baked, not fried, and filled with a pasty gray mush that looked and smelled like under-cooked oatmeal; perhaps it was.

"It's a plot," he told Cal as they hovered around the appetizer table. "The administration is trying to kill us all off—it'll save them the trouble of firing us."

Three other doctors swiveled around to glare at Plato. One of them eyed his vegetable roll dubiously and set it back on the table.

"It was just a *joke,* guys." He watched them hurry into the auditorium. "Geez—what's gotten into these people?"

"It's not very funny, under the circumstances." Cal gestured to the other staff members scattered around the alcove—all keeping a safe distance from the Marleys. "Haven't you noticed? Everyone's kind of edgy, and they're acting like we chiefs have the plague."

"Why?" Plato frowned. "It's not like *we* have any control over the layoffs."

"They're not nervous about the *layoffs,*" she replied. "They're nervous because we keep *dying.* It doesn't seem safe to be a chief these days. Sandra Jarvis was offered the position of acting chief of surgery, and she turned it down."

"That's crazy," Plato complained, fighting a shiver. Whistling in the dark. "Silly superstition."

" 'Seven little Indians, standing in a line,' " Cal quoted, remembering Cy Kettering's words during the camping trip. " 'One went home, and then there were six.' "

"Maybe we should take a little vacation," he suggested, then frowned. "Except our jobs would be gone by the time we got back."

"Better to be unemployed than dead," she observed pragmatically.

"That's my Cal—always looking at the bright side." He grabbed a Chinese oatmeal roll and stuffed a pumice biscuit into his pocket. "Come on, let's head inside and make people nervous."

The first half of the meeting was the same old ritual—a droning recitation of last month's minutes by the medical staff secretary, the annual argument about how much money the staff should contribute to the senior residents' graduation party, and a rambling report about the declining rate of postoperative infection among patients on the orthopedics ward, together with suggestions for implementing similar preventive measures on all the hospital wards.

But things got more interesting when Plato saw a familiar figure bounding up the stairs to the podium like an exercise instructor launching into an aerobics class. Frank Evans hadn't let yesterday's setbacks dull his enthusiasm for Riverside's planned face-lift. The marketing director ran through much the same presentation he had given yesterday—the architectural improvements, the mission statement, and the new name and logo.

Judging by the response, most of the medical staff seemed to wish they had brought some of the rotten fruit inside the auditorium. Early on, Evans dodged the flurry of scornful criticism and skeptical questions with the good grace that had earned him the marketing director's post. But as his presentation continued, the legendary enthusiasm finally began to flag. And when the last slide flashed onto the screen, Evans looked positively relieved.

Cal giggled when the new logo lit up the screen.

"Looks like a cockroach with a weight problem," she whispered to Plato.

"I thought it looked like a pregnant termite," he replied.

"I can see that." She nodded thoughtfully. "What's it *supposed* to be?"

"A mother and child."

"You're kidding." She frowned at the screen. "That's

a really fat mother. If Botticelli's women ran a nursery, that's what they'd look like. Where are her arms?"

Plato pointed.

"Oh." She giggled again. "I thought those were antennae."

"So did I."

Up at the front of the auditorium, the medical staff's Oldest Member was standing with yet another question. Dr. Silas Gundleford, a gastroenterologist who had supposedly worked in Kellogg's original clinic, pointed his cane at the phrase beneath the logo.

" 'RiversEdge Cares,' " he read. "Cares for *what*?"

Frank Evans tugged at his necktie. "Well, umm, just *cares,* I guess. You know, cares about, uhh, *people*."

"People's *money,* more like." Gundleford swiveled his cane to the marketing director. "Fancy marketing crap, that's all this is. Phony baloney. Why don't you save the money and hire us some more floor nurses?"

"That's hardly my responsibility," Evans replied. "I have no control over—"

"What's all this going to cost you folks—three million? Five?"

"Seven million dollars, sir." Evans was reddening now. "But the tax situation with regard to capital improvements is extremely favorable, and—"

"Seven million bucks." Gundleford shook his bald freckled head in disbelief. "You know how many nurses you could hire for seven million bucks?" He swiveled his gaze to the audience and raised his voice even more. "What—a hundred or so?"

"Two hundred," someone near the back shouted. The doctor—one of Riverside's neurologists—punched a few more numbers into his calculator and glanced up. "A hundred-fifty, if you throw in benefits."

"A hundred-fifty nurses," Gundleford mused aloud. "Or just fifteen nurses, for ten years. And I've got patients ringing call buzzers for twenty minutes, waiting for a nurse while they're drowning in—"

"I appreciate your input," Evans interjected. He swallowed heavily, combing a hand through his frizzled red hair. "I'll be happy to pass it along to the administration." He set his remote down on the podium in defeat. "That concludes my presentation. Thank you for your time."

He limped from the stage and shambled out the door of the auditorium like a doctor leaving the bedside of a dying patient.

David Inverness returned to the podium, a slight smile on his lips. "Thank you, Dr. Gundleford." He looked around the auditorium. "I'm sure Mr. Evans will convey your—er—*feedback* to the people in Administration."

The medical staff cheered. From the front row, Silas Gundleford stood again and waved his cane triumphantly.

"That just about concludes our business for tonight," Inverness continued. He stared down at the podium and swallowed. "But I do have one more piece of news."

Something in the tone of his voice sent a hush throughout the auditorium.

"It has been my pleasure to serve the doctors and patients of Riverside General for the past eight years as medical director and chief of staff." He glanced up. "During that time, I've made quite a few friends—and maybe a few enemies, too, but I hope you all realize that I have always acted with the hospital's best interests at heart."

The medical staff fidgeted and whispered like a courtroom audience before a decisive verdict.

"My goal was always to serve our institution well— to leave our hospital better off than when I started my tenure." He shook his head. "Unfortunately, that's not the case—and I'm sorry for that. But I've done all I can."

Plato glanced over to his left. Sitting beside him, Marta Oberlin was crying openly and cursing under her breath.

"And so I regret to announce my resignation from the positions of chief of staff and medical director at Riverside General Hospital," he finally said, putting a special emphasis on the hospital's name. "I look forward to devoting more time to the internal medicine residency, where I will continue as chief. I thank you all for standing by me during my tenure. I've enjoyed working with you."

In the shocked silence that followed, Riverside General's former chief of staff folded his papers into his pocket, switched off the microphone, and stepped down from the stage. Rather than walking through the aisle to the back, he turned to exit through the same door Frank Evans had used.

But Silas Gundleford stopped him with his cane. The white-haired gastroenterologist creaked to his feet, grabbed Inverness's hand, and shook it warmly. The rest of the audience applauded soberly, rising to their feet and shaking Inverness's hand or patting his back as he headed up the aisle and out the back door of the auditorium.

Marta Oberlin started to stand, to follow him, then slumped back into her chair. The rest of the assembly suddenly erupted in confused speculation and angry words. Following the others out, Plato overheard several physicians angrily—and mistakenly—blaming poor little Frank Evans for the news. Others more wisely pointed the finger at Godfrey Millburn, and especially his assistant, Quentin Young.

Marta Oberlin was one of them. Walking beside Cal, the obstetrician explained how she had tried to talk Inverness out of quitting, but he had insisted. Lowering her voice, she told Cal and Plato that Quentin Young had been plotting to call for David's resignation.

"David still has a few friends in Administration," Marta explained. "So he sidestepped Young, and put in his resignation early. There was nothing else he could do."

"But could they force him to resign?" Cal asked incredulously.

"Maybe not—that would depend on the hospital trustees." Marta shrugged. "But Young and Millburn could make life awfully unpleasant for him—for all of us."

"I'm still surprised," Plato confessed. "I never expected him to—"

"Don't count him out yet," the obstetrician advised. "They're going way too fast with all this. I think David has something planned."

Marta Oberlin sounded oddly confident, as though she already knew David's strategy. Perhaps she did.

She flashed her feral grin— like a leopard stalking a wounded antelope. Plato shuddered, remembering that moment on the bus, when she had thought he was responsible for the Camp *Success!* trip.

For the first time ever, he felt a pang of pity for Millburn and Young.

Chapter 16

Plato arrived at his office early the next morning, hoping to get some work done. Instead, he spent a full hour answering questions for Jeremy Ames and his counterpart in the Lake County sheriff's office. The two detective reviewed every event, every moment of the hours preceding Surfraire's and Kettering's deaths. Plato was surprised that they hadn't asked about Wallace's death as well, since the Geauga County coroner had found evidence of murder, but Jeremy explained that Plato would be visited by yet another detective—from Geauga County—once *that* investigation got underway.

Plato felt like Ebeneezer Scrooge fretting over his three astral visitors: couldn't he just see them all at once and get it over with?

But they finally left, and Plato dove back into his paperwork. For a few minutes, anyway. Just until the royal summons arrived.

His nurse, Hilda, had fielded the message and taken it to his office. She stood in the doorway and watched him read it, a ghastly pallor showing through her layers of rouge.

"Is it true, Plato?" She pursed her lips. "About the teaching programs?"

He shrugged. The hospital was a hornet's nest of buzzing rumors this morning. Plato had heard that geriatrics and pediatrics would be cut first, and that the residencies would get the ax by the end of the academic year in June.

"Don't worry, Hilda," he bluffed. "It's just a rumor—you know how they are." He smiled. "Besides, you've got enough seniority to transfer to any floor you want."

"And you?" She folded her arms, unwilling to let him off so easily. "What will *you* do? And Cal?"

"We'll open a doc-in-the-box," he teased. "With a great guarantee—if I can't cure my patients, Cal will give them a free autopsy."

"And *I* will be your nurse," she promised. One corner of her mouth turned up slightly—about as much of a smile as Hilda ever permitted herself. She slipped her arm over Plato's shoulder like a minister walking a convict to the electric chair. "Good luck, Plato."

"Thanks." Walking to the elevator, he knew he would need it.

Plato kept up his brave front all the way downstairs, until he reached the tunnel. Once he was alone, he realized that his knees were shaking, his pulse was pounding, and a cold sweat was trickling down his forehead.

His joke about a doc-in-the-box had carried more than a grain of truth. If Millburn tossed him out on his ear today, Cal's salary alone wouldn't be enough to pay their bills, the mortgage, and the student loans. He would have to find another job, and fast.

It might very well mean staffing an urgicare center for a while, or moonlighting in an emergency room. If Plato got lucky, he might eventually find a slot in a group practice, though those opportunities were getting harder to find. More likely, he would end up in an HMO—seeing patients on an assembly line, having his competence judged by quotas and billing statements, and by his ability to move people out the door as quickly—and as cheaply—as possible.

He would hate it. Plato loved teaching, and the relative freedom of clinical care in an academic setting. The chance to spend as much time as his patients needed, to do the job right. He even enjoyed research, when he had the time.

Entering the tiny unmarked portal to the administration wing, Plato felt a sudden surge of nostalgia for Lionel Wallace and his blundering incompetence. At least his heart had been in the right place.

Godfrey Millburn's office suite occupied one-quarter of the first floor—a corner section facing out over the river. The anteroom was big enough for a game of half-court basketball. Colorful banners and airy tube sculptures hung from the high ceiling. Two rows of desks flanked a broad stretch of plush carpet leading up to Millburn's secretary. She sat behind the enormous altar of her desk and glared at Plato, looking for all the world like a high priestess eyeing the latest sacrific—and thinking the natives were getting a little stingy these days.

Shrugging, she leaned over to her intercom and announced his presence in an apologetic voice. "Dr. Marley is here to see you, sir."

"Excellent, Madeline!" The voice was bluff and cheerful—apparently Godfrey Millburn reveled in the opportunity to fire people. "Please send him in."

Frowning, the secretary glanced at Plato and sighed. She waited a long moment, as if to consider her boss's outlandish request, then finally stood and gestured.

"This way, Dr. Marley." She ushered him into Millburn's office and softly closed the door behind him.

Millburn was parked behind a spacious teak desk, leaning back in his tall leather chair, a languid smile on his face. To Plato's surprise, the CEO's office was plain, almost spartan. In contrast to the rest of the administrative wing, the area was floored with polished oak and a few scattered throw rugs. Pale pine book-cases lined the walls, and slate-blue curtains framed the windows. Along with the usual collection of books and journals necessary to certify Millburn as a serious administrator, the shelves housed an odd assortment of carved ducks and geese, stuffed fish, family photos, and trophies. Hunting bows dangled from two of the walls—an ancient longbow and a modern, deadly look-ing crossbow.

Sitting behind his desk, Millburn followed Plato's gaze and chuckled. "Archery is a passion of mine. Sit down, sit down."

He gestured to a single chair across from his desk. Like the bookcases, the desk and chairs and matching sofa were made of knotty pine and simple quilted cush-ions. Plato slid into a chair and realized that the office was remarkably similar to Millburn's home, if a bit more sparsely furnished. Although he couldn't swear to it, Plato thought that the sofa's upholstery pattern was identical to the furniture he had seen at Millburn's house.

Must be nice, Plato thought. The CEO probably got a volume discount on his home furniture.

"I feel like I'm back at your house," Plato confessed.

"That's the idea," Millburn agreed. "We just moved into the new office yesterday—I may need a few more pieces to fill up this place." He grinned. "But it's a nice touch of home." He gestured to a photo on his desk. "Helps keep my mind on my family, so I don't spend *too* much time here."

"Good thinking." Plato studied the family portrait—Millburn, his wife, and a teenaged daughter. Contrary to his expectations, Millburn's daughter didn't look like a miniature undertaker or an extra from *Night of the Living Dead*. The girl was gorgeous.

"My daughter, Elizabeth." Millburn gestured to another photo, as though he were introducing her in person.

Gorgeous was an understatement. Apparently, the students at her high school were equally impressed—a sash across her shoulder announced that Elizabeth Millburn had been Geauga Valley High's homecoming queen. Her straight black hair was reminiscent of Marlo Thomas in *That Girl*, and the satin evening gown looked like something from Plato's senior prom, but with her flashing eyes, dazzling smile, and rhinestone tiara, she was still absolutely stunning.

"You must be very proud," Plato said. He couldn't help staring at the photo and wondering how the CEO had fathered such a beautiful child. Apparently, Elizabeth Millburn got her looks from her mother.

And then, despite his hopeless predicament, Plato grinned. Maybe there was hope for his and Cal's children after all. Provided they took after their mother.

If they ever had any.

"*Very* proud," Millburn agreed. He gestured around the room. "Most of these trophies are Elizabeth's—she taught *me* how to shoot." A faraway look came into his eyes, and he was silent for several seconds. Finally, he blinked and glanced back at Plato. "But we're not here to discuss Elizabeth, are we?"

"I guess not." Plato shrugged, not really minding. After all, the longer they talked about Millburn's daughter, the longer Plato would remain employed.

"We're here to talk about *you*," the CEO said. He leaned forward and grinned, licking his lips in anticipation.

Here it comes, Plato thought. He realized he was clutching the arms of the chair, bracing himself like a prisoner facing a firing squad. *Do I get a last cigarette?*

"I think you have a bright future ahead," Millburn continued.

Yeah, right. With some other hospital.

"That's why I'd like to promote you."

Plato swallowed, blinked, and rubbed his eyes. Millburn was still there, still talking. He slowly flipped through a file on the top of his desk—Plato's employment record, presumably. It was a thick folder, since Plato had done both his residency and fellowship at Riverside.

Plato winced, remembering. It was a checkered history at best; Plato especially hoped the CEO hadn't read the part about Rupert Jameson. As an intern, Plato and his fellow scut-monkeys had endured a month of slavery at the hands of their senior resident. Jameson had badgered and harassed and tormented his interns, running the house medicine floor like a military prison and driving his two junior medical students to tears. At the end of the month, the entire group had rebelled, trapping their senior resident in the catacombs of the hospital's lowest level and cutting the power to the lights. It took Rupert Jameson three hours to escape, and he'd never been the same since.

But apparently the story had never made it into Plato's records at all. After sifting through the file once more, Millburn was still talking, still smiling.

"An *outstanding* record," he concluded. "And that's why I would like to offer you the post of medical director here at Riverside."

"M-m-m-m?" Plato stammered.

"Of course, the positions of medical director and chief of staff would now be split," Millburn continued smoothly. "Anyway, you lack the seniority to be chief of staff. I expect Tony Jeffries, the vice-chief, to take over that aspect of Dr. Inverness's duties as chief of staff."

"M-m-m?"

"But I think the post of medical director falls well within your capabilities. Certainly, our department will be happy to provide guidance." He shrugged. "And eventually—who knows? Perhaps you might make chief of staff as well."

Plato finally untangled his tongue from his teeth. "I don't think I understand."

"It's quite simple, really." Millburn leaned back and folded his hands together, a praying mantis at rest. "The medical director post is now a free-standing position. Dr. Inverness obviously had too many responsibilities as both chief of staff *and* medical director— especially since he was also the chairman of the internal medicine residency." He nodded. "You'll be salaried at the same level Dr. Inverness was—that is, one hundred and eighty per year."

"A hundred-eighty *thousand*?" Plato asked, stunned. His current salary was less than half that figure.

"I assume that's satisfactory," Millburn said smugly.

Plato needed time to catch his breath, to shift gears and slow his racing thoughts. He had entered Millburn's office fully expecting to be canned. The sudden turnabout was incredible, unbelievable.

In fact, Millburn's proposal was *too* unbelievable. Plato's first reaction to the offer was a wary skepticism. Why had the CEO chosen him, of all people? He was only a few years out of fellowship, with just a few months' experience as chief of his tiny geriatrics department. Riverside General had dozens of doctors with more administrative experience, with the political pull and savvy necessary to do the job well.

In a sudden flash of insight, Plato realized that his lack of experience was an *asset* to Millburn. By hiring an unproven, inexperienced junior doctor as Riverside's medical director, Millburn would have a pawn with little political power of his own. The move would kill any hope of organized opposition by the medical staff.

Insulting, but probably accurate.

Plato tried to weigh the alternatives. On the one hand, if he turned the job down, he probably wouldn't be employed much longer. But if he accepted the position—and if Inverness's prediction about Riverside's coming demise was true—Plato's new job wouldn't last long either.

Besides, if David Inverness had given up the fight against the administration, did Plato have any chance at all? Most likely he would last only a few months and end up as the administration's scapegoat.

"What about my fellowship?" Plato asked, stalling for time. Were the rumors about the teaching programs really true? "Would I still be able to teach?"

Apparently not. Millburn grimaced, then shook his head.

"I'm afraid you may not *have* a fellowship to teach in," the CEO replied. He smiled sympathetically. "I'm sure you're already aware of the hospital's financial problems."

"I've heard rumors." Plato shrugged. "But on Tuesday, you spoke about a commitment to education here at Riverside."

"Believe me, Plato—I've *tried*." Millburn spread his hands helplessly. "I realize you have responsibilities to your fellows and residents—you all do. But we have to look at the overall solvency of the hospital, too. As medical director, you'll come to understand our predicament much better."

"I'm sure I would," Plato said ironically.

He stared out the window, considering. Apparently the decision had already been made, and the rumors were true. Geriatrics was getting the ax, and probably most of the other residencies as well. Medical education at Riverside General was a thing of the past.

"I'll speak to the Board," Millburn promised graciously. "Perhaps I can talk them into keeping the fellowship open until the end of the academic year—as a condition of your accepting the post." He sighed. "Otherwise, I can't make any promises."

"I see." Plato could see very well indeed. He would be blackmailed into taking the position—his four geriatrics fellows would have a very rough time finding positions partway through the academic year; they'd be lucky to find slots in time for *next* year. He could either accept Millburn's offer and take the fall when the hospital closed, or refuse and lose both his job and the entire geriatrics program immediately, leaving his fellows out in the cold.

"Of course, you may want some time to consider the offer," Millburn advised. "But we could easily appoint you acting medical director as of today. Approval by the Board of Trustees is really a formality—Quentin Young and I both hold seats on the Board and we've been very successful in pushing our plans through."

I bet you have, Plato thought. Several of the trustees were contractors or businessmen who reaped large benefits from the hospital's business. They were likely to keep approving Millburn's plans as long as the money continued to flow into their pockets. Plato imagined that many of them would somehow profit from the Vista takeover as well.

Although Plato had a friend or two on the Board, he doubted he could sway enough opinions to oppose Millburn, even if he became medical director. But perhaps he could string Millburn along for a while, buy enough time to find positions for his fellows elsewhere. Enough time for *him* to find a new job, as well.

"You're right," he finally agreed. "I need to think it over, to talk with Cal and see how she feels."

"Of course, of course." Millburn smiled genially. "Take your time. You can meet with Quentin on Monday; I'm heading home early and taking the weekend off." He glanced at the photo again. "Getting together with the family."

Plato nodded. "Going away somewhere?"

The question seemed to throw him off guard. He frowned in apparent confusion, then nodded slowly. "As a matter of fact, yes."

Millburn stood; the interview was obviously over. Plato followed him to the door, glancing at the trophies and knickknacks as he walked. The biggest, grandest trophy stood almost two feet tall, filling a shelf of its own beside the door. Plato studied it with admiration: a muscular silver archer was stretching a huge longbow to the breaking point, sighting down the shaft with practiced confidence, ignorant of the fact that he was standing atop a ridiculously narrow pedestal and would surely topple over from the kickback if he ever fired. At the base of the marble pillar, a silver nameplate proclaimed that Elizabeth Millburn had won the state championship for all-around archery.

"Quite a trophy," Plato said. He had won his only trophy in second grade: his baseball team had placed third in the city's pee-wee league. The trophy was four inches tall and plastic. Cal kept trying to banish it from the bedroom dresser.

"Elizabeth's biggest award," Millburn said. He chuckled in that odd, atonal way, like a robot learning to laugh. "She was really proud of it. We all were."

"I bet." Plato nodded once more, wondering if he and Cal would ever have children, what it would be like. "Seems like she's a fantastic kid—you're very lucky."

"Hmm?" He frowned slightly, then nodded. "Yes. I certainly am."

He reached out to squeeze one of the archer's arms in a familiar gesture, perhaps a good-luck ritual; Plato could see that the silver paint was already rubbing off that arm.

"A wonderful girl," Millburn said softly. "I can't wait to see her again."

Chapter 17

Cal was waiting down in the atrium, wringing her hands and pacing anxiously around the fountain. She hurried to Plato's side when he appeared.

"I came as soon as I heard," she said, giving him a quick hug.

He glanced down at her, surprised. "Heard what?"

"It's okay." She shook her head firmly. "It's not your fault—it's this damned administration."

"*What's* not my fault?"

But Cal wasn't listening. She bit her lip and turned away to watch water cascade over the fountain's pink marble tiles. "First David Inverness, and now you." She glanced back at him again, then squeezed his hand. "But we'll be all right. We'll get through this somehow."

Millburn's secretary crossed the alcove, bearing a sheaf of papers and a grimace. But she brightened when she spotted Plato. "Congratulations, Dr. Marley."

Cal watched the woman disappear down another corridor, then growled. "Congratulations? For losing your job?"

"I didn't lose my job," he explained. "Not yet, anyway."

She grabbed his hands and beamed. "You mean they're keeping the fellowship open? That's *fantastic*, Plato."

"Not exactly." He shook his head, trying to collect his thoughts.

Dulcimer music filtered down from speakers at the top of the atrium. The fountain burbled and gushed and roared. A pair of administrative suits sauntered in from the parking deck, talking and laughing. They sobered suddenly, eyeing Plato and Cal with the wary suspicion of natives spotting white settlers.

"Let's go someplace where we can talk, okay?" He took her hand and walked back toward the hospital entrance. "This is kind of a long story."

"I know the perfect spot." She led him downstairs and through the hospital's catacombs, to the quietest place at Riverside. The morgue was Cal's semiprivate retreat, her refuge from the hustle and hurry of the pathology labs, the endless buzz of overhead pages and high-priced analytic machinery. On especially rough days, Cal even ate her lunch in the cool quiet of the morgue, among the inert bodies and glittering countertops—a stainless steel sanctuary.

Plato often accompanied her to the morgue on evenings when she was really backed up; he'd sit at the small desk in the corner and finish his dictations while she carved away at a corpse or two. Domestic bliss; a home away from home. These days, they seemed to carry on more conversations over dead bodies than over the dinner table.

As usual, the area was deserted. Cal opened the cooler, saw only one blue-footed specimen waiting patiently for his appointment, and nodded with satisfaction. She rounded up a couple of chairs and poured Plato a cup of coffee. He sipped gratefully, collecting his thoughts.

Finally, he began his story—starting with the summons at his office, and ending with Millburn's fantastic offer. Cal choked on her coffee, sputtering and wheezing.

"Medical director?" she gasped.

"That's exactly how I felt," he confessed. "Good thing I wasn't drinking coffee. Here I expected to be fired, and he offers me—"

"Medical director?" Cal repeated. She eyed Plato suspiciously. "You're putting me on, right? An April Fool's joke or something?"

"Not at all," he protested. "Why do you think his secretary congratulated me?"

"That's right." She shook her head, and the corners of her mouth turned up. "Then Millburn can't be serious. Medical director? Gah!"

"Thanks, Cal." He frowned petulantly.

"No, really." She giggled, patting his knee. "I could just see Riverside General after they put *you* in charge. Three-day work weeks. Video games in the ICU, and a basketball court in Maternity so the new dads don't get bored."

"Not a bad idea," he mused. "The moms could play, too—it might speed up deliveries."

"Close the hospital library, and install a swimming pool instead."

"Now you're talking."

"You could take a dip with the nursing students any time you liked."

"Ouch." He squinted at her. "Something tells me you don't think I'm medical director material."

"Oh, you could do the job all right," she conceded. "And you might even get to be pretty good at it, once you learned the ropes. But they won't give you enough time to do that."

"I know." Plato nodded. "It's a setup."

"I'm glad you see it, too." She sighed, relieved. "Did you turn him down?"

"It's not quite that simple, Cally." He told her about Millburn's promise to keep the geriatrics fellowship open until June if Plato accepted the position, and his threat to close it immediately if Plato refused.

"Blackmail." She shook her head. "Either you screw your geriatrics fellows, or you take the rap for Riverside going down the tubes."

"Right." He sighed. "I was hoping you might see another way out."

"Sorry." She leaned closer, shaking her head and frowning earnestly. "You *have* to decline, Plato. The fellows can get other positions somewhere eventually. But if your record is ruined, you'll have a hard time finding work changing bedpans, let alone teaching geriatrics at the fellowship level."

"I know." He leaned back in his chair and folded his arms defiantly. "But I'm going to try to stall, at least for a little while. To buy some time for my geriatrics fellows. Even a week or two would help."

She nodded. "And maybe *you* can find another job, too."

Plato swallowed heavily as it finally hit him. It really was over.

He had started his first rotation at Riverside General as a medical student, almost ten years ago. Virtually all of his clinical education had taken place here, including residency and fellowship. He had worked here as an attending physician ever since, caring for many of the same patients over the years, working with the same colleagues, sweating over the fledgling geriatrics program, and watching his students arrive and learn and move on. He had even met Cal here, in this very autopsy lab, of all places.

Riverside General was home. But it was time to move on, to say good-bye.

"Dan Homewood could use some time, too," he

noted. Dan was his partner in the geriatrics program—second in command of the fellowship and his partner in the office practice. "And Hilda, my nurse."

Cal touched his arm. "I'm sorry, Plato."

He glanced up to see a tear sneak down her face before she could wipe it away.

"Hey!" He grinned. "Look at the bright side—we'll finally have enough time to start a family. I can stay home with the baby while you work."

"You and a baby?" She chuckled, wiping another tear away. "It's easier to see you as a medical director than a househusband. You'd have the baby drinking beer from the bottle."

"Why bother with a glass?"

She groaned. "Besides, I don't know if we can support a baby and a mortgage and a bazillion dollars in student loans on just my salary."

"Maybe we won't have to." He flashed a sly grin. "If I can stall long enough for Millburn to get bumped off, we'll be just fine."

"*Plato!*" she scolded. "That's not funny."

"I know." He sobered. "Speaking of which, I have to go to Andre Surfraire's funeral this morning. I promised Gabrielle I'd be there."

She nodded. "I wish I could come, too."

"Why don't you?"

Cal eyed him sullenly. "I have to study for my exam."

"Exam?" Plato frowned. Cal had another year or two before she was due to take her pathology board exams again.

"ACLS," Cal explained gloomily. "I have to renew my certification."

"Hah!" Plato burst out laughing. "Now, that *is* funny."

Certification in ACLS—advanced cardiac life support—was a requirement for all members of Riverside's medical staff, and for many of the nurses as well. The skills included basic life support techniques like CPR, as well as the fantastically complex algorithms for medications and electroshock treatments to be given in cases of cardiac arrest. Passing the certification tests was always a bear, a matter of rote memorization and recall under pressure. And it didn't get any easier with repetition, since new algorithms and guidelines were drawn up every year or two.

For anyone else, Plato would have felt only sympathy. But he couldn't help laughing at the fact that Cal—who spent all of her time in the hospital basement, dissecting dead bodies—should be required to pass the ACLS exam.

"What's so funny?" she asked indignantly.

"You—having to pass ACLS." He shook his head and gestured toward the cooler. "Like maybe you'll need it for that guy in there."

She sniffed. "I see live patients once in a while."

"What—once a year?"

"At least every few months," she huffed. "Anyway, ACLS training is a medical staff requirement. And we can't afford to have both of us out of work."

"You're right." He dug the ACLS review text from a stack on her desk and smirked. "Better start studying."

"Thanks for your support." She curled her lip at the text, as though it were a particularly disgusting biopsy specimen. "And just when is *your* next ACLS exam?"

"Next year." He chuckled as he walked away. "But I won't need to renew."

"Why not?"

He smiled gleefully. "Because househusbands don't need ACLS."

*   *   *

Andre Surfraire's funeral was far less elaborate than the former CEO's—a quiet graveside affair with just a handful of mourners and not a single reporter. Andre Surfraire himself wasn't even there, or not very much of him. According to his wishes, the surgeon had been cremated yesterday, immediately after the autopsy. He now occupied an astonishingly small brass urn atop a granite monument bearing his name.

Gazing at the urn while the minister said his final blessing, Plato couldn't help wondering—did they really put *all* of Surfraire's ashes in there? Were they really the surgeon's ashes at all? How would anyone know the difference, unless they actually watched the cremation—something he imagined most family members would prefer not to do?

Gabrielle Surfraire still seemed to be taking it rather hard. Behind her gauzy black veil, the widow seemed to hang on the minister's words, clinging to them for some small shred of comfort. She had allowed herself to sob, twice, on the shoulder of the tall dark woman standing beside her. The lady looked enough like Gabrielle to be a sister or perhaps a cousin.

Thankfully, Surfraire's first wife didn't seem to be present, nor were her brothers. Most of the other members of the tiny gathering seemed to be Andre's friends from Riverside General; Plato recognized several surgeons and surgical residents, along with a nurse or two. He was surprised Annie Nussbaum hadn't attended. Perhaps she couldn't break away.

The minister closed his book and bowed his head, intoning a final blessing that floated away on the wind. He lifted his head and the assembly offered a last "Amen." Finally, the minister patted Gabrielle's shoulder and handed her the urn.

To Plato's surprise, the widow didn't leave the urn at the grave. Instead, she tucked it firmly under her arm and made the rounds of the mourners, thanking them all for coming and inviting them to her house for tea. She reached Plato last of all.

"Dr. Marley—Plato." She smiled faintly and lifted the veil. "I'm so glad you came."

She turned to the woman beside her and gestured to Plato. "Angelique, *je veux te présenter mon ami*, Dr. Plato Marley."

The woman nodded somberly. She looked like she hadn't smiled since Kennedy was shot.

"My sister," Gabrielle explained. "Angelique."

Plato nodded and offered a careful smile, scouring his memory for the old phrases he'd learned in high school. *"Je suis enchantée*, Angelique."

The woman's face lit up. She raked him with a barrage of rapid-fire French, of which Plato understood perhaps one word in six. He glanced helplessly at Gabrielle.

"High school French," he explained. "I know 'hello' and 'nice to meet you' and 'peanut butter sandwich.' After that, I'm kind of lost."

Gabrielle giggled, then explained his problem to Angelique. The woman shrugged and smiled graciously, then replied to her sister.

"She wants me to thank you for trying," Gabrielle interpreted. "She says it's rare to meet an American who bothers."

"That's because they don't often serve peanut butter sandwiches in French restaurants," Plato replied, inwardly grimacing at the lame joke.

But Gabrielle interpreted that as well, and her sister laughed aloud.

"I hope you'll be coming back to the house with us?" Gabrielle asked.

Plato nodded. "Certainly." And then he remembered one more phrase. *"Avec plaisir."*

* * *

An hour later, he and Gabrielle were standing on the banks of the duck pond, watching a flotilla of Canadian geese ply the water and poke their bills into the green muck beneath the surface. Although it was only early April, spring had already established a firm beachhead on the back corner of the Surfraire estate. Cattails and lily pads had sprung to life, the grove of pear trees surrounding the banks was awash in a riot of pink and white blossoms, and Plato could hear faint *cheep-cheeps* coming from the nesting grounds in the weeds lining the opposite shore.

"I'm grateful to you for coming here with me." Gabrielle was holding the brass urn and watching the geese. She might have been speaking to her husband's ashes, or his spirit, but she suddenly turned to glance up at Plato. "I didn't want to do this alone, but I did not want to bring Angelique along. She didn't quite—*approve*—of Andre."

"I'm sorry for that," he replied. And he *was* sorry. Standing here with Surfraire's widow, seeing the surgeon through her eyes, he realized how little he had known the late chief of surgery—how little he knew *most* of the doctors at Riverside. With their busy schedules and limited contact, few doctors at the hospital made or maintained close friendships. Plato honestly wished he had known Surfraire better.

"It was his age, mostly," Gabrielle explained. "That, and his first marriage. As a strict Catholic, Angelique could never sanction his divorce."

Plato nodded his understanding.

"Even though his wife was a raving lunatic," she continued. "Even though the Catholic church would surely have annulled such a union."

"Still," he replied, "I'm glad she came here for you."

"And I, too." She shrugged. "I have very few friends

of my own here, as you can see. But I didn't want Angelique out here now. She wouldn't understand."

Slowly, reverently, Gabrielle unscrewed the lid of
the urn and set it on the ground. She glanced up at
Plato. "This was Andre's wish—to be cremated and
scattered here. It was his favorite place." She gave a
sad smile. "Sometimes, on summer evenings, we
would sit together and watch the geese, listen to the
wind moving through the trees."

She lowered her head and glanced at the urn. "When
he told me about it, how he wanted to be cremated, I
laughed. We laughed together—it was such a big joke,
something that would happen many years—decades—
from now." She looked up at Plato, her dark eyes shin-
ing. "That was only last fall."

Gabrielle hiccuped and sobbed and sniffled. Plato
pulled a Kleenex from his pocket and offered it to her,
patting her shoulder awkwardly. She leaned closer,
pressing her head into his shoulder and sobbing. He
patted her back, muttering soothing words and feeling
the hard coldness of the urn between them. Finally,
Gabrielle pulled away, dabbing at her eyes.

"Thank you." She smiled and clutched his hand.
"Really. You are a good friend, Plato."

She turned away, carrying the urn toward the marshy
edge of the pond. She nearly slipped in the soft mud, so
Plato gallantly offered her an arm. Together, they
squished to the very edge of the water and halted. As
they sank in the mud, Gabrielle muttered a few words
to herself, or to Andre, then shook the dark ashes into
the grass and the water, watching them flutter away to
merge with the pink and white pear blossoms floating
on the calm surface of the pond. She led Plato along
the shore for a few steps and shook out more ashes, cir-
cling half of the pond before the urn was empty.

They stood and watched the ashes drifting out toward

the center of the pond before finally sinking. A few gray-white chips of bone floated along as well, bobbing in the wakes of the cruising geese. One especially large chip refused to sink, and the leader of the Canadian flotilla steered his charges over to investigate.

Plato frantically scanned the marshy banks for a rock or stick to throw at the predatory goose, but he came up empty. Finally, he dug in his jacket pocket and discovered one of the pumice biscuits from last night's medical staff meeting. Taking careful aim, he flung it across the water and caught the leader squarely in the neck.

The goose gave a raucous honk before pivoting neatly and discovering the biscuit floating behind him. A vicious fight ensued, a deadly melee of flapping wings and nipping bills and fluttering feathers. By the time it was over, the last of Andre Surfraire's mortal remains had finally sunk to the bottom of the pond.

Gabrielle turned and squeezed his arm fondly. "That was very well done." She glanced up at the sky. "I'm sure Andre got a good laugh out of that."

"I hope so."

"Do you always carry food in your pockets?" she asked, cocking her head curiously.

He nodded. "I never know when I'll get time to eat."

She smiled. "Andre was just the same way. And he *loved* to eat."

"I know." Plato grinned, remembering Andre's enthusiasm for the breakfast treasure hunt at Camp *Success!*

"Perhaps we should head back to the reception," Gabrielle said reluctantly. She replaced the lid of the urn and tucked it under her arm again, casting one last fond look out over the pond.

"I know," Plato agreed. "And I've got to head back to work."

"Yes—I'm sure you have a lot of work to do."

He nodded. *Like looking for a new job.*

Walking back to the house, Gabrielle was quiet and thoughtful. Perhaps more at peace with herself and with the loss of Andre. She certainly seemed more relaxed. Hopefully, the healing had begun.

But before they reached the house, she turned to Plato and frowned. "I was thinking about Andre—about the time he told me he wanted to be cremated." She paused on the path and glanced up at the house. "It happened one evening, on our way home from the theater."

Plato nodded.

"I drove the car, because Andre was sleepy—he had been up the whole night before with an emergency surgery." She bit her lip. "I thought he was asleep, so I took the shorter route—up Waite Hill Road. But he woke up just as we started up the hill."

Gabrielle stared at Plato, her forehead wrinkled in confusion. "He was very upset, even frightened. By then, I knew better than to tease him about it. I just apologized, and we came home." She glanced down at the urn in her hands. "But it was that same night that he told me he wanted to be cremated. Plato—it's like he *knew* what was going to happen!"

"That *is* strange," Plato agreed.

"I can't help thinking it must have something to do with his murder," Gabrielle insisted.

Plato nodded. Maybe she was right. The police had so far found no important leads in any of the murders; the killer had hidden his or her tracks extraordinarily well.

Jeremy Ames had even checked the past ten years of accident records for Waite Hill Road. Despite the large number of crashes, most were minor, few involved any serious injury, and *none* mentioned Andre Surfraire.

Maybe they just needed to look a little harder.

Chapter 18

Plato decided not to go straight back to the hospital. Yesterday, Hilda had telephoned all of his scheduled patients for this afternoon and informed them that Dr. Marley was sick and wouldn't be in. She had been very surprised—and rather annoyed—when Plato had shown his face in the office this morning.

So his afternoon was basically free, though he planned to return to the hospital later and talk with Dan Homewood and the rest of the department about Riverside's plans to close the geriatrics program. He had quickly told Dan and Hilda about his strategy that morning, just before rushing out to Andre Surfraire's funeral. He wasn't looking forward to this afternoon's meeting, and he didn't want to go back to Riverside any sooner than he had to.

Besides, his conversation with Gabrielle had sparked another memory—one that he was surprised he had forgotten. Her comment about Andre's eating habits had brought the whole Camp *Success!* fiasco into clear focus again for Plato. He remembered the surgeon's incredible appetite, and his almost childish disappointment over the meager fare they were served last Friday night. The rest of the evening came back as well—Surfraire's and Wallace's earth-shattering snores, Plato's decision to sleep in the living room, his peacemaking visit with Cal, and his return to bed an hour or two later.

And one more thing—the person that Plato had seen leaving the bedroom just a moment before he reached the door.

He hadn't given the incident much thought since then; after all, Lionel Wallace's death had been considered accidental until just yesterday afternoon. But Plato's guess about someone switching tablets in Wallace's pill dispenser was probably on target. The market offered dozens of penicillin preparations; with the proper information, a killer could have easily found a pill that resembled one of Wallace's medications. According to David Inverness, the late CEO had taken only three pills on a regular basis—two for high blood pressure and one for depression—and all three pills were taken in the morning.

The killer *could* have made the switch before bedtime, but he or she would have been taking an incredible risk by searching Wallace's belongings while everyone was awake. The switch would have been far safer after the campers were asleep.

That left only one conclusion. Plato must have seen the murderer leaving the room last Friday night.

Too bad he hadn't recognized Wallace's nighttime visitor. But the cabin was so dark at that hour that Plato couldn't even be certain whether it was a man or a woman. The figure had been just a blur in the darkness as it darted into the bathroom.

On the other hand, considering that three murders had already been committed, perhaps it was best that Plato *hadn't* been able to recognize the killer. If he had, the killer would probably have recognized Plato as well.

And would have done something about it by now.

Plato watched the hills and valleys of Geauga County flit by—silos and farmhouses, scattered country retreats of wealthy Clevelanders, miles of woodland coming to life with that first hint of green among the brown. Tractors dotted a few of the fields, turning the soil in preparation for planting: the first sure sign of spring in Ohio. Hopefully, this week's freeze would be the last of the year.

As he approached Camp *Success!*, Plato wondered who Wallace's nocturnal visitor might have been. Obviously, he and Cal were ruled out, as were Millburn and Surfraire and Wallace. And, of course, the late Cy Kettering.

That left Annie Nussbaum, Patty Kidzek, Marta Oberlin, and David Inverness. Plato couldn't imagine that the killer was one of the three women—despite Marta's avowed intention to disembowel Plato with a gynecologic speculum—nor could he believe that David Inverness would hurt a fly. The former medical director was allergic to harsh *words*, never mind physical violence.

An outsider, then?

Perhaps. After all, the cabin had several entrances, and Plato doubted that any of the doors were locked. A rear corridor led from a back door to the sleeping areas, so the killer could have entered without having to sneak past Plato and Cal as they dozed on the living room sofa. But who would have risked visiting the cabin that night?

Who even knew they were there?

Plato spotted the dingy sign marking the entrance to Camp *Success!* He swung his car onto the dirt road and headed toward the main cabin. It was hard to believe that only a week had passed since Claude Eberhardt had driven the ten of them here on the bus. So much had happened that it felt more like a year; Plato had almost expected Camp *Success!* to look different, somehow.

But it didn't. The entrance was marked by the same

rickety wooden sign, the ancient dirt road was just as narrow and rutted, and the trailheads bore the same inane slogans as before. One of the Camp *Success!* buses was parked in front of the main cabin, a sprawling, modern-looking structure that Plato had seen only briefly, after Wallace had been carried off in the ambulance.

Hopefully, Claude Eberhardt would be here today, and would have some time to answer a few questions.

The guide wasn't hard to find; Plato bumped into Eberhardt just as he was dashing out the front door of the main cabin. He offered a quick apology, then glanced at Plato again, his eyes widening in recognition.

"Dr. Marley." He smiled politely. "How nice to see you again."

From his tone, Eberhardt might as well have said, "Please go away, I'm busy." Plato ignored it.

"You're just the person I was looking for," he replied. "I was hoping to ask you a couple of questions, about last week."

"Sorry." The guide glanced at his watch and frowned over at the bus. "I'm just leaving to pick up my retreat group. Maybe some other time."

"This will only take a couple of minutes," Plato promised. "It's about Lionel Wallace."

"I figured as much." His shoulders slumped. "The police were here already today. They're saying he was murdered."

"He was." Plato nodded.

"How?" Eberhardt asked, his brows narrowing with sudden curiosity. "Last week they said it was *allergies*. Was he poisoned or something?"

"No. It *was* allergies." Plato gestured to the door. "I can explain it, if you're interested."

"The police didn't tell us anything," the guide complained. "They just said that Dr. Wallace was murdered. And then they asked a bunch of crazy questions, mostly about you folks." He glanced at his watch again, then nodded. "I've got a few extra minutes, anyway. Come on inside and have some coffee."

He led him to his office, a tiny cubicle near the back of the building. A small sheet-metal desk, its chair, and a rickety canvas seat nearly filled the room. A sagging bookcase took up the rest of the available space. Plato squeezed into the canvas chair and glanced out the window. At least Claude Eberhardt had a lovely view: a hilltop vantage looking down over the mossy green top of the blooming forest. Beyond the woods, he could just make out a bare grassy clearing: the start of the camp's challenge course.

Plato sipped a can of Diet Pepsi while he told Claude the story of Wallace's murder. He also explained his theory that penicillin had been substituted for one of Wallace's pills in the seven-day dispenser Friday night.

"Then it must have been somebody from your group," Claude observed.

"Why?" Plato asked quickly. "Were the doors locked that night?"

"Nope." He shrugged, then gestured out the window toward the empty woods. "But it's not like there are crowds of people out here, just waiting to break into a cabin. Besides, how many people knew you folks were out here this weekend—or which cabin Dr. Wallace was in?"

"That's true," Plato conceded reluctantly. "We had a hard enough time finding our cabin in broad daylight."

"It's not as tough as it seems." The guide chuckled, then sobered. He leaned across his flimsy desk and frowned. "I've been following the stories in the papers—three doctors murdered so far, right?"

"So far." Plato nodded. "And only seven of us left."

Six, he amended to himself—if one member of their

group was the killer. And that seemed more likely than ever. But they still hadn't ruled out an outsider—a killer who knew the campground, and knew where Lionel Wallace would be staying.

"If somebody *did* know where we were," Plato persisted, "they could just drive in late at night, right? And then sneak up to our cabin?"

"Nope." Claude Eberhardt shook his head. "We've got a fence and a pair of metal gates up at the entrance. Nobody notices them, but we close them up at night. And we've got a night patrolman who keeps an eye on the road and the main cabin here. He'd have caught anyone who tried to sneak in from outside." He waved a hand at his window again. "Nothing but woods for miles around; somebody would have to hike at least three or four miles to get into camp without using a car."

"But I *saw* somebody that night," Plato said. He had been saving that tidbit for the police, but he didn't see any reason to hold it back from Eberhardt.

"What?" The guide lurched forward in his chair, frowning at Plato. "Where?"

"In our cabin." Quickly, he told Eberhardt about the figure he had seen leaving the bedroom last Friday.

"Did you see whether he came in from the outside?" Eberhardt asked. He was biting his lip and drumming his fingers on the desktop. Anxious, or just eager to follow up the lead? "Did he go *back* outside?"

Plato shook his head. "I really didn't think about it that night. The person just darted into the bathroom. I was practically asleep before I realized it wasn't somebody from our room."

The guide nodded slowly, satisfied. "Then it could have been anyone—probably somebody from one of the other rooms." He leaned back in his chair again and sighed. "No reason to suspect somebody from the outside."

Plato shrugged. No reason, except he couldn't see David or Marta or Patty or Annie as killers.

But Eberhardt was right. Who could have known they were there—and found their cabin in the dark? A murderer couldn't have gotten past the night patrolman. Not unless he or she was already in the park—

Plato sat up eagerly. "What if they were already here?"

"You mean, somebody drove in and *hid* here until dark?" The guide gave a thin smile. "For one thing, all the cars are registered. For another—"

"No, I mean somebody with another group," Plato replied. Now he remembered *why* they had been stuck in the run-down Henry Ford Lodge; the other two lodges, newly refurbished, were already booked. "Who else was here that weekend?"

"Two other parties." Eberhardt stared at the ceiling. "They weren't mine, so I didn't know much about them—just what the other guides told me." He glanced at Plato and shrugged. "One of the groups was an advertising agency, from Columbus, I think. And the other one was some management corporation."

"Not a hospital?" He sat back, disappointed.

"Nope. They had a funny name." The guide closed his eyes, then shook his head. "A day care, or maybe an exercise clinic."

Plato's ears perked up. He leaned forward, trying to hide his eagerness. "Could you just check the name for me? I'm sure the police will end up asking anyway— once I tell them what I saw."

"I'm not supposed to give out that kind of information." Claude took a deep breath, considering. He still seemed a bit nervous, or maybe it was just claustrophobia. By extending his arms, he could have easily touched the window and wall simultaneously. But he finally stood, shrugging. "You're right—the police will have to know anyway. Just don't tell anyone *I* told you."

He edged past Plato and led him down the corridor to another door. Inside was a large conference room, lined with bookshelves and plants and inspirational posters. One of the walls was filled with tall windows that faced out over a deep, rock-filled ravine. At the front of the room, a large whiteboard held yet another inspirational quote, scrawled in huge multicolored letters.

THE SECRET OF SUCCESS IS CONSTANCY TO PURPOSE.
—*Benjamin Disraeli*

Claude caught Plato gazing at the whiteboard and sighed.

"Our quote of the day. We've been working on Disraeli lately."

Plato frowned sympathetically. "You have to memorize them?"

"Of course." He tapped his temple. "I've got dozens of those quotes floating around in here."

He turned away to scan one of the bookcases, then pulled out several large ring binders. They looked identical to the syllabi Plato and Cal had received on their arrival at Camp *Success!*

"We always have a few extra manuals, from the no-shows," he explained. "We just rip out the front pages and put new ones in. Saves paper."

He flipped open the first binder and grunted. "Hammond Advertising Agency—based in Columbus." He opened the next. "Same with this one."

Plato glanced at the syllabus. It *was* identical to the one he'd received. "The programs are the same for all the groups that come here?"

"Basically." Claude nodded. "The McDonald's approach to management consultation. We try to personalize our lectures a little bit, but it's kind of a cookie-cutter approach." He looked up at Plato, grinning as if to challenge him. "Surprised?"

"Not really." He sat down across the table and glanced at the whiteboard again. *Not at all.* "Claude—do you really buy all this stuff?"

Eberhardt gazed at him a long moment, sizing him up. Finally, he gave a satisfied nod.

"Some of it. A little of it." He glanced back at the closed door and lowered his voice. "This program's great, for some groups. And it's pretty lousy for others." He shrugged. "But mostly it's an excuse for managers to spend money, to feel like they're doing something productive. You wouldn't *believe* how much they charge groups to come here."

Plato blinked. He hadn't expected such honesty from a Camp *Success!* guide.

"You want to know *my* favorite quote about success?" Claude Eberhardt leaned closer, lowering his voice even further, as though Big Brother might have a camera hidden in this very room. Perhaps he did. " 'Success depends on three things: who says it, what he says, and how he says it; and *what* he says is the least important thing.' "

Plato grinned, thinking of the changes at Riverside, Millburn's "reforms," and Frank Evans's forced enthusiasm. He shook his head. "Doesn't sound like the kind of thing General Patton would say."

"John Morley," Eberhardt replied. He shrugged. "This job is just temporary. I've got one more year to go on my M.B.A., but I ran out of money."

"With all your contacts, you shouldn't have any trouble finding a job."

"You got it." He flipped through another binder and shook his head. "Know what I'd do, if I was one of these big-shot administrators? I'd spend all that extra money on computers instead, so the secretaries would stop bitching. Or give all my top administrators a free weekend at some nice resort. *That's* how you spark employee loyalty."

Plato nodded. "I wouldn't mind working for you someday."

Claude Eberhardt grinned. "Maybe you will."

He opened the last binder in the stack and nodded. "Here it is. Funny name—RiverEdge Wellness Management Group."

Plato scurried around the table and studied the page. Apparently, the hospital's new name wasn't quite as secret as he'd been led to believe.

"How many people were in this group?" he asked calmly, trying to hide his interest.

"It was a pretty big gathering—maybe twenty people," Claude replied. "They were in the Harvey Firestone Cabin—just up the road from yours. Why? Do you know these people?"

"I think so." Plato scanned the rest of the page and nodded. "Yes, I do."

Only one name was listed on the page—the name of the group's ranking member, the liaison between the RiversEdge group and the Camp *Success!* staff. An associate vice president at Riverside Hospital.

Quentin Young.

Plato pointed at the name. "Did Mr. Young attend the retreat last weekend?"

"Of course." Claude nodded quickly. "He's the person who set it up." The guide peered at the group's name again. "RiversEdge Wellness Management. Now what do you suppose these people *do*?"

Plato shook his head. "To tell you the truth, I honestly don't know."

Chapter 19

Cal was in the cafeteria when it happened. She was having a late lunch with David Inverness and Marta Oberlin, thrashing out Plato's quandary and the dismal prospects for the rest of the teaching programs at Riverside.

Most of the cafeteria was empty, but the few doctors who were still dining had given the trio a wide berth, casting furtive glances at Cal and David and Marta from several tables away, as though they expected the chiefs to be fired at any minute.

"Which one of us will be next?" Marta mused.

"Fired, or murdered?" David asked. Despite their gloomy situation, Riverside's former medical director and chief of staff looked more content than he had in years. His suit was freshly pressed, his eyes were clear and bright, and his straggly gray hair was even tamed into some semblance of order.

"*Fired,*" Marta replied. She shivered. "I hope we're done with that other business."

"Patty Kidzek," he answered. "No doubt about it." He shook his head sadly. "I talked to her this morning, to try to get her ready for it."

"You're that sure?" Cal asked.

"Plato's program and Patty's were losing money. Especially Patty's—with that outreach program for poor kids." David spread his hands. "The rest of us were at least breaking even. Not that it'll help us much in the long run."

"The administration's latest claim is that medical education is a *distraction* from the main mission of the hospital." Marta clenched her teeth. "That mission being to make money, of course."

David nodded.

"Distraction!" the obstetrician seethed. "Stupid little shits."

"Easy, girl." He patted her arm.

"Maybe that murderer *isn't* done yet." She grimaced. "Godfrey Millburn was on that camp-out with us, right? Why doesn't somebody bump him off? That would be a nice distraction."

Cal couldn't help chuckling; Marta and Plato had at least one thing in common. So did the rest of them. Right now, Cal would have gladly paid someone to bonk Millburn over the head. Not to kill him, exactly, appealing though that might be. Just to put him out of action for a while—a one-year coma, perhaps. With the housekeeping staff watching over him in the ICU.

"Just give me some time, kid." David gave a sinister grin, an expression Cal had never seen before. A bitter, vengeful smile, totally uncharacteristic of their meek medical director. "They've gone too far. *Way* too far."

The cafeteria suddenly fell silent. David glanced over at the door, and his face fell. All the other diners were watching the door, too.

Patty Kidzek had just shuffled into the physicians' dining room. Head down, shoulders slumped, the normally buoyant pediatrician looked like a stuffed animal that had lost its stuffing.

She wove her way through the tables, looking more shocked than defeated. Her eyes were glazed, and she moved with the dumb automatism of a shell-shocked soldier.

Dr. Silas Gundleford hobbled over to her side. He asked her a question, received a quick nod of the head, and stomped his cane in frustration. He asked another question, and Patty shook her head and flashed a skeletal smile. Gundleford muttered something, then stomped away out the door.

The other diners frowned sympathetically, then burst into a babble of anxious speculation as Patty shuffled to the table. Wordlessly, she slumped into a chair beside Marta and stared at her hands. Her breaths were coming in quick gasps, as though the trip across the cafeteria had been the last yards of a marathon, the toughest steps she had ever taken.

Finally, she glanced up at David Inverness and nodded. "You were right."

Marta Oberlin reached out to squeeze the pediatrician's arm. Kidzek patted her hand and smiled weakly.

"How long?" David asked.

"They told me to clear my desk by two o'clock."

Cal gasped.

Even Inverness seemed nonplussed. "They're not giving any notice?"

"Oh, they'll *pay* me for another ninety days, just like it says in my contract," Patty replied bitterly. "And the residents are getting sixty days' pay. But they have to be gone by the end of the day, too."

"What about your patients?" Cal asked. "How will Riverside staff the floors?"

The hospital had three pediatrics floors as well as a neonatal intensive care unit. Many of the patients were followed by private pediatricians who weren't on the hospital staff. But many others—the indigent patients, especially—were cared for by the house staff: the interns and residents and medical staff of Patty's teaching division.

By eliminating its teaching programs, Riverside

General Hospital would shed most of its burden of uninsured patients.

"You haven't heard the worst of it," Patty replied. She shot an angry look at Cal, then turned to David, ignoring Cal completely. "Even *you* didn't think they'd go this far."

"They're not closing the floors," he said.

"Oh, yes, they are," she replied. "House patients are being transferred immediately to other area hospitals. Private patients can be followed here until their discharge, or until they are stable enough to be transferred." She stared at her hands and hiccuped, allowing a single tear to trickle down her cheek. "And as of June first, Riverside General will no longer be a pediatric hospital."

More tears came, and she swiped them away angrily, staring at her sleeve. "I said I wouldn't do this. D-d-*damn* it all!"

"That's the spirit," Marta comforted. She leaned over to put her arms across Patty Kidzek's shoulders and pulled her close. "This isn't your fault. Remember that."

Marta turned to glare at Inverness. "I'd gladly strangle Godfrey Millburn myself, if he had the nerve to walk through that door right now."

But Patty Kidzek pulled away, shaking her head. "It wasn't Millburn."

They gaped at her in confusion.

"Of course it was," Inverness insisted.

"No." The pediatrician pulled a box of Kleenex from the voluminous pockets of her lab coat. She shot a bleary-eyed glance at David and shook her head again. "It was Quentin Young."

"It may have been Young who *told* you about it," Cal said. "But it must have been Millburn's decision."

"It was Quentin Young's decision," Kidzek insisted,

still looking at Inverness. "Young told me that Millburn had left it up to him, that it was his first important decision as a senior vice president." She slapped the table angrily. "He said his people had been doing cost studies on our floors for the past three months, found we're losing too much money. So instead of just shutting the residency, his decision was to kill the whole department. Everything."

"I can't believe it," Inverness muttered. He turned to Marta. "They've gone too far this time. Aside from our contracts with the residents, they can't close the floors without some kind of medical authorization. They'd need a medical director's approval to make a move like that, and they don't have it."

"They've *got* the medical director's approval," Kidzek said. She glared at Cal.

"What are you talking about?" Cal asked, genuinely puzzled.

"As if you don't know." She turned to David Inverness. "Guess who took over your job—and approved the closing of our entire pediatrics division?"

Inverness frowned. "Patty—"

But Kidzek wasn't listening. She swiveled her gaze back to Cal and spoke, her voice dripping with venom. "Your husband. Our new medical director."

Before Cal could reply, the chief of pediatrics stood. She turned to David and Marta and smiled grimly.

"You're wrong, Patty." David shook his head earnestly. "Plato would never—"

"I've got to run—I have to pack up my office before two o'clock." She turned to Cal. "Be sure to tell your husband I said thanks."

Unfortunately, Cal didn't have time to run after Patty Kidzek and explain. She was already late for the ACLS exam; she'd be lucky if the written test hadn't started already. After David promised to explain things to the pediatrician, Cal rushed over to the ACLS training room.

Luckily, the test hadn't started yet. Looking around at the other examinees assembled there, Cal wondered how many would still have jobs by the time their current certification expired. What was the point? After the scene with Patty Kidzek, the last thing Cal wanted to do was take an exam.

But rules were rules. And Cal didn't want to give the administration any more ammunition than they already had, any more reason to justify firing her. Especially since Plato was about to lose *his* job.

Apparently, many other members of the medical staff felt the same way. Several internists were there, along with Plato's old friend Nathan Simmons. The family doctor flashed a nervous smile at Cal; he was probably still worried about her veiled threat to tell Leah about the St. Patrick's Day party. She smiled back, and Nathan shivered.

Even Silas Gundleford was there, frowning over some study notes that were—honest-to-goodness—yellowed with age. How the old gastroenterologist managed to pass these exams with outdated notes was a mystery to Cal. Maybe the protocols hadn't changed as much as she thought they had.

The remaining members of their group included a scattering of residents and medical students and a pair of nurses from the intensive care unit.

The room itself was quite large—big enough to hold twenty desks for the written part of the test, as well as three testing stations for the practical exam. The testing stations were impressively realistic—three hospital beds complete with red metal heart carts, electronic defibrillators, mock medication syringes, and three "Annie" dolls. The full-sized human dolls were specially designed for teaching life-support procedures; their chests were equipped with pressure-sensitive devices that determined whether trainees were performing chest compressions and artificial respirations properly. The accuracy of a trainee's technique was printed on a paper readout that scrolled out of the side of each Annie's head.

But basic life support—chest compressions and respirations—was only a small part of the test. The written exam focused on all those complicated algorithms and flowcharts and medication protocols that Cal had been cramming into her head for the past two days. And the practical exam included a very realistic Annie-based code blue, where Cal would have to run a mock lifesaving attempt based on EKG readings—calling out the correct doses and types of medications at the proper times, administering CPR or respirations as necessary, and deciding when to deliver the defibrillating shocks to the heart—and at which voltages.

The whole thing was very intimidating, almost as nerve-racking as medical board exams. In these final minutes before the test began, every nose in the room was buried in a pile of notes or an ACLS book, cramming those last few details or flow charts into their heads before the test actually began.

Every nose except Cal's. Years ago, she had found that last-minute cramming often made things worse, mixing last-minute details into the information she'd so carefully filed away.

Besides, she had a clear plan, based on an easy-to-remember acronym. For cardiac arrest, it was E.B.A.—which stood for epinephrine, bicarb, and atropine. Simple. And for ventricular fibrillation—

Or was it E.A.B.? Did atropine come *before* bicarb? Or was that the protocol for ventricular fibrillation?

And what about calcium chloride? Had they done away with that?

Cal panicked. She tore her book open and scanned the algorithm for asystole—full cardiac arrest—then breathed a deep sigh of relief. She was right the first time; she never should have doubted herself.

But what about ventricular tachycardia?

"Please close your books and place them under your desks." Unnoticed, the exam leader had entered the room and crossed to the desk at the front. It was the director of the intensive care unit herself, a pulmonologist who seemingly had been at Riverside since the dawn of time. Dr. Geraldine Paige was almost as old as Silas Gundleford, which meant she had probably witnessed the introduction of penicillin and the marvels of the iron lung. The intensivist spent virtually every waking hour in Riverside's unit, guarding over her charges and scolding residents and interns—and even attendings—when they made the slightest deviation from accepted life-support protocols.

Paige was an iron-fisted dictator. Residents and interns dreaded their ICU rotations, although they admitted that they learned more from Paige than they would have ever thought possible.

Every test-taker's worst nightmare was that Paige might preside over their ACLS exams. The ICU Dictator only did it once every year or two, but she supposedly flunked most of her examinees during the practical, dreaming up incredibly complex situations that were never covered in the manual.

And if Cal flunked, she would have to repeat the exam *next* month. And memorize this nonsense all over again. If she was still employed.

She sighed. There was nothing for it but to try. And to hope some kind of miracle might save her from having Paige oversee *her* practical exam. After all, it was only a one in three chance.

The written part of the exam was surprisingly easy. Having taken the test every few years since medical school, Cal had learned which questions to expect and had prepared accordingly. She finished the written exam quickly, then glanced around the room to see most of her fellow examinees still scratching away with their Number Two pencils.

So Cal looked over the exam once more, double-checking her answers and making sure the ovals were filled perfectly. She had almost finished when Paige finally called an end to the test. Two medical students near the door groaned as the Dictator wrenched their half-completed tests from their grasps.

Paige glanced at the tests and fired her gray eyes at the students. "You're not even close. Might as well skip the practical." She jerked her head toward the door. "Better luck next time."

With a forlorn sigh, the medical students slunk from the room.

Paige and her two assistants collected the rest of the exams and led the remaining examinees over to the testing stations. The Dictator called for a quick head count and herded the crowd into three groups.

Before Cal knew it, she found herself standing across from Paige herself, at the first testing station. The old woman gave a tight smile, as though her dentures were paining her.

"Now, Dr. Marley, as an *attending physician* here at Riverside, I'm sure you'll be able to show the others how it's done. Right?"

"I haven't spent much time in the ICU lately," Cal confessed. She shrugged helplessly. "By the time they reach my department, all my patients are already dead."

The rest of the crowd tittered gleefully. Even Paige chuckled. Then she gestured at the sheet-covered Annie doll. "And so, to all intents and purposes, is this lady. But your task will be to bring her back to life."

She glanced at the ceiling thoughtfully, then snapped her fingers. She licked her lips, then grinned at Cal. "The patient, a sixty-seven-year-old female, was admitted with an inferior wall myocardial infarction and a resultant type one second-degree atrioventricular block. I assume you're familiar with Wenckebach periods, Cal?"

Cal nodded dumbly. She didn't have the slightest idea what Wenckebach periods were, and second-degree atrioventricular blocks of any type were as unfathomable to Cal as the Dead Sea Scrolls. Why couldn't Paige have asked about a simple ventricular tachycardia? She could do ventricular tachycardia in her sleep.

"The patient's condition stabilized after supportive therapy," Paige continued, "and she was transferred to the general medical floor. But on the third day of hospitalization, a nurse walking past the room heard a weak cry for help." She waved her hand, sketching an imaginary nurse in the air. "She hurried inside to discover our patient, out cold. Naturally, she tried to rouse the patient before calling the code."

Without looking down, the Dictator tore back the sheet and shook the Annie doll, reciting the standard litany taught in basic life support classes across the country: "Annie, Annie, are you all right?"

Cal didn't look down either; her attention was riveted on Paige's face, on the woman's words. She was trying to remember the difference between second- and third-degree AV blocks, trying to recall her carefully memorized protocols, trying to guess what appalling surprise the Dictator had in store for her next.

But Cal could never have guessed the surprise that was waiting for all of them.

"Of course, Annie is *not* all right," Paige continued blandly. "She's in full cardiac arrest, and the nurse calls a code blue."

Somebody in the crowd gasped, and another person shouted, "Oh, my God!"

Paige cut her eyes to the others and then glanced down at the Annie doll.

The only trouble was, it wasn't an Annie *doll* at all. Staring up at the Dictator with glazed eyes and a tortured grimace was Riverside General's chief of nursing services. Her face was pale blue and waxen, and the bedsheet behind her head was stained with a spreading butterfly pattern of dried blood. Her shirt had been yanked up to her shoulders, and a dozen or more perfectly circular burns showed up clearly against the fish-belly pallor of her chest—one set grouped just over the sternum and another at the left side of the rib cage. The poor woman might have been stampeded by a herd of very angry pogo sticks.

Defibrillator marks. The paddles had been positioned correctly, but the device had obviously been used to *cause* cardiac arrest rather than treat it.

As Geraldine Paige had said, Annie was *not* all right.

Annie Nussbaum was dead.

Chapter 20

"Four to six hours," Cal pronounced after examining the body.

Jeremy Ames scribbled a note on his pad and looked up. "That puts the time of death between eight and ten this morning."

Cal gave a tired nod. It had been a long afternoon.

At least the police had arrived in record time. To Cal's surprise, Jeremy was the first officer to appear. The detective hadn't had to go far; he had been upstairs, questioning Cy Kettering's staff about Wednesday's murder.

Despite the presence of Geraldine Paige—the ICU Dictator—as well as a dozen highly trained ACLS examinees, nobody had bothered to attempt resuscitation. For one thing, Annie Nussbaum was stone-cold dead; her skin had chilled almost to room temperature, and blood had started settling into dependent areas—livor mortis. For another, rigor mortis was already well advanced; Annie's arms and legs were moderately stiff, and her clenched fists were as cold and rigid as a pair of stones.

Along with confirming that the chief of nursing was long past hope of resuscitation, the signs helped Cal estimate the time of death. Not that she was entirely sure about the time; even her two-hour range was probably too narrow. Pinpointing the time of a death was far more an art than a science—the onset of physical signs like rigor mortis could be delayed or hastened by dozens of factors ranging from ambient temperature and movement of the body to disease processes and physical activity before death.

The use of electrical defibrillation as a murder weapon made Cal's estimate especially tricky. She had never autopsied anyone intentionally killed by a defibrillator before, had never even *heard* of such a case. But Cal knew that victims of electrical shock often developed rigor mortis far more quickly, because electrically induced muscle spasms depleted the muscles' energy reserves. On the other hand, high levels of muscle activity could also produce heat and slow the body's cooling.

So Cal's judgment that Annie Nussbaum had died four to six hours ago was far more of a guess than a certainty. But her guess was based on years of experience.

Though she couldn't be sure about the timing, Cal was at least certain about the *cause* of Annie's death. The nursing chief's head had bled freely, but the wound showed no evidence of a depressed fracture or other signs of a fatal blow. And Annie's eyes were open, implying that she had awoken from unconsciousness—momentarily—when the defibrillator was applied.

More important, the victim's chest bore perhaps two dozen burn marks, signs that the paddles had been used several times to ensure that the heart was stopped. The defibrillator's cardiac monitor—the device that detects a heart rhythm in a patient—had been overridden, and the charge was set to 360 joules, the maximum jolt deliverable through the paddles.

That high level of shock was rarely used more than a few times in resuscitations. For people with normally functioning hearts, a jolt of even *half* that voltage could trigger a fatal arrhythmia. Multiple 360-joule shocks could burn through the heart's fragile conduction pathways like lightning strikes shorting out a VCR.

Needless to say, the ACLS exam had been halted immediately when they found that one of the Annies was real. Cal had quickly cleared the room and called security, closing the door and examining the body while she waited for the police to arrive.

Jeremy Ames and a detective from the city homicide division had taken statements from the examinees while a pair of uniformed cops checked the room for fingerprints and trace evidence. The fingerprint check was hopeless; Cal expected the cops to find dozens of different prints, while the killer had probably used gloves. But they dusted the defibrillator and the rails of Annie Nussbaum's bed, hoping the killer might have slipped up.

The missing Annie doll was quickly found, standing in a closet in the corner.

Cal almost had an opportunity to put her ACLS training to good use after all; the cop who opened the closet door had screeched like a banshee when the Annie doll tumbled out into his arms. It hadn't helped that the Annie was wearing a glazed smile and a bright red bikini, and had half a roll of EKG recording tape sticking out of her head. Apparently, she had last been used for the poolside lifesaving program and hadn't changed back into her usual jogging sweats.

The plump cop had needed several minutes to catch his breath and steel himself to check through the other closets. His partner had teased him mercilessly for the rest of the investigation.

But finally they had wrapped up their work, the crime scene photographer had come and gone, and the coroner's crew started packing the body away for transport to the morgue. Jeremy Ames pocketed his notebook and glanced up at Cal. "I've got to go question some more people. You going to be okay?"

"Sure." She shrugged. "I want to ask around a little, too."

"Listen, Cally." The detective moved closer and latched on to her elbow, guiding her into the hallway and out of earshot of the other investigators. "Ten people went on that camping trip last weekend. Ten hospital chiefs. And four of them are dead."

"I *know*, Jeremy." Cal sighed impatiently, ignoring the fear welling up in her chest. She was all too aware of that deadly arithmetic, all too certain that the killer was targeting Riverside's division chiefs—a group of which she and Plato were still members.

But Cal had never backed down from a fight, never learned how to tackle problems other than head-on. To turn away now, to try to run and hide, would make her even more frightened than she already was.

Besides, Annie's murder had made Cal even more certain that she was right—that the killer had some reason for choosing such odd methods. Death by defibrillator was both bizarre and tremendously impractical. The killer had taken a huge risk, and this time, he or she hadn't bothered trying to stage the death as an accident or suicide.

Each piece of the puzzle, each successive murder, seemed like another attempt to act out a bizarre fantasy, or perhaps to extract some strange form of justice.

"I'll be careful," Cal told her friend. "I promise."

"You'd better be." Jeremy grinned. "Plato would never forgive me if—" He broke off, frowning. "Where *is* that slacker, anyway? Taking another day off?"

"He went to Andre Surfraire's funeral." Cal glanced at her watch: three-fifteen. He should have been back by now. She had paged him half an hour ago, but he hadn't called back yet.

"You'd better make sure *he* stays out of trouble, too." The detective waggled his head, like a bulldog shaking himself dry. "I've got enough on my mind with these murders without worrying about the two of you." He watched the coroner's crew wheel Annie Nussbaum's sheet-covered body out the door and down the hallway. "Best thing would be for you and Plato to head home and take it easy. I'll call you tonight."

Cal nodded. "Sure thing, Jeremy."

He frowned at her dubiously, then touched her arm again. "Whatever you do, stay away from Quentin Young."

Cal glanced up at him sharply. Having Quentin Young implicated would be too good to be true. "Why?"

"A few reasons." Jeremy shrugged. "For one thing, that stuff you told me about the hospital's sale to Vista Health Management. Seems to me, Young stands to make a pile of change if this deal goes through. And from what I've heard, Wallace and Nussbaum were dead-set against it. So was Surfraire." He waved a hand. "And Millburn's leaving Riverside to work with Vista's competition, right?"

Cal nodded. Quentin Young certainly seemed to have a clear motive, though it still didn't explain the bizarre murder methods. On the other hand, perhaps the deaths themselves were some kind of smear campaign against the hospital—a drunken chief of surgery and a suicidal chief of psychiatry certainly didn't help Riverside's image with the community.

"But why kill Cy Kettering?" Cal asked.

"Who knows? Maybe Kettering still had influence with the Board, or maybe he knew something about Young."

"Was Quentin Young one of Cy's patients?" she asked quickly.

"Now, Cally," he replied, grinning mysteriously. "You can hardly expect me to answer *that*."

Especially since Jeremy probably had no access to Kettering's charts, she realized. Strict confidentiality would be maintained even after the psychiatrist's death—regardless of the fact that the murderer might have been one of Kettering's patients. But maybe the police had learned something from the psychiatry staff upstairs.

"Anyway, we have a much more important reason for suspecting Quentin Young," Jeremy continued. "Something we just found out from Nussbaum's secretary." He moved closer and lowered his voice. "Apparently, Quentin Young came over to her office early this morning. They had an argument—about staffing, according to the secretary. They went down the hall to a conference room, and she didn't see either of them after that."

"Did anyone else see them together?"

"A maintenance worker spotted Nussbaum alone down here, just after she met with Young." He frowned. "But we haven't found anyone else who remembers seeing them together. Not yet, anyway. He *could* have been following her."

Cal was puzzled. The ACLS testing station occupied a largely deserted corridor on the first floor of the hospital. "She was seen down *here*?"

"Right in this same hallway," Jeremy replied. "But there's nothing else in this section besides storage and the exam room, right?"

Cal nodded. They were standing in the west wing of the hospital, a long and narrow addition that had been built back in the 1930s. Unfortunately, the wing extended just a little too close to the banks of the Cuyahoga River. The cinder block walls of the basement below were stained with high-water marks from the various times in history that the Cuyahoga had seeped over its banks. The basement of this wing was completely deserted—abandoned to the cockroaches and mice and the Cuyahoga River. Even up here on the first floor, the atmosphere smelled faintly of algae and ripe fish.

Which probably explained why this area was only used for storage and occasional ACLS classes. The two floors overhead had long ago been converted to offices for the medical and nursing staffs, as well as the headquarters for the various teaching divisions.

So why had Annie Nussbaum come down here this morning?

"It may not be connected with her death, but it's quite a coincidence." The detective shook his head. "Regardless, we've got an APB out for Quentin Young right now."

"What time did he meet with Annie?" Cal asked.

"Nine o'clock." Jeremy stretched his thin lips in a triumphant grin. "And nobody's seen him since." He squeezed her shoulder. "So now you know why I want you to stay out of the way. And you'd better tell Plato the same thing."

"I will," Cal promised.

Heading back to her office, she only wished she knew where Plato *was*.

Cal was halfway down the basement stairs before she realized what she had done. Even though the stairs were dimly lit and dank with mildew, they were the quickest way to the rest of the hospital from the west wing. Although the first floor had an elevator at its far end, the car only went *up*, not down—probably to keep its occupants from drowning if the basement flooded again.

Anyone with an upstairs office in the old west wing had two choices—they could either trek back along the second- or third-floor corridors to the main part of the hospital, where elevators would take them to any floor they wished, or they could come down the small elevator in this wing, which stopped at the first floor corridor where the murder had been committed.

Staffers had little reason to use the rickety old elevator, unless they were taking the ACLS exam. The first floor of the west wing opened into the laundry and food-service areas, a bustling hive of carts and trays and machinery. To reach the main part of the hospital, you would have to thread your way through a maze of corridors and hope you weren't squashed by a runaway forklift.

It was obvious that anyone with an upstairs office in the west wing would have a much easier time reaching the hospital by traveling along the corridors upstairs, then using the main elevators to reach the other floors.

Unless they were heading for a certain part of the basement: Medical Records.

For reasons Cal couldn't begin to understand, the gods of Riverside had long ago decreed that Medical Records would be placed in the western part of the hospital. Not in the west wing, of course, or the charts would have mildewed long ago. But Medical Records was very near the west wing, in a portion of the basement that was otherwise dedicated to maintenance—the heating and electrical plants.

Annie Nussbaum must have been heading for Medical Records when the maintenance worker spotted her on the first floor. By taking the old elevator down to the ground level and then taking the stairs to the basement, she would have saved herself ten minutes of walking.

She had no idea *why* Annie Nussbaum would need to visit Medical Records; nurses didn't need to dictate hospitalization summaries the way doctors did. Perhaps it was something perfectly routine—a quality assurance check, or an incident report about one of her nurses. Or perhaps it wasn't routine at all.

So rather than heading east, to her office and the morgue, Cal hurried down the narrow corridor that led to Medical Records. And she was just about to ring the bell, to summon the medical records clerk and learn whether Annie Nussbaum had indeed visited the chart room this morning, when her pager went off.

Cal groaned, glanced at the number, and saw that it was an outside line. Maybe it was Plato. She hurried to a telephone and dialed. Plato answered on the first ring, his voice fuzzing over a line that popped and crackled with static.

"I'm calling from a pay phone," he told her, his voice muffled by the *whoosh!* of a passing car. "On Route 6, near Kirtland—I'm on my way back from Camp *Success!*

Before she could break the news about Annie Nussbaum, he told her how he had remembered seeing someone leave his room in the cabin last Friday night and decided to drive out to the camp and investigate. Cal tried to break in, to cut his monologue short, but every time she tried another car *whooshed* by and drowned out her words.

Plato touched on the high points of his interview with Claude Eberhardt—especially the seminar for RiversEdge Wellness Management.

"Then Quentin Young was *there* last weekend?" Cal asked, surprised.

"Uh-huh." A fuzz of static drowned out the rest of his comment.

"What?"

"I said, I had an interesting chat with Gabrielle Surfraire, too. After the funeral."

"Tell me about it later," Cal said finally. "I've got to tell *you* something. Some bad news."

"Oh, no."

She took a deep breath. "Annie Nussbaum is dead."

"Oh, my *God*!" Even thought this was the fourth murder in a week, he still sounded genuinely shocked. "How?"

Cal told him about the ACLS exam, Annie's head injury, and the apparent use of a defibrillator as the murder weapon.

"There's a really *sick* person out there, Cal." His voice sounded tight, nervous. "Maybe you should just head home early—okay?"

"I will," she promised. "I want to check out one thing first."

She told him about her theory, that Annie Nussbaum had been headed toward Medical Records when the maintenance worker had spotted her on the first floor.

"Makes sense," Plato agreed. "That's how I get down to Medical Records whenever I'm over there. First, they pink-slip me for delinquent charts, then I go to the medical staff office in the west wing to apologize, then I head downstairs to Medical Records to dictate them."

Plato was an old veteran with delinquent charts. His record was eighty-seven overdue charts. Some joker had put up a WANTED! poster of Plato in the medical staff office.

"You take the elevator and then the stairs?" she asked.

"Yeah. I can't think of anywhere else she could have been going." He sighed. "Speaking of going, I'd better move along. I just didn't want you to get worried—"

"I need to tell you one more thing first." She braced

herself to be calm, to be supportive. After all, if Quentin Young really *was* the killer, he'd soon have more problems on his hands than misrepresenting Plato. "It's more bad news."

Quickly, she told him about the closure of the pediatrics floor, and Young's claim that Plato had approved the move.

"He said *what*?!" Plato's voice cracked with anger. "Goddamn him to hell! Him and Millburn both!"

An odd noise like the bellow of a wounded grizzly bear rumbled over the line.

"Plato?" Cal was concerned. She had never heard him this angry. Incoherent noises—crashes and bangs and more outraged growling—crackled through the receiver. If he wasn't foaming at the mouth, he was awfully close. "Plato? Are you there?"

"I'm going to kill them," he said suddenly. His voice was deadly calm, with that undertone of controlled insanity that you sometimes hear in sports figures and psychotic killers. "I'm just going to *murder* them."

"Now, Plato—" She was genuinely worried. What if he *did* do something violent? Would he? Could he?

"No—I won't kill them," he continued. "That would be too kind. I'll just sue their pants off."

"That's more like it," she agreed, relieved.

"Matter of fact, I'm just up the road from Millburn's house." He sounded calm now, determined. "I'm tempted to go there right now and tell him I'm not accepting the medical directorship, not on any terms. Give it to him in writing, so they can't weasel out and claim I actually took the job."

He had a point. By declining the position today, it would be clear that he could not have approved the closure of the pediatrics ward. If he *didn't* decline the job—and quickly—Millburn and Young might make

any number of awful decisions in Plato's name, perhaps pretending that he had been appointed temporary
medical director.

The significance of the congratulations from Millburn's secretary was beginning to hit home.

"What are you going to write it *on*?" Cal challenged.
"The back of a parking ticket? An old candy wrapper?"

"Good point," he agreed. "Maybe I'd better type it
up on some official Riverside paper."

"You got it." She nodded, relieved. Somehow, she
wasn't sure she trusted Plato at Millburn's house. It
would be disastrous if he lost his temper, lost control.
She didn't really want Millburn hurt. Not *much*, anyway. "Just hurry back to the hospital, okay? And page
me when you get here."

"You bet." He hung up.

She turned back to the counter and rang the bell.
To her relief, the records clerk who answered was
someone with experience. Mabel Rogers, the plump,
ageless grande dame of Medical Records, had served
up charts from behind the counter ever since Cal could
remember.

But Mabel wasn't her usual cheerful self. She
frowned and shook her head. "You heard the news
about poor Annie Nussbaum?"

Cal nodded. "I'm going to miss her."

"Terrible thing, terrible." She huffed a huge sigh and
shook her head again. "It's so hard to believe—
specially since I just saw her this morning."

"You did?" Cal was stunned. She hadn't even had
to ask.

"Yeah. She came in to pull some charts."

"What did she want to see?" Cal asked, trying to
sound casual.

Mabel looked down at the counter, as though she
weren't sure if she should answer. "I been meaning to

tell the police about it. Maybe I should talk to them first." She glanced up at Cal and beamed. "Course, you're *with* the police, ain't you? Being a coroner and all."

Cal nodded. It was only a *white* lie. "I'll be sure to pass it on to Lieutenant Ames."

"Sure thing, Dr. Marley—just lemme find the chart for you. We haven't put it away yet." She riffled through some folders behind the counter, dug lower, and finally emerged with a small manila envelope. *Two* envelopes, actually. "Here they are."

She handed them over to Cal. "Maybe you can tell me if they're worth bothering the police about."

Cal almost pushed them back, expecting the charts to be active files, protected by confidentiality rules. But of course they weren't. These records were on microfilm, indicating that the patients had died long ago. As if to drive the point home, both envelopes also bore somber black stickers.

She took the records to the microfilm reader and switched it on. The name on the first envelope wasn't at all familiar—Jennifer Lawrence. Even on microfilm, the record was thick, covering several hospitalizations, most of them for psychiatric problems. Cal slid up to the registration page and gasped when she saw the listing for next of kin.

Jennifer Lawrence was Godfrey Millburn's wife.

The second chart was more straightforward—one flimsy sheet covering a single hospitalization. *That* name was certainly familiar.

Elizabeth Millburn. Cal checked the summary sheet at the front of the folder. Discharged, deceased.

Godfrey Millburn's daughter had died twenty years ago.

Chapter 21

After hanging up, Plato had suddenly realized that he had a whole sheaf of Riverside letterhead paper sitting in his briefcase. He always carried it back and forth from work, in the slim hope that he might actually get some memos written at home. It never happened, of course.

But the paper would come in handy now. In longhand, Plato wrote an official-sounding response to Millburn's job offer, declining the post of medical director and expressing his hope that Riverside would locate another suitable candidate soon. He signed it *and* dated it, moving the time back a couple of hours so that Quentin Young wouldn't have a leg to stand on. Then he started the Corsica and headed for Millburn's house.

Plato was relishing the prospect of a face-to-face meeting with Millburn, of telling him exactly what he thought of the administration's policies, of informing him that he should expect a call from his lawyer.

Not that Plato actually *had* a lawyer. But it sounded good. And if he really decided to go through with a lawsuit, his cousin Homer—an assistant prosecutor— could probably recommend some good ones.

And if they won, maybe he wouldn't *have* to look for another job.

Plato was so busy planning out exactly what he

would say that he nearly missed the turnoff to Millburn's house. It was a small side street off of Route 6, a little dead end that had probably once been a farm back when Kirtland was too far from Cleveland to be considered a suburb. The freeways had brought it a lot closer.

Millburn's house was the last one on the street, just before a rutted turnaround useful to lost travelers. Plato skidded into the driveway, hoping Millburn would be home—hoping his *family* would be there, too, so they could witness his embarrassment. It was too bad Quentin Young wouldn't be there also—he was probably in jail by now. Maybe Plato could go and make faces at him during his murder trial.

He sped up the gravel drive, skidding back and forth to avoid the ruts, spitting rocks and pebbles all over Millburn's pristine front lawn, and rehearsing his lines one more time. The garage door was open, and only one car was parked inside—Millburn's gold Lexus. Apparently, the CEO was home alone. Too bad.

Plato fishtailed his car to a stop just inches from the rear fender of the Lexus, spattering gravel into the garage and hearing it spang against the luxury car with a satisfying clatter. He jumped out of the Corsica, slammed the door, and spotted Millburn standing behind the barn near the back of his house.

The CEO was holding a pose identical to the one on his daughter's trophy. Though Millburn was only a few dozen yards away, he seemed completely oblivious to Plato's arrival. The bow was stretched to a half-circle, the arrow pointed directly at a target almost a hundred yards away.

Plato noticed that a stiff wind was blowing, ruffling Millburn's hair and tugging at the sleeve of his coat like an impatient child. He pivoted slightly into the wind, still maintaining the tension on the bow. He paused for a long moment, shoulders lowering as he breathed out. After that, the only motion came from the bow itself. One second Millburn was holding it taut, then suddenly the ends of the bow sprang forward and the arrow was gone. Millburn watched it fly, freezing his body in precisely the same pose until it struck.

The arrow buried itself in the gold circle at the center of the target, just an inch or two from the true center. Millburn shrugged, slung the bow over his arm, and turned to Plato.

"Dr. Marley!" he called, still the jovial host. "Good to see you."

He paced across the lawn and beamed at Plato. "Have you come to tell us you've accepted our offer?"

"Hardly that," Plato growled. He pulled a slip of paper from his pocket. "I've come to officially decline the position of medical director at Riverside General Hospital, both verbally and in writing." He stuffed the paper in Millburn's hand. "And to say that you and Quentin Young are two of the most twisted, lying, cheating, filthy skunks I've ever had the displeasure to work with."

Plato didn't actually *know* whether skunks were prone to lie and cheat, but it certainly sounded good.

"Expect to hear from my lawyer *very* soon," he concluded.

"Well, now!" For all his faults, Godfrey Millburn certainly knew how to take an insult. He beamed, shaking his head and slapping Plato on the back. "You sure gave it to me, didn't you?" He shrugged. "And you may just be right. But would you mind telling me what I've *done* to deserve all this?"

Plato gazed at the CEO dumbly. He felt like Michael Dukakis debating Ronald Reagan—insults just seemed to slip off of Millburn's skin like butter off Teflon. He'd mapped out the entire conversation based on the assumption that Millburn would get riled, angrily protest his innocence, order Plato off his property—*something*. Instead, the CEO actually seemed to admire Plato's outspokenness, though he was puzzled by the comments.

To his chagrin, Plato felt his carefully kindled anger start to slip away. Maybe Millburn really *didn't* know what Quentin Young had done. After all, Millburn had supposedly left the decision in Young's hands, hadn't he?

"You don't know?" Plato finally asked. "About the pediatrics floor?"

"I knew Quentin was probably going to close the residency." He frowned at Plato. "Why? What has he done?"

Plato could see no other course but to take Millburn on faith. He told the CEO about Kidzek's firing, her scene in the cafeteria, the news that the whole pediatrics department had been closed.

"The entire *department*?" Millburn seemed genuinely surprised. "My, but that boy does move fast."

"There's more," Plato said. As if that wasn't enough.

Millburn pulled his coat tighter around him and leaned into the wind. He jerked his head toward the house. "Come on inside for some coffee and you can tell me the rest of the story. I'm starting to *freeze* out here."

He was right; the rising winds had brought a chill— perhaps Ohio *hadn't* seen its last freeze of the spring. Plato shrugged, still dazed by Millburn's attitude, and followed the CEO around to the front door.

The house was much like he remembered it—a monument to country living. Stone geese, ornate quilts on the walls, a few mounted animal heads. Two deer, a moose, and even a bear. Plato spotted a few other items he hadn't noticed before—a portrait over the sofa that he now recognized as Millburn's wife and his daughter, Elizabeth. It was a summertime scene done in oil, reminiscent of Monet, with the bright red barn he'd just seen as a backdrop and bright flowers bursting to life all around the subjects. The artist had done quite a nice job; Plato had first thought it was an old impressionist painting rather than a contemporary portrait.

In the kitchen was a large copy of the same family photo that stood on Millburn's desk. Seeing it again, Plato realized that Elizabeth Millburn had indeed inherited her good looks from her mother. Millburn's wife had the same dark hair and oval face, the same soft features and bright smile. She might have been Elizabeth's older sister rather than her mother.

Glancing at the cadaverous CEO as he poured the coffee, Plato smiled to himself. Elizabeth Millburn probably uttered a daily prayer of thanks that her looks had come from her mother rather than her father.

"Now, Plato." Millburn handed him a cup of coffee and led him to the family room. "Have a seat and tell me all about this other thing."

Plato told him all about it—Quentin Young's assumption that he had accepted the medical directorship, his incredible arrogance in claiming that Plato had taken the position and approved the closure of the pediatrics department, and the potential damage to Plato's reputation and standing in the community.

"I don't even think it's *legal* to close entire divisions without following some sort of procedure," Plato protested.

"It isn't." Millburn closed his eyes and shook his head gravely. "Quentin Young has made a very serious mistake. I'm truly sorry."

"Well, his *mistake* has cost a top-notch physician her job," he replied. "And I wouldn't be surprised if Dr. Kidzek sued you folks as well."

"Poor Quentin." Millburn sighed. "I thought he was ready to take the reins. Apparently, I was wrong. Not that it really matters now."

"Not that it *matters*?" Plato felt his temper heating up again.

"There's nothing I can do about it, Plato." Millburn gazed at him with an oddly sad look. "I told you, I'm going to see my family today."

"What does that have to do with anything?" Plato shot back. "Call Patty Kidzek today and apologize. You can wait until Monday to fire Quentin Young." He folded his arms. "And I'd like some kind of statement issued to the staff, apologizing for Young's claim that I had approved the closure of Pediatrics."

"You don't understand, do you?" The CEO leaned forward. "I won't *be* here on Monday. Quentin Young will be taking over as CEO."

"You're going to St. Louis?" Plato gave a puzzled frown. "I thought that wasn't for another month."

"I changed my mind about that." Millburn stood, staring down at Plato with that same melancholy expression.

Seeing the CEO standing before the portrait of his daughter and wife, Plato suddenly realized that Elizabeth Millburn *had* inherited something from her father after all. Godfrey Millburn's huge, dark eyes seemed to be watching him from Elizabeth's face. If Millburn's daughter had been about to cry, her eyes would have looked just like her father's.

Seeing him there, Plato suddenly began to understand.

"Come with me," Millburn urged. "I'd like to show you something."

His voice had changed somehow. It was still Godfrey Millburn, but *younger*, and warmer. The soft tone a
patient father might use with a favored child.

He led Plato to a doorway in the corner of the family
room. During their entire visit last Tuesday, that doorway had remained closed. It looked like the entrance to
a first-floor master bedroom.

And that's exactly what it was. Except it obviously
wasn't Millburn's room. The place was clearly Elizabeth's, judging by the pink canopied bed, the stuffed
animals tucked in beside the pillow, the cheerleader's
pom-poms hanging from the closet doorknob.

Millburn gestured around with a fond smile. "Elizabeth fell in love with this room when we first moved
in. She was so happy, Jennifer and I couldn't turn her
down. So we took one of the bedrooms upstairs."

Plato shivered. Godfrey Millburn was changing before his eyes. He was no longer the ruthless CEO of
Riverside General Hospital; perhaps he never had been.
He was a doting father, a loving husband. A family
man. He flashed an innocent, proud smile at Plato.

Looking away, Plato gasped. The room *itself* was
strange—a perfectly normal girl's bedroom, except for
some odd inconsistencies. Like the Polaroids on the
bulletin board, which were almost faded to white, and
the school newspaper tacked between them, yellowing
and curled as though it had been printed on parchment.
A record player—a real *record* player, complete with
an eight-track tape deck—was parked in the corner beside a collection of albums. Fleetwood Mac's *Rumours*
album topped the pile. A stack of eight-tracks towered
beside it.

Either Millburn's daughter was really poor, or she
was an antique collector.

A row of trophies filled the bookcase beside the door.

Archery trophies, much like the one in Millburn's office. Plato glanced at an inscription:

> *Lake County Archery Association*
> FIRST PLACE, ALL-AROUND TEEN
> ELIZABETH MILLBURN
> 1976

Plato stared at the date, rubbed his eyes, and read it again. It didn't change.

He turned away to see yet another photo on the far wall. Elizabeth Millburn and her mother, grinning into the camera and holding the identical trophy Plato saw on the shelf. He moved closer. Millburn's wife looked vaguely familiar. He had noticed it in the other photos as well, but even more in this candid shot.

"I *thought* you might recognize her," Millburn said. He gestured to the photo. "My wife, I mean. You've met her before."

Plato glanced blankly at the CEO.

"Before she died." Millburn's sad smile faded away, leaving a menacing grimace. "Before you and the other doctors killed her."

Chapter 22

"So I've got an APB out on the wrong person," Jeremy complained.

"Look at the bright side," Cal replied. "I don't think Millburn has anyone left to kill."

"Unless he starts taking out his grudge against the whole *hospital*." The detective shrugged. "After all, he's got plenty of reason to hate Riverside. And he's got a couple dozen screws loose—we don't know what he's going to do next."

She nodded. Godfrey Millburn had clearly gone off the deep end, and with very good cause. Riverside's CEO did indeed have plenty of reasons to bear a grudge against Riverside, even if the cause was two decades old.

Hopefully, the cops would catch him before he could do any more harm. Millburn's secretary had told the police that her boss was at home, taking the rest of the day off. And of course Riverside's surviving chiefs had been warned—all of them except Plato. And he'd be back soon.

"Lucky thing you stumbled on those charts at all," Jeremy mused.

Cal nodded. Lucky for her, but unlucky for Annie Nussbaum.

But the unluckiest one by far was Godfrey Millburn's daughter. Elizabeth Millburn's medical record chronicled an incredible run of bad luck, a disastrous series of accidents and oversights that had turned a benign hospitalization into a complete catastrophe.

A catastrophe that began on the day of Elizabeth's senior prom, twenty years ago. Jennifer Lawrence had taken her daughter out for a last-minute visit to the hair salon that afternoon. They were returning home along some back roads in Waite Hill when they were sideswiped by a drunk driver.

Their little Datsun had bounced off the other car and slipped off the road, plunging halfway down a steep cliff before slamming into a tree. Jennifer Lawrence had been driving that day; she suffered only a mild concussion requiring an overnight hospital stay for observation. Elizabeth had been less fortunate; she sustained a number of scrapes and bruises, a broken nose, and several cracked ribs.

The girl missed her senior prom, of course. She was admitted to a local suburban hospital but transferred to Riverside just a few hours later, when doctors began to suspect a bruised or ruptured spleen. Cal understood the reasoning behind the transfer—aside from getting better care for his daughter, at least theoretically, Godfrey Millburn would be saving a substantial pile of money. He was only a middle manager at Riverside back then, but hospital employees received a hefty discount on their charges, and doctors often waived employees' fees entirely.

That policy had changed, of course, over the past few years.

But at the time, the Millburn family probably saved a great deal of money by transferring their daughter to Riverside. And they were probably grateful that they had, for Elizabeth Millburn's spleen had indeed been bruised. On her second day at Riverside, the teenager burst into tears and started screaming, clutching the left side of her abdomen. Her blood pressure plunged, and she was rushed to the operating room. During emergency surgery, the doctors discovered and removed a ruptured spleen, along with two liters of fresh blood.

Injuries of the spleen were especially tricky, Cal knew. Even in the current era of CT scans and MRIs, doctors still had trouble deciding whether a bruised spleen needed to be removed. A small bleeder might seal itself, but torn arteries might also continue to ooze over several days, pumping the tough splenic capsule full of blood like an air compressor overfilling a basketball. And yet the patient often felt little or no pain until the rupture actually occurred.

Luckily, Elizabeth Millburn's ruptured spleen was caught in time. The operation went well, and she bounced back with the characteristic vigor of youth—until the second day after her surgery.

Spiking fevers and chills pointed to a postoperative infection—which was all the more serious in a patient whose spleen was missing. The surgeon made the correct diagnosis, drew blood cultures for identification of the guilty germ, and started empirical therapy with high-dose intravenous penicillin. The drug was a reasonable choice at the time, except for one small problem.

Elizabeth Millburn was profoundly allergic to penicillin.

Almost immediately after her first dose, the girl suffered a life-threatening allergic reaction that quickly progressed to anaphylactic shock. She went into full cardiac arrest before she could be rushed to the intensive care unit. A code blue was called.

Doctors and nurses rushed to her bedside from all points of the hospital, administering cardiopulmonary resuscitation and injecting drugs to reverse the allergic response and start her heart pumping again.

But despite their efforts, Elizabeth Millburn's heart failed to start again. The resident running the procedure charged the defibrillator and shocked the patient.

And nearly killed himself in the process.

As it turned out, the device was old and outdated, and improperly grounded as well. Rather than a standard dose of 360 joules, the patient received the full line voltage, several times the proper amount. Her chest was burned from the jolt. The intern's lab coat had only brushed the bed rail, but he passed out from the shock.

Naturally, Elizabeth Millburn didn't recover. A peer review of the incident concluded that Lionel Wallace, the attending surgeon on the case, had committed an "understandable oversight" by administering penicillin, since the patient's allergies hadn't been documented in the records that were sent from the outlying hospital. The reviewers *did* cite the floor's nursing supervisor, Anne Nussbaum, for failing to test the defibrillation unit twice weekly, according to the manufacturer's guidelines. She was suspended for three days, then returned to her normal duties.

"So he murdered every person who was involved in his daughter's death," Jeremy mused. "Killed them just the same way he thinks they helped kill her. Poetic justice."

"An eye for an eye," Cal agreed.

"A shock for a shock."

He was right. Andre Surfraire had been the drunk driver who caused the accident, Cal now knew. Jeremy had checked with the Waite Hill police, who dug deeper in their files to uncover a record of the event. Surfraire had been cited for driving while intoxicated and causing a nonfatal accident; he had paid a stiff fine and had his license revoked for thirty days—a relatively stiff penalty at the time.

Jeremy had learned one other interesting fact from the police report—Andre Surfraire had actually been the chief surgeon at the suburban hospital where Elizabeth Millburn was first treated. Perhaps his position at that hospital contributed to the Millburns' decision to transfer their daughter to Riverside. But as it turned out, she would almost certainly have been safer at the other hospital.

Or perhaps not. After all, the other doctors hadn't documented Elizabeth's allergy in the first place.

In any event, Surfraire had eventually come to Riverside as well. Cal wondered if the surgeon had ever known that the victim of his carelessness eventually died.

Probably not, or he would have been far more uncomfortable around Godfrey Millburn. Lionel Wallace certainly was oblivious to Millburn's hidden anger. The absentminded CEO had trouble remembering the names of his current department chairs; he was hardly likely to recall an event that had happened twenty years ago. It was undoubtedly just one in a succession of professional failures.

Annie Nussbaum was most likely to remember the tragedy; perhaps she did. But she obviously hadn't made the connection between the murders and Elizabeth Millburn's death. After all, she couldn't have known that Andre Surfraire had caused the accident, and she probably didn't realize or remember that Lionel Wallace had prescribed the lethal penicillin.

Not until too late, not until she visited Medical Records this morning.

"Surfraire caused the crash," Jeremy said, raising one finger, "so he gets killed in a car wreck in exactly the same spot." He lifted another finger. "Wallace prescribed penicillin and caused the kid's allergic reaction, so he gets bumped off the same way." The detective frowned. "Funny that he wouldn't check the kids for allergies, when he was allergic to the same drug himself."

"Lionel Wallace's allergy wasn't picked up until last year," she reminded him. "Still, he should have asked. But Lionel Wallace was always very absentminded."

"How did he get to be CEO?"

"Politics." Cal frowned. "The Board of Trustees liked him—he was the ideal figurehead. Somebody who was a doctor but who wouldn't fight much over changes. Anyway, they probably knew that Millburn would really be running the show."

"But they didn't know how Millburn really felt about his boss," Jeremy pointed out. "How long do you think he's known about what really happened to his daughter?"

"Not very long." Cal shrugged. "Maybe not until he was appointed vice president last fall."

Jeremy nodded, and lifted a third finger. "To continue—Annie Nussbaum didn't catch the faulty defibrillator, so she gets zapped the same way Elizabeth Millburn did." He frowned. "But what about Cy Kettering?"

Cal picked up the second chart. The entries were much more recent, ending just ten years ago.

"He was Jennifer Lawrence's psychiatrist," she replied.

"Oh, no."

She nodded.

"Godfrey Millburn has a pretty radical approach to health care reform."

"Very funny." She flipped Jennifer Lawrence's record into the microfilm reader and moved to the last page. Like her daughter's record, the bottom line read *Discharged, deceased.* Cal glanced up at the detective.

"Jennifer Lawrence suffered from major depression. Chronically, for several years."

Jeremy grimaced. "Let me guess—ever since her daughter died?"

"Exactly. She blamed herself for her daughter's death. She felt responsible."

"Even though the accident was Surfraire's fault?" He grunted. "That doesn't make any sense."

"Guilt doesn't have to be *rational*," she pointed out. "How many assault victims blame themselves for being in the wrong place at the wrong time?"

He shrugged. "Sometimes they're right."

"Come on, Jeremy. You know what I mean."

"I know."

"The same thing sometimes happens with car crashes," Cal continued. "If one person lives and the other dies, the survivor often feels responsible."

"Especially if she was driving." He folded his arms and leaned against the counter. "But just where does Cy Kettering fit into all this? He didn't *cause* her death, did he?"

"Not exactly," Cal replied. "But Jennifer Lawrence attempted suicide several times. Always the same way—in her garage, with the motor running."

"In her car," Jeremy repeated. He closed his eyes. "Replaying the accident, maybe?"

She nodded. For a cop, Jeremy had a good grasp of psychology.

"But somebody always caught her in time—usually her husband. And she was always hospitalized until she got over it."

"Until the last time."

"Right. Cy Kettering discharged her from the hospital, maybe a little earlier than he should have. Or maybe Jennifer Lawrence had just decided she'd had enough."

Cal sifted through the record of Jennifer's last complete hospitalization—the one immediately prior to her successful suicide attempt. She scanned the chart itself, curious whether the woman had really been discharged early. Had Cy Kettering made a mistake? Until now, Cal had only read the discharge summaries without actually looking at the hospital record itself.

A medical student had written the final floor note, in a scrawling, nearly illegible hand.

"Just a two-day hospitalization," Cal noted. "Practically an overnight stay—but the insurers were getting tight with their money by then."

She frowned at the medical student's writing. It looked familiar, somehow. *Very* familiar.

It was a standard SOAP note—a progress note covering the areas of Subjective assessment, Objective findings, Assessment, and Plan. Exactly what you'd expect from a medical student doing one of his first clinical rotations:

> SUBJECTIVE: *Patient reports feeling much improved today, no longer bothered by suicidal thoughts or plans. Displays much insight into her feelings of guilt and remorse, related to daughter's fatal car accident ten years ago. Has promised to contact Dr. Kettering if suicidal thoughts recur.*
>
> OBJECTIVE: *Afebrile, unremarkable physical exam, vital signs stable.*
>
> ASSESSMENT: *Patient stable s/p recurrence of major depression and suicide gesture. Ready for discharge.*
>
> PLAN: 1. *Discharge today per Dr. Kettering's instructions.*
>   2. *Continue imipramine treatment at 100 mg b.i.d.*
>   3. *Follow-up visit with Dr. Kettering scheduled for tomorrow a.m.*

Cal gasped when she reached the end of the note. It was cosigned by Dr. Kettering. And the medical student who wrote it was Plato Marley.

Chapter 23

"We didn't have any other children," Godfrey Millburn said with an odd smile. "Jennifer and I had a saying about that. We only had one child, but that was okay, since we got the *best* one."

That wasn't just a father's pride, Plato now realized. Even allowing for the distortion of the years, the curious way memory sees only the good things, like a weak flashlight reflecting only the brightest objects in its path, Elizabeth Millburn was an extraordinary kid.

National Honor Society, class valedictorian, athlete, a published poet, and an artist. Issues of *Ploughshares* and *Triquarterly* containing her poetry were tacked up on the bulletin board beside the school newspaper. The painting of Elizabeth and her mother hanging above the sofa in the family room was her own work, a portrait given to Jennifer on Mother's Day, just a few weeks before Elizabeth died.

As if that weren't enough, the girl had been a top volunteer worker at the local hospital. She started a reading program that paired sick kids with elderly volunteers who came in twice a week to read and spend time with the children. The program was copied in hospitals throughout the state.

For all those reasons and more, she had been awarded a full four-year scholarship to Harvard, the mecca of learning that her father could never afford for himself. She had enrolled in their premedical program, because Elizabeth Millburn's fondest ambition was to become a doctor.

"Ironic, isn't it?" Millburn asked. He stared at his hands. "That with all her incredible talents, she chose *medicine*? But then, she wouldn't have been an *ordinary* doctor."

"I'm sure that's true," Plato agreed nervously. He studied the former CEO, looking for signs of the insanity that must be lingering just beneath that calm, paternal surface. For Godfrey Millburn had undeniably gone over the edge. Riverside General's chief executive officer was chairing his last meeting. His next hospital appointment would be to a rubber room somewhere.

If they ever caught him.

Millburn had told him the whole story of his daughter's tragic accident, her disastrous treatment at Riverside General Hospital, and the fatal code blue where a defibrillator had short-circuited and killed Elizabeth Millburn rather than rescuing her.

They were still in Elizabeth's bedroom, the shrine to a lost daughter. Millburn was huddled in a chair beside her desk while Plato stood beside the door, wondering what to do next. The logical move—getting the hell out of there and calling the police—wasn't as simple as it seemed, for one particular reason. Aside from old photos and trophies and pictures, the room contained yet another memento of Elizabeth Millburn.

A wicked-looking crossbow was perched on the desk beside the CEO, loaded and cranked, ready to spring. The tip of the bolt was especially intimidating—a trio of straight razors tapering to a perfect point. Just *looking* at it made you want to bleed.

Every time Plato edged toward the door, Millburn would reach for the crossbow and pat it lovingly.

Recalling the CEO's deadly accuracy with a bow, Plato decided to stick around and listen.

While Millburn recounted the story of his daughter's tragic death, he had picked up a remote and aimed it at the room's only concession to modernity—a small combination television and video player. The tape was a copy of the family's silent home movies—Elizabeth as a baby, as a toddler, as a Brownie and then a Girl Scout. Camping trips and Christmases, swimming and ice skating. Elizabeth as she worked on the painting that now hung over the soda. The two parents singing happy birthday as the daughter blew out eighteen candles and swigged a beer, making a face at the taste.

Plato suspected the hospital CEO had watched the tape scores of times, perhaps every day. In the brief pauses during his story, Millburn would turn to the silent television, absently mouthing each word, parroting each gesture of his daughter and wife, as though he might somehow bring them back to life if he could just get their movements down *perfectly.*

"She was very much like my wife," Millburn mused. "Jennifer was a nurse, as I'm sure you know. Another irony."

"I don't think I ever met your wife," Plato protested. Millburn had never brought his wife to any of the hospital functions. Plato would have recognized her, remembered her. Still, she *did* look vaguely familiar.

"Of *course* you met her," the CEO chided. "She was one of Cy Kettering's patients. Back when you were just a medical student."

Watching Millburn's wife on the television screen as she opened her Mother's Day present, Plato finally began to remember.

"Jennifer Lawrence." Millburn reached forward to touch the screen fondly. "She kept her maiden name."

Plato remembered, vaguely. She had been hospitalized

on the psychiatric floor—a chronically depressed, chronically suicidal woman. Plato had started his psychiatry rotation—his first clinical assignment—on the day Jennifer Lawrence was discharged; he'd met her only once for a brief predischarge interview.

Later that same month, he heard that Jennifer Lawrence had finally killed herself, using the same technique she had always tried before—starting her car in the garage with the door shut. Usually, she did it just before her husband came home from work, counting on him to find her and rescue her in time. A cry for help. Each time, she would go back to the hospital for more intensive therapy, for a change of antidepressant drugs, for another course of electroconvulsive treatment.

Except this last time, Godfrey Millburn had unexpectedly worked late. Jennifer was already long gone by the time her husband came home.

"She didn't kill herself," Millburn told him. For the first time, his bitterness began to show. The dark eyes flashed. "*Grief* killed her. Grief over the loss of our only child—at the hands of incompetents like Lionel Wallace and Annie Nussbaum. And Andre Surfraire."

Plato finally understood. Certainly Andre Surfraire had been at fault in Elizabeth's death. So had Lionel Wallace and, to a much lesser extent, Annie Nussbaum. Perhaps even Cy Kettering could have done something differently—kept Jennifer hospitalized for another week, or altered his therapy somehow. Still, it didn't make sense for Millburn to blame Kettering for his wife's death.

But Millburn's killing spree had little to do with logic. Plato had learned enough psychiatry to realize that most of all, Millburn probably blamed *himself* for his wife's death. Like so many relatives of suicide victims, Godfrey Millburn surely thought he should have done something differently, too—should have been able to find better treatment for his wife, should have kept a closer eye on her.

Should have come home sooner on that last day.

But for Millburn to blame himself was just as wrong as blaming Kettering—or Plato.

"I didn't *know* about all this," Millburn continued. "I didn't *realize* it until I was appointed vice president." He shrugged. "I was curious, and I wondered sometimes whether Wallace had covered something up. But I trusted the peer review committee's findings. Until I was able to pull the charts, and read them myself."

"You could have read them anytime," Plato pointed out. "You could have had your lawyer go over them, to see whether malpractice—"

"Do you think I cared about *money*?" He took a deep breath, calming himself with obvious effort. "Besides, Lionel Wallace was a very powerful man, even then. And Cy Kettering was chief of staff. I was a *nobody* then—I didn't want to risk challenging them. But when I found out what really happened, it was different. Much different."

Plato nodded.

"Nobody ever *told* me Elizabeth was given penicillin." Millburn leaned forward and switched off the television as it displayed one last lingering shot of Elizabeth. The girl's face grew smaller and smaller, fading to a laser-bright point at the center of the screen before vanishing altogether. "Nobody ever explained that the defibrillator was *broken*—they just told me she arrested and they couldn't bring her back."

Plato was stunned—until he remembered that Elizabeth Millburn had died twenty years ago. Compared with the current system, the medical field had been far more tight-lipped about problems and shortcomings, far more paternalistic, and far less likely to reveal accidents and errors. The current emphasis on patient rights and malpractice litigation had changed much of that—or at least made it harder to sweep problems under the rug.

"I nearly *died* when Andre Surfraire joined our staff," he continued. "But that was *nothing* compared to how I felt when the Board appointed Wallace chief executive officer. The same bumbling nitwit who killed my daughter."

He licked his thin lips and gave a ghastly smile. "But I showed him—showed him just how it felt. Poetic justice."

"You switched penicillin for his heart medicine," Plato observed, trying to keep Millburn talking, to keep him calm.

He nodded. "And I staged Surfraire's accident, too. I was going to do it at the hospital, perhaps next week, but he had left his hat here. Came back to get it, so I took the opportunity—knocked him over the head and shot him full of Smirnoff's." He glanced at Plato. "I started off as a phlebotomist, you know. Worked my way through school doing blood draws for snot-nosed interns who didn't know the radial artery from an antecubital vein."

As he talked, Plato studied the crossbow again, wondering whether Millburn was planning to dispense yet another dose of poetic justice.

"Same thing with Cy Kettering and Annie Nussbaum," he added. "Poetic justice."

"Annie Nussbaum didn't have any control over the defibrillator," Plato pointed out. "It was an old, outdated model, you said so yourself. Just because she didn't test it often enough doesn't mean it wouldn't have broken down anyway."

"Maybe so." Millburn shrugged. "But she *knew*—about me. Somehow, she must have remembered my daughter. I caught her looking at me strangely the last few days."

She was probably expecting to get fired, Plato thought.

"I happened to be downstairs, leaving the cafeteria just as Annie Nussbaum was leaving Medical Records," he continued. "I saw her there, and I followed her upstairs, wondering what to do. And that's when I saw the defibrillators." He leaned toward Plato, trying to make him understand. "It was like Elizabeth was guiding me. Elizabeth and Jennifer both. I could almost *hear* them telling me what to do."

He spoke as though his actions were perfectly logical, perfectly rational—even though Annie Nussbaum had made her mistake twenty years ago, even though she had become one of the most competent nursing professionals in the city.

"I hadn't *planned* on killing her at first," Millburn explained, as though he knew what Plato was thinking. "But when she began to suspect, and when I passed the training room, I understood what I had to do."

He patted the crossbow and smiled at Plato. "I've learned to believe less and less in coincidence. My rise to the top at Riverside, learning what really happened, having the opportunity to make them pay—it can't be an accident." He cocked his head and frowned, as though he had heard something. "Elizabeth and Jennifer are here, now. They're very near."

Slowly, gradually, Plato inched toward the door. Millburn glanced back at him instantly, and slid the crossbow along the desk.

"No, Plato." He shook his head. "You'll stay. There's a reason for you to be here, too."

Right, Plato thought. *Bad luck. Bad karma. Maybe I didn't help enough little old ladies across the street when I was a kid.*

"They didn't want me to be alone," Millburn continued. "Not now. Not right at the end."

He turned the crossbow completely around, so the razor-tipped shaft was aimed directly at his chest.

"So many times, I've wanted to do this. Sat in this room late at night, just like this, with my finger on the trigger." Another copy of the family portrait was propped on the desk, just behind the crossbow. Millburn smiled at it. "But I had so much to do first."

Plato couldn't move fast enough. He was running across the floor, watching Millburn's bony finger whiten on the trigger as he hunched over the crossbow with his arms outstretched, like a galley slave tugging his oar. The desk was only a few feet away, but it might as well have been a mile. Plato's steps seemed impossibly slow, as though his feet were buried in a pool of Jell-O.

In spite of it all, Plato finally got there, just in time. He dove, lashing out at the bow and knocking it free from Millburn's grasp.

But the marksman had already shot his bolt. The arrow pinned Millburn to the chair, the mangled, bloody tip ripping through his chest and popping out the back of the seat. The force actually knocked the chair itself back several feet. The empty crossbow clattered to the floor as the swivel chair drifted to a stop.

Plato hadn't imagined the wax-skinned CEO could get any more pale, but he did. A thin trail of blood trickled down the front of his sport shirt. And yet Millburn somehow looked more alive, less like a cadaver, than ever before.

He stared at Plato with Elizabeth's eyes, smiled with Elizabeth's smile.

"You came," he croaked. A trickle of blood seeped from the corner of his mouth. "I *knew* you would."

Plato nodded, though he knew Millburn wasn't talking to him. He checked the man's neck for a pulse, then reached forward and gently closed his eyes.

Godfrey Millburn had joined his family at last.

Chapter 24

INTEROFFICE MEMO

From: David Inverness, M.D., Medical Director and
      Chief of Staff
To: All Department Chiefs
Date: Tuesday, April 7
Re: Hospital Remodeling

All department chiefs are requested to attend a meeting on Monday, April 13, regarding the revised plans for Riverside's construction and remodeling project. Allocation of space for the various teaching departments will be discussed, along with long-term plans to build a new pediatric wing and child outreach center. Attached is a summary of the initial plans for the pediatric extension project, presented by Dr. Patricia Kidzek, Chief of Pediatrics. Please review it before the meeting.

The day after Godfrey Millburn's funeral, Cal worked late. She pulled into the driveway at eight o'clock, walked through the front door, and stopped dead in her tracks. Something was different.

An unmistakable aroma flooded her nostrils—a scent she hadn't known for months. The heady bouquet of a home-cooked meal.

Cal tossed her jacket onto the banister and sniffed deeply. She had slogged through another busy day, skipping lunch as usual, and snacking on peanut M&M's and Ritz crackers throughout the afternoon.

Her stomach growled like a caged tiger. She drifted toward the kitchen, breathing deeply, floating across the foyer on a fragrant cloud of simmering supper.

And not just *any* supper, she realized once she reached the doorway. Plato was stirring a saucepan full of finely chopped vegetables and flour while a smaller pot seethed and bubbled over a blue flame. Slowly, he stirred its dark red contents into the larger saucepan, smiling with satisfaction. He turned the burner down, covered the pot, and spotted Cal in the doorway.

"Chicken Madeira?" she breathed raptly.

He nodded. "Surprise."

Cal hurried across the kitchen and into his arms, pulling him close for a long, lazy kiss. Finally, he lifted his head and grinned.

"Wow. What was *that* for?"

"A tip, for the chef." She pressed herself against him and smiled fondly. "The first time you made Chicken Madeira—that's when I knew I was in love."

He raised an eyebrow. "And here I thought it was my sex appeal."

"That, too." She unbuttoned his shirt and slipped her hands inside. They kissed again, drawing even closer as he leaned down to nibble her neck, unzipping the top of her dress just enough to slip it down over her shoulder. He leaned over and nuzzled that tender hollow just above her collarbone.

But just as things started getting interesting, the oven timer pinged.

Cal pulled away gently. "Better get that."

"Huh?" Plato breathed in her ear. "Whazzat?"

"The *chicken*." She drew back and grinned. "Supper. Vittles. Eats."

"I'll just turn the oven off." He dragged her close again. "We can eat later. Afterwards."

"Beforewards." Cal scurried away again and rustled

up a pair of oven mitts, squinting into the oven with approval. Chicken breasts in puff pastry, brushed with an egg glaze and then baked to a delicate golden brown. "Looks just right."

Plato folded his arms. "You really do like this stuff, don't you?"

"Almost as much as I like you," she replied, pulling the pan out of the oven. "Anyway, I'm *hungry*."

"Me, too," Plato confessed. He strained the Madeira sauce into a serving bowl and lifted the lid of a casserole. "Voila! *Broccoli a la Velveeta et Potato Cheeps.*"

"*Splendide!*" Cal crowed.

"And the crowning touch," he added, brandishing a wine bottle. "*Le cheap vin rouge!*" He glanced at the price tag. "Actually, not all that cheap. A nice Merlot the wine guy recommended. Cuvaison."

Cal set the table while Plato uncorked the Cuvaison and poured. They touched glasses and sipped.

"Very nice," Plato said. He set his glass on the table and smiled. "I've got a bit of news for you."

"And I've got some news for *you*," she replied.

Last night, after Godfrey Millburn's funeral, Cal and Plato had sat down for a long talk about the future. As a condition of David Inverness's reappointment, the Board had promised that Riverside's educational programs would remain open indefinitely. The *Plain Dealer* had run a long story detailing Vista's planned takeover of Riverside and the potentially disastrous impact on health care among Cleveland's urban poor. Quentin Young had been given two weeks' notice; it was rumored that he would apply for Millburn's job in St. Louis.

So Plato's position was secure. But he wasn't looking forward to continuing the endless grind of chiefhood, the long hours and endless demands of the department chairmanship. Cal had felt the same way about *her* job at Riverside, too.

They concluded that they needed to do something, to cut back at work somehow, to be able to spend more time together. To start living a seminormal life again.

But neither of them had been ready to commit themselves, to make a decision about their jobs. The discussion had ended vaguely, with some halfhearted promises to talk again later, when they had time. And so they both looked forward to more of the same—more late workdays, more frozen dinners, more ships passing in the night.

Today at work, Cal had finally realized that she and Plato would *never* have enough time. Their jobs were like some powerful addiction, a habit that grew and consumed them, one they would never be able to break.

"I've decided to step down as chief of geriatrics," Plato announced suddenly.

"You *what*?" Cal's jaw dropped. "I thought you *loved* that job!"

"I love *teaching*, and taking care of my patients." Plato shook his head. "But I *hate* administration—and all the time it takes. All the meetings, and the paperwork. I hardly have time for my patients anymore. Or for the geriatrics fellows." He shrugged. "Dan Homewood's been itching to run the department for years now."

He doled a chicken puff onto his plate and ladled the Madeira sauce over the top, then handed the bowl to Cal.

"But the most important thing is having more time for *you*." He frowned at her. "What's wrong? I thought you'd be happy."

"I *am* happy, Plato." She bit her lip. "But you're not going to like this."

"Like what?"

"I told them I was stepping down as chief, too." Cal took a deep breath and continued. "And I really wish I could quit Riverside altogether. The medical school just asked me to take a formal position as associate director of the anatomy lab."

"That's *wonderful!*" he cried. "Think about how much more time you'd have with two half-time jobs instead of three." He grinned. "The Riverside job was more like a full-time position in itself."

"You're not upset?" she asked. "It would mean less money—the medical school won't pay enough to make up for Riverside."

"We'll get by." He patted her hand. "We've almost got the credit cards paid off, and the second mortgage on the house is finished this summer. And our first round of student loans is paid off, too." He tilted his head quizzically. "But why? Last evening, you sounded so committed to the Riverside job."

"I know. I like teaching the residents, but I enjoy the medical school more." She shrugged. "And working at the coroner's office. Something had to give."

She took a chicken puff and drowned it in Madeira, then forked the first bite into her mouth. Sheer ecstasy.

"I'll have more time for you—and maybe *I* can learn how to cook a dish or two." She stared at her plate shyly. "Plus, if we're going to start a family, I'll need some flexibility."

"What?" Plato tugged his ear. "It sounded like you said something about a *family*."

"I did."

"Children?" He held a hand above the floor. "Baby humans?"

She nodded.

"But you always said we weren't ready yet."

"*I* wasn't." She grinned at him. "But *you* certainly were."

It was true. Plato loved children, and loved the idea of having kids of his own. Walking through shopping malls, he would spot a toddler and point him out to Cal like a boy yearning for a puppy. *Wouldn't it be nice to have one like that?* To Cal, it was always mildly irritating, and more than a little scary.

But lately Plato's teasing hints hadn't bothered her so much. And over the past few months, on the rare occasions they were out together, she found herself starting to catch his enthusiasm.

It was time to quit hitting the snooze button.

"I'm *always* ready," he replied with a lascivious wink.

"I know." She giggled, then sobered. "I guess I was always scared. Of having some problem with the pregnancy, or not being a good mom, or not having enough time. Or changing my mind once it was too late—realizing I'd made a big mistake." She gazed at Plato and took his hand again. "I wanted to be *sure*. And now I am."

Plato nodded. "I think that was on my mind today, too." He sighed. "I didn't want to end up like David Inverness."

Cal laughed. "I think Marta Oberlin may cure some of his workaholism."

Rumor had it that David's ex-wife had broken things off completely when she heard that Inverness was returning to his old position. Cal had little doubt that, with David permanently and completely free, Marta Oberlin would help him realize that there was at least one other fish in the sea.

Plato was quiet for a long moment, frowning down at his plate.

"What are you thinking about?" Cal asked, though she already knew.

"Godfrey Millburn." He glanced up at her and shook his head. "I keep seeing him."

Cal nodded. The late CEO's story had occupied many people's thoughts in the past few days. Millburn's suicide and his implication in the string of deaths had been front-page news; Plato had declined several newspaper interviews and two television appearances. He had told the whole story only to the police and to Cal.

Telling Cal about it that night, Plato had gotten very choked up—the full impact of Millburn's tragedies didn't really hit until it was all over. In a newspaper interview, Quentin Young had also filled in many of the details—how Millburn had never really claimed that his daughter was alive, but had acted as though she were. How he had started to change after Lionel Wallace was appointed Riverside's CEO, becoming increasingly erratic and reclusive, prone to angry outbursts and disjointed comments.

It was quite understandable, since Wallace had been promoted over Millburn's head—the very man whose incompetence had caused his daughter's death. Until Wallace's appointment, Millburn had probably been able to displace his anger and guilt into his work. But once Wallace was named Riverside's CEO, that outlet was denied to Millburn. He could no longer contribute to a system that had made such a horrendous mistake.

Apparently, Millburn had planned to leave Riverside, to leave his memories behind. But he became completely unhinged before he could move to St. Louis. And the killing began.

"What if that ever happened to *us*?" Plato asked quietly. "How would it be to lose a child—or to lose *you*?"

"It would be pretty awful," she conceded. "For either of us. But I like to think you're more solidly grounded than Godfrey Millburn."

"Coming from you, that's high praise." He shrugged. "But don't count on it. My aunt Thelma spent half her life at Massillon State—the big psychiatric hospital. Obsessive-compulsive disorder." He shook his head and shuddered. "She was always washing and cleaning. Terrible thing."

"Don't worry—you don't take after *her*."

"Very funny." He sighed. "I just keep seeing Millburn's face, when he was watching that tape. Locked in the past."

Cal squeezed his hand. "There's an old saying— 'You'll never *have* a chance if you don't *take* a chance.' "

Plato groaned. "Don't tell me—Benjamin Disraeli?"

"Nope." She shook her head. "My mom."

"Point taken." He sighed, then forked a sprig of *Broccoli a la Velveeta* into his mouth.

"Speaking of Camp *Success!*," Cal mused, "there's one thing that I still don't understand."

"What's that?"

"It's about the person you saw in the cabin Friday night." She soaked up the last of her Madeira sauce and leaned back, patting her stomach with a satisfied smile. "Godfrey Millburn was already in bed, right?"

"Yeah." A ghost of a smile flickered across his face.

"So who *was* it?" She grimaced. "Or was it just your imagination?"

"It wasn't my imagination," he replied. "It was Claude Eberhardt."

"Eberhardt?" she gasped. "How do you know?"

"He called me at work today." Plato shrugged. "He was worried that the police might find out about him, so he confessed."

"Confessed?" Her eyebrows knotted with confusion. "Confessed to *what*? Don't tell me Millburn hired him to—"

"Nope. *Wallace* hired him." Plato chuckled. "Don't

you remember how the two of them spent so much time chatting together that night?"

"Yeah." She eyed him askance, certain now that it was all a joke.

"Lionel Wallace paid him fifty bucks to bring him a cheeseburger."

"A *cheeseburger*?" Cal scowled. "You're kidding."

"Don't you remember how hungry we were that night? The camp only planned on having six of us there. The rest of us had celery sticks and carrots."

"I remember. *Believe* me, I remember." She folded her arms and huffed, feeling the anger welling up. Administrators! You couldn't trust them for a minute. "A *cheeseburger*!"

"With onions."

"With *onions*!" Cal fumed. "What about *team spirit*? Remember Wallace's talk about *shared adversity*? What a crock!"

"Easy, Cal," Plato said calmly. He snickered. "Wallace is dead, remember?"

"As if *that's* an excuse." She shook her head in awe. "Fifty bucks, huh?"

Plato nodded.

"That kid's going to be a great businessman someday."

He grinned. "I think he already is."

Cal started clearing the table, setting the plates beside the sink and packing the precious Madeira sauce into the refrigerator.

"After we finish the dishes, I'll write my resignation letter." She frowned. "And then we can go to sleep early—I've got a seven o'clock meeting tomorrow morning."

As she passed by, Plato reached out and swung her neatly into his lap. "Aren't you forgetting something?"

"What?" She frowned innocently.

He slipped his arms around her waist and breathed

on her neck. "You said something about starting a family, remember?"

"Tonight?"

"The dishes can wait." He slid his hand under the hem of her dress and up along her thigh. "And you can dictate your resignation letter at work tomorrow."

"We can't get pregnant *yet*, you know." She smiled. "I'm still taking my pills."

"There's an old saying," Plato murmured, finding that hollow beside her neck, then moving down, down. "Practice makes perfect."

"Good thinking. And we may need *lots* of practice. To get it just right." Cal wrapped her arms around his neck and sighed. "Ahh, teamwork."

Plato grinned. "It's the gateway to success."

Here's a preview of the next
mystery featuring
Cal and Plato Marley,
Mind Over Murder

Chapter 1

"Dr. Marley," said the cadaver in a soft, oily voice, "it's so *good* to see you again."

Cal Marley, deputy coroner and anatomy professor, had seen a lot during her career. She had dug bodies from the frozen wastes of Lake Erie and the muddy banks of the Cuyahoga, carved up hundreds of corpses in the county morgue, and embalmed dozens of cadavers here at Siegel Medical College.

Cal Marley knew cadavers. And one thing she knew for certain was that they never talked. Sometimes an occasional cadaver would make an odd noise, shifting in its stainless-steel sarcophagus here in the anatomy lab, settling into its winding sheets or burbling as the oily embalming fluid trickled through its flaccid blood vessels.

But the cadavers had never, ever talked.

Which was why Cal spilled her coffee all over the embalming room floor. Just minutes ago, she had undressed the lab's latest donation, flushed his arteries with saline fluid and then "juiced" the body, pumping its blood vessels full of preservative embalming fluid. And while the pump did its work, she had stepped next door for a cup of coffee. She returned just a few minutes later, planning to tie off the cadaver's arteries, package him neatly in a shroud and a man-sized plastic baggie, and slip him into place beside his comrades on the wall rack.

It had been a good day; the body rack already held two cadavers that Cal had embalmed earlier. The anatomy lab's body count was almost up to its quota for the upcoming fall semester.

But when Cal had returned with her coffee, one of the freshly embalmed cadavers up in the wall rack had spoken. Which, she knew, was patently impossible.

But that didn't stop the cadaver from sitting up from the rack, smacking his head on the next "bunk" overhead, and smiling ruefully.

"These things sure aren't very comfortable."

That was when Cal noticed that there were now *three* cadavers in the rack instead of two. And this third "cadaver" was fully dressed—overdressed, actually. For instead of the *de rigueur* shroud and baggy, this fellow was wearing a three-piece suit. The very suit Cal had just removed from the body on the table.

Stiffly, the visitor rolled over and climbed down from the rack. He shrugged his massive shoulders and shook his pant legs down, but it didn't help. Although the body on the table was enormous, the borrowed suit was far too small for the visitor. The jacket's sleeves stopped halfway down his forearms, and the cuffs of the pant legs dangled a good four inches above his ankles. The buttons on the dapper vest strained with the pressure of each breath, and the shirt collar squeezed the man's neck like a well-tailored noose.

The visitor looked like the Incredible Hulk just before he pops his clothes.

"I hope you don't mind my borrowing the suit, ma'am." He shrugged at the cadaver on the metal table and smiled his vacant smile—a grin which was oddly reminiscent of the cadaver's, as though they were sharing in the same joke. "I figured *he* didn't need it anymore."

It was like part of a nightmare—a crazy dream that was all the more terrifying because it made utterly no sense. The man was talking now, blathering on about the cut of the dead man's suit and the chilliness of the steel racks.

" 'Course, I guess it doesn't *matter* much how cold those racks are, when you think about it. I mean, these bodies can't feel anything anymore, can they?" He frowned at Cal, as though he expected her to answer, but continued before she had a chance. "That's something I've always wondered. I used to ask my mom about it sometimes before she died, but of course she couldn't tell me *then*. 'Course she could tell me *now*— at least, if she *could* tell me, you know what I mean?"

He paused again for just a second, then turned to the cadaver on the table and started muttering in a low undertone. Cal caught a few words, could hear the intruder asking the dead man the exact same question, pausing in just the same place, as though he expected the *cadaver* to answer.

"How about you, huh? I mean, you can't feel anything anymore, can you?" His voice trailed away and he chewed his lip thoughtfully. He jerked his head up at Cal and frowned. "You ought to put some *clothes* on this guy, you know that? What'd you take them off for, anyway? Huh?"

He took a step closer to Cal. She wanted to scream, to turn and run, to call security—*anything*. But she forced herself to remain calm, take a few deep breaths, and smile up at the intruder. Even if he hadn't dressed himself in a dead man's clothes and climbed into a cadaver rack for a nap, this guy was obviously ten watts short of a bulb. That odd smile, the glazed look in his eyes, the pressured, flighty speech—he was either psychotic or flying high on drugs. Either way, it wouldn't pay to alarm him. The best thing to do was to stay calm, to keep cool. To wait until she had her chance and then run like hell.

"Can I help you?" She smiled politely, as though talking cadavers commonly showed up in her anatomy lab.

"My name is Jimmy," the man responded. He took a step closer, towering over her. "But I bet you know that already."

Keep calm, she told herself again, taking a quiet step back and forcing down a scream. Cal was just five-feet-two-inches tall and barely topped a hundred pounds dripping wet. And she was down in the basement of a small medical college on a summer evening when the place was all but deserted. Screaming wouldn't do any good; the security guard would never hear her.

"Don't you remember me?" Jimmy asked with a frown.

"Sorry, no," she replied. But as the man stepped closer again, she frowned. His face *did* look vaguely familiar somehow. A face from the past, from several years ago—except he looked *younger* than the person she pictured, which didn't make a bit of sense. Somebody's brother? Somebody's son? She took another step back and shrugged. "Should I remember you?"

"I would think so," Jimmy replied. Quick as a flash, he lashed out and grabbed her wrists, locking them in a death grip. He smiled at her. "You're the one who sent me to prison."

Cal screamed.

"Where the hell's your wife?" Homer asked impatiently.

"Embalming cadavers," Plato Marley replied. He shrugged at his cousin. "Take it easy—she should be home any minute."

Homer Marley was pacing around the kitchen like a bear before feeding time. The burly assistant prosecutor opened the oven and peered lovingly at the simmering tray of burritos, then took a whiff.

"Maybe we should start without her," he suggested hopefully.

"No way," Jeremy Ames replied. The county homicide detective shook his grizzled gray head; he was a stickler for procedure. "We all eat *together*—that's the rule."

Nina Ames, the detective's fourth and final wife, nodded firmly. "It's *tradition* that we should wait."

Homer Marley harrumphed but sat down. Nina Ames was right. It was poker night at Plato and Cal's, a Saturday evening tradition for the past three years. Once a month, the five of them assembled at a designated house for a long evening of dinner and beer and penny-ante poker. When it was her turn, Nina Ames generally cooked meals from her homeland—*saltimbocca alla romana*, *vitello alla parmagiana*, and her own *lasagna con pollo*. Plato prepared more traditional fare—grilled steak and baked potatoes, homemade chili, and Homer's favorite—triple cheese and chicken burritos.

Homer, the perennial bachelor, typically treated his guests to take-out pizza.

"How about some more chips and salsa?" Plato suggested.

"I'm chipped out," Homer complained. He sighed mournfully. "But I'll take some anyway."

"I'll get it," Nina insisted. She hurried over to the pantry for a fresh bag.

Jeremy Ames followed his wife like a fond puppy trailing its master, then turned his schnauzer nose back to Plato. "Maybe you should try paging Cally, huh?"

"I *tried*," Plato replied. He waited for Nina to refill the bowl, then shoveled a chipful of salsa in his mouth.

"I paged her three times in the last hour. Her beeper's on the fritz."

"What about calling the school?" Homer asked.

"Maybe I should," he agreed. It wasn't like Cal to be this late without calling—especially on poker night. She liked Plato's burritos almost as much as Homer did. "Cal promised to be home an hour ago."

But just as he reached for the telephone, a pager went off. Plato, Homer, and Jeremy all glanced at their belts. Jeremy grinned and studied the display.

"It's mine—the homicide office downtown." He stood and dialed the number. "They probably forgot I'm on vacation this week."

"I didn't know you ever *took* vacation," Homer muttered.

"He doesn't," Nina replied. She shook her blond head and turned her wide brown eyes to the ceiling. "On our cruise last year, I thought Jeremy would *kill* somebody just so he could solve the case." She smiled fondly at the detective. "My husband is a very restless man."

Restless was an understatement. Detective-Lieutenant Jeremy Ames had the bulging eyes and jittery manner of a hyperthyroid patient, or maybe a meth addict. The human bloodhound worked as much overtime, nights, and weekends as the sheriff's department could dish out. During his few off hours, he taught police procedure and Tai Chi at the community college.

And since he had given up smoking, Ames was even more jumpy than usual. He had worn out his first three wives like a savage mustang tossing novice riders, but Nina was somehow able to handle him. The gorgeous, sloe-eyed Mediterranean beauty could tame her husband with a simple look or gesture.

But nothing could tame Jeremy Ames now. He hung up the phone and whirled, eyeing first Homer and then

Plato. His eyes bulged like a tadpole's, and his long snout twitched at the air anxiously. His pale face was completely drained of color. He swallowed heavily.

"That was a friend of mine from the Homicide Division," he explained, pulling a tab of Nicorette gum from his shirt pocket. "Something awful has happened. Jimmy Dubrowski has escaped."

"Oh, my God!" Homer breathed.

Plato glanced at his cousin blankly. "Jimmy Dubrowski?"

"Don't you remember him?" Jeremy asked. He popped the gum into his mouth and studied Plato skeptically. "The West Side Strangler?"

"Killed five people before they finally caught him," Homer said. "Guy was a total nutcase. Guilty by reason of insanity—ended up in a mental hospital down near Massillon."

The story was familiar now; the whole thing had happened right around the time Plato met Cal. Three years ago now, though it seemed like a lifetime.

He frowned at his cousin. "But why should I remember him?"

"Your wife helped send him up the river."

"Oh, no." Plato closed his eyes, feeling his heart pounding in his chest. *Cal!*

"That's not the worst of it," Jeremy continued mercilessly. He was chewing the Nicorette furiously and drumming his fingers on the countertop. "The wardens searched Jimmy's room after he broke out, and they found a scrapbook."

"A scrapbook?" Homer asked.

"Full of news clippings." The detective glanced up at Plato. "Clippings about your wife. Every single case she's handled for the past three years." He grunted. "The doctor wouldn't say much in the interests of *confidentiality*. But he claimed Jimmy Dubrowski is 'obsessed' with your wife. And that he should be considered extremely dangerous." Ames rolled his eyes. "Like we didn't already know that."

"Holy Mary," Nina Ames breathed.

Plato glanced at the clock on the wall. Cal was almost ninety minutes overdue now, yet she hadn't called. It wasn't like her, not at all.

"Oh, my God!" Plato murmured in a shaky voice. He couldn't move, couldn't *think*.

"I already sent the cops over to the medical school," Jeremy continued. "They should be there any minute."

"We should start praying, I think," Nina suggested.

"You pray," Jeremy told his wife. "Stay here and pray—and answer the phone."

"And you?" she asked.

"We're going to the medical school," the detective replied simply. He spun on his heel and headed for the front door.

Homer grabbed Plato's arm and followed the detective, seeming to understand his cousin's helplessness.

"Don't worry, Plato," he said in a soft voice. "Cal's a tough girl—she'll be all right."

"You got it," Jeremy agreed with a sickly, unconvincing grin. He scrambled into his car and waited for Homer and Plato to pile in the other side. "I bet she's just fine."

"But what if she *isn't*?" Plato asked quietly. "What if she *isn't*?"

Jeremy Ames spun the wheel as they roared into the street, tires screeching. He leaned across Plato to open his glovebox and pulled out a heavy, black police-issue revolver. The detective glanced at the cylinder to make sure it was loaded, then set it down on the seat beside him.

"In that case, Jimmy Dubrowski will be dead." His voice was cold as steel.

Plato stared dully out the window as the trees and houses flashed by. He knew Cal was in trouble; he could *sense* it somehow. And there wasn't a damn thing they could do about it. By the time they got there, it would be all over.

If it wasn't already.

Behind him, Homer reached up to pat his shoulder. "Don't worry, pal," he repeated. "She'll be just fine."

Plato wished he could believe him.